VICTORIA DAHL

So Tough to Tame

H HARLEQUIN® HQN™

Recycling programs
for this product may
not exist in your area.

ISBN-13: 978-0-373-77789-1

SO TOUGH TO TAME

Copyright © 2013 by Victoria Dahl

Printed in U.S.A.

3 1907 00309 8497

This book is for Jif,
who tries very hard to keep me almost sane.

So
Tough
to
Tame

CHAPTER ONE

RAIN SNAKED DOWN the windshield of his F-150 in lazy rivers as Walker Pearce waited for the stoplight to turn green. Jackson Town Square was deserted, but the light waited for nonexistent tourists to make their way across the street. He hit the windshield wipers, wishing they could wipe the phantom trace of her fingers from his skin, as well. The cab of the truck still smelled like her perfume.

Ignoring the rain, he cracked his window, then pulled forward when the light turned.

It wasn't that he hated her. It was just that he'd thought she'd really wanted to talk when she'd called. But, of course, that wasn't what Nicole had wanted from him. It never was.

He knew his scruples weren't exactly sound. He'd kissed her, yes. In fact, they would've had sex one night if they hadn't gotten spooked by a near interruption. So no, he couldn't pretend that he was above such things, exactly. But somehow, messing around with the ranch owner's wife had felt less wrong when it had been…happenstance. An unexpected moment alone in the tack room. An accidental meeting after a summer party. He hadn't meant it. Neither had she. Or so he'd told himself.

But now that he was no longer working at the Fletcher Guest Ranch, Nicole couldn't leave it to chance. She'd called and asked him to meet her by Old Warm Springs. It was important, she'd said. She'd needed to see him. He'd liked that. Feeling important to a woman like her. But he'd mistaken the word.

Walker scrubbed a hand over his mouth, thinking he'd have to shave his beard if the smell of her skin wouldn't wash off.

He hadn't had sex with her this time, either, despite the way she'd climbed onto his lap and pressed herself against him. He wasn't sure why he was so determined to protect her marriage. She didn't seem to care all that much. Before he'd gotten fired from the ranch, Walker had told her they couldn't do it because he worked for her husband, because they'd be doing it under the man's roof, because he'd be fired if they got caught. But those things didn't matter now, so why did he feel even less tempted?

Maybe she'd just picked the wrong meeting spot. The springs had reminded him of junior high, and swimming with girls who'd made his head spin with fascinated lust when sex had seemed unattainable and dangerously romantic.

Sex was no longer unattainable and there was nothing romantic about the danger with Nicole. She just made him sad. And he was worried that everyone at the ranch suspected. He'd been fired for yet another paperwork screwup, but being fired over paperwork wasn't one of the most common stories told around a campfire. It had been an excuse. Walker had known that and so had his manager. Walker had no idea if that meant Nicole's husband knew, or if it was a matter of rumors just becoming too much for management to ignore.

Whatever the reason, seeing her felt wrong now, but his refusal had seriously pissed Nicole off. Maybe she wouldn't call again.

He felt only relief at the idea as he parked his truck in front of his apartment and got out. But instead of heading into the building, he crossed the lawn and walked toward the old saloon next door.

Truthfully, he missed the ranch. He missed his dog. He needed a drink, and fast.

"Hey!" Jenny Stone called from behind the bar as soon as he walked in. "You're just the man I was looking for!"

Walker couldn't help the wide grin that spread across his face. Jenny was a damn cute blonde. "Oh, yeah? Is there something Nate ain't giving you, darlin'? I'd be happy to oblige."

Jenny rolled her eyes. "You wish."

"True enough. But I do try to steer clear of a woman whose boyfriend carries a gun. Tends to leave a mark." He took off his hat and grabbed a stool.

"The usual?"

When he nodded, she drew a beer and shot a nervous look toward the back of the saloon. Walker turned to look, but the place was nearly empty at 3:00 p.m. on a rainy Tuesday.

She slid him his beer and leaned close. "You remember Charlie Allington?"

For a moment, Walker had no idea who Jenny was talking about. He'd worked with a damn lot of cowboys in his day, some who'd come and gone so quickly that he'd never even learned their names. "Charlie," he repeated, looking for a memory. The one that popped into his head shocked the hell out of him. "Oh, *Charlie!* Of course."

He and Charlie Allington—known as Charlotte only if you were trying to irritate her—had gone to high school together. In fact, she'd been his tutor for all of his junior year. "It's been a long time," he said.

"So Charlie is Nate's cousin. Once removed or second cousin or however that works."

"Is she doing okay?" Last he'd heard, she'd moved to Vegas for a big job.

"She's great. She's back in town, working at one of the Teton resorts as a security manager, and she called Nate to ask if he knew a place she could stay."

"And you suggested my place?" he asked with an automatic wink. But he felt guilty as soon as he said it. The last time he'd seen Charlie she'd been a sweet teenage girl whose number-one interest had been the track team.

"Oh, I know your door's always open, but I need something else."

"What?"

She smiled and cocked her head. "A favor."

He eyed her fluttering lashes suspiciously.

"Rayleen has been complaining about the Stud Farm being invaded by a swarm of women."

"I'd hardly call Merry a swarm."

"Yeah, well, she's still pissed that Grace moved out and talked Rayleen into letting Merry stay. She was hoping to pack the place with nothing but big hotties again this winter." She nudged his elbow. "As usual."

He gave her another grin. Old Rayleen owned the apartment building next to the saloon. She had a long history of only renting to young men, and since the house had once been the Studd homestead before it'd been broken up into apartments and modernized, the town had started calling it the Stud Farm.

Last year, Rayleen had reluctantly broken with her lecherous tradition and let her great-niece move in. Then her niece's best friend.

"What does this have to do with Charlie?" Walker asked.

"Um…I was hoping you might talk Rayleen into renting to your old friend Charlie. You know, just another cowboy looking for a place to crash for the winter."

"Another— Oh, no. No way. Rayleen likes me."

"Rayleen loves you!" Jenny interrupted. "That's why she'll let Charlie move in without even seeing her. And by the time she's moved in, even Rayleen wouldn't be mean enough to evict her. Not to mention it'd be illegal to blatantly kick out a tenant for being female."

"What about kicking out a tenant for lying about a new renter?" he grouched.

"She'll forgive you. You're too big and handsome and sexy for her to hold a grudge." She fluttered her eyelashes again.

"I like it a lot better when you don't have an ulterior motive for calling me sexy."

"But that's the only time I call you sexy, so catch-22."

He grinned. "You sure about that, Jenny?"

Jenny rolled her eyes. "Save your magic for Rayleen, cowboy."

"Hey, I've got an idea. Why don't *you* trick her into renting a place to Charlie and leave me out of it?"

"No way. Rayleen's my boss. She can fire me. She can't fire you." Jenny nudged his half-empty beer. "That beer's on the house if you do it."

"One beer? I haven't been out of work that long. I'm not desperate."

"One beer and the gratitude of Deputy Nate Hendricks. That could come in handy. A cop on your side. And think of your old friend Charlie!"

Yeah. Cute little Charlie. She needed a place to stay. And the Stud Farm was one of the few cheap, nice options in this tourist town. "Shit," he muttered.

"Yea!" Jenny cried, confident she'd won him over.

Walker shook his head and scrubbed a hand through his hair. It was too long and starting to curl over his collar. He'd meant to shave his beard and get a cut weeks ago, but now it was turning cold and he couldn't bring himself to shear any of it. Still, it would've given Nicole less of a hold if he'd gotten rid of it.

He downed the rest of his beer. "I'm not going to lie to an old lady. But I'll do what I can, all right?"

"All right. Thanks. You're the best, Walker."

"That's what they say."

"You're also incorrigible. Good thing, because here comes Rayleen."

He grimaced and nudged his glass toward Jenny. "Free refill?"

"I thought you weren't desperate."

"I'm not. I'm scared."

"All right," she laughed. "Free refill. *After* you pull it off."

Walker took a deep breath and turned with a grin to meet the harmless-looking white-haired woman. "Well, if it isn't my favorite landlord. Hey there, Miss Rayleen."

"Turn back around, Walker," she snapped. "I wasn't finished looking at your ass."

"I'd think you'd have it all mapped out by now. You look often enough."

"There's no such thing as enough when it comes to a fine piece of tush, fool."

"Why, thank you, ma'am." His smile came more easily now. He really did love this menace of a woman. "I was just asking Jenny here where you were hiding."

Rayleen raised a silver eyebrow and settled into her normal seat at a table at the corner of the bar. "You finally decided to up your cougar game? Ten-year age difference no longer a challenge?"

Walker felt his cheeks heat a little at that. Was she talking about Nicole? Did everyone know? But he shook it off. She was kidding, and if he didn't want to own up to his actions, then he'd do better to behave well in the first place. "Nope. I wanted to ask about the apartment across from mine. Is it still vacant?"

Her eyes narrowed. "Maybe. Why?"

"My old friend Charlie is looking for a place."

"Hmph. Just how old a friend is Charlie? Some dried-up cowhand?"

"Nope. My age, give or take."

Her eyes sparked with more interest now. "Yeah? Is he a cowboy?"

"No. More of a security expert, I believe. Works at a resort."

She stuck a cigarette between her lips and let it dangle there. He'd never actually seen her smoke one. She just liked having them on hand, apparently. Her gaze darted down his body and then back up. "How tall is he?" The cigarette bobbed.

Walker cleared his throat and shifted. "Aw, hell, Rayleen. I don't know. Shorter than I am."

"Hm."

Everyone knew Rayleen liked a lot of eye candy hanging around. Walker didn't care. He was just happy for the chance to get a decent place at a decent price. And he could use her fondness for his ass to his advantage now. "I have heard the word 'cute' bandied about on occasion."

"Oh, yeah? Well, then." She shuffled a pack of cards with a flourish and started dealing out her first solitaire game of the day. "That snowboarding instructor I'd hoped to rent to broke his damn leg or something. Won't be here this season. A shame. He was almost as big as you. Not sure about this whole cute thing."

Walker shot Jenny a look and she made a hurry-up motion with her hands.

"Well," he tried again. "I've known Charlie a long time. Since high school."

"Charlie who?"

Walker rolled his shoulders. This was it. "Charlie Allington. You know the Allingtons?"

She shrugged. Charlie had left town for college, so she might never have been around after reaching legal drinking age.

"Charlie's one of Nate's cousins," he clarified.

Rayleen made a noncommittal noise, but she liked Nate. Maybe that would work in their favor. Rayleen flipped over another card. Jenny hovered close by, rubbing a slow circle into the bar with a rag.

Finally Rayleen shrugged. "All right. I am getting a little tired of these seasonal workers. That last one really tore up my wood floors. What the hell was he doing in there? Playing hockey?"

He shook his head sympathetically. They'd all had to listen to Rayleen complain about refinishing those floors, but he'd heard the real reason for her anger was that the kid had called Rayleen a nasty old bitch when she'd kept his security deposit. Walker shook his head at that. What kind of punk would say something like that to a woman?

She flipped another card. "How long does he want to rent the place?"

Walker met Jenny's eyes. "Through the winter?" She nodded.

"So he'd be up for a six-month lease?" Rayleen asked.

"I'm not sure. Probably."

"Okay. Tell him to come on by. No pets. No water beds. A month's rent as a security deposit up front. If I like the looks of him, I'll offer a six-month lease. If I don't, it'll be month to month and he can get gone before the skiing starts."

"Thanks, Miss Rayleen."

She shrugged. "I ain't doing anyone any favors. I'm just looking to fill in the next couple months of dead time before the season."

"Aw, you're sweeter than you let on."

She snorted. "Not hardly, boy."

Shit. "Here's the thing...."

The cigarette went still between her lips and her eyes rose to meet his with a hard gaze. "What?"

Walker glanced at Jenny, who shook her head, but Rayleen would find out sooner than later, and his mama hadn't raised him to lie to old ladies. "My old friend Charlie? Charlie is actually short for Charlotte."

"Charlotte?" She cackled. "What kind of a name

is that for a…" The amusement left her face and was quickly replaced with tight anger. "No," she said firmly. "No, sir. I don't care how fine your behind is in those jeans, I ain't letting one of your floozies move in here."

"She's not one of my floozies! I haven't seen her since high school!" He frowned at his beer and muttered, "Not that I have floozies."

Rayleen snorted. "I said no, and that's that."

"Come on. Charlie is a great girl. And she'll take good care of the apartment, not like some twenty-something snowboarder looking for a place to party with his friends."

"He's right," Jenny finally jumped in. "The last two seasonal renters were a nightmare. And you say all the time how disgusting men are."

"Hmph." She took up her cards again. "They are disgusting. And idiotic. That's why I don't keep any in my own house. But they're nice from a distance."

Trying not to imagine that he and the other residents were just exotic animals in a zoo, Walker ducked down and met Rayleen's eyes above her hand of cards. "It's just for a few months, Rayleen. Please? As a favor to me? I'll make sure she doesn't play hockey in there. In fact, if she does, I'll kick her out myself."

Rayleen scowled. "Goddamn women. They're starting to breed like rabbits in there. Every time I look up, there's another."

"Please?" he repeated, folding his hand around hers, cards and all. "For me?"

She jerked her hand away. "Fine. Just cut the shit.

She can move in, but she'd better not put up any pink paint. Or frilly curtains. It ain't a damn henhouse."

Walker leaned in and kissed her cheek before she could get away. "I owe you, Rayleen."

Her face went pink as she shoved him away. "Oh, go on. Stand by the bar and look pretty before I change my mind." She was grumbling as he moved away, but Walker tossed Jenny a big smile.

"Refill?" he asked, pushing his glass toward her.

"I can't believe you pulled it off!"

"Aw, she's just a big softie."

Jenny laughed so hard she had to brace herself on the bar. "Yeah. Sure. You keep telling yourself that."

But Walker knew he was right. Rayleen was harmless, and she was going to love Charlie. He was sure of it.

"Oh, Charlotte, there you are!"

Charlie gritted her teeth at the sound of Dawn Taggert's voice, but she made herself smile as she turned around to greet the other woman. She'd known her boss would likely be at this baby shower. After all, the mom-to-be was one of their old friends from high school, another girl like Dawn and Charlie who'd been invited to all the after-school clubs and none of the parties.

They'd all been good girls back then, and so far, Charlie was the only one who'd fallen from grace. Dawn had yet to miss a chance to remind her.

As Dawn closed the distance across the crowded living room, Charlie realized that Dawn had the mom-to-be in tow. Charlie forced her smile wider. "Sandra! Congratulations! Thank you so much for inviting me. It's been so long."

"It has," Sandra said, hugging Charlie past her hard belly.

"You look amazing." She did. She had a smooth bob similar to Dawn's, though several shades darker than Dawn's blond hair. And despite the amazing bulge of her stomach, she looked as if she hadn't gained weight anywhere else.

"You look great, too."

"Thanks." Charlie smoothed a self-conscious hand over the cardigan sweater she'd pulled on over her dress. She didn't feel great. She felt dowdy and unnatural and thin as a stick in her modest clothes and ballet flats. She hadn't dressed like this since she'd interviewed for college, but she'd been trying to change her image. Besides, Dawn had insisted her head of security couldn't wear heels and be effective. Charlie wanted to protest that she felt much more badass in heels and a tight skirt, but unfortunately she wasn't in a position to argue.

"Your house is beautiful," Charlie said to Sandra.

"Thank you. Peter bought it as a surprise when I made partner."

Partner. Right. They both cleared their throats and shifted uncomfortably, but Dawn jumped right in. "Speaking of work, Charlie, will you come in early tomorrow? You're going to need to put in a few extra hours in the next weeks before the grand opening of the resort."

Charlie ground her teeth together as she watched Sandra look away. Sandra was uncomfortable, yes, but she was also trying to hide a smile. "I've been in early every day this week. It's not a problem."

"I know, although I'm surprised, considering the hours you keep." She turned to Sandra. "I thought she would've settled down after that mess in Tahoe, but…"

Both women turned to look at her with pity, but their pity looked suspiciously avid. Scandal was so delicious, after all. Or it was as long as you weren't involved. Charlie had enjoyed scandals and gossip herself, up until a few months ago.

She didn't want to be defensive, but she was under attack yet again, and it grated against her bones. At least Dawn was masking her distaste in politeness this time. "All my late nights since I moved here have been spent working," she said slowly, carefully.

"Right," Dawn answered with a sly smile. "That's why the facilities manager was in your place until ten last night."

Charlie's smile slipped as her heart thundered. She'd been worried her suspicions had been paranoia, but this was the confirmation she'd been looking for. Dawn had been watching her. Spying on her.

"We were working," she finally mumbled.

"Oh, I'm sure," Dawn replied.

Sandra reached out to pat her arm. "Well, Charlie, we're just happy to see you on the right track again."

The right track. Sure. That was why she'd come back here, wasn't it?

For a few months, she'd been lost. Utterly lost. Shut up in an apartment in Tahoe she could no longer afford and terrified about her future. But she was setting it right now. Working hard, toning down her life. Losing the heels. Keeping her head down. Biting her tongue and biting it hard.

"I'm doing my best with her," Dawn said, as if Charlie was her new pet project. Considering the effort she put into spying, the idea wasn't too far off. But Charlie couldn't be her project anymore. Anger was boiling beneath her skin. She wanted to bolt, but she couldn't.

She was trapped, and the urge to fight back was getting harder to suppress. But she couldn't lose this job. She couldn't.

Her phone vibrated just in time, providing a reason to escape. "Excuse me. I'd better get this. It might have something to do with work."

Before she was out of earshot, she heard Dawn saying, "I just don't know what happened to her. She had so much promise."

Charlie closed her eyes, took a deep breath and answered her phone. It was her knight in shining armor, otherwise known as her cousin Nate, calling with exactly the news she needed.

"Oh, my God," she whispered. "You really did it? I'll be there in twenty minutes. Don't move!"

This time when she turned back to the party, it wasn't hard to smile. Not at all.

"Sandra!" she called out, hurrying back for one last fake hug. "I have to run, but congratulations again. You're going to make a great mom."

She was. Sandra seemed great at everything. Unlike Charlie, she'd actually lived up to her promise.

Before Dawn could ask where she was going, Charlie made her escape and rushed out to the valet to get her car. She pulled away with a groan of relief. Freedom. For a few hours, at least.

When she'd moved back to Jackson, she'd thought reconnecting with old friends would be good for her. After all, she really *was* trying to get back on the right track. At first, she'd been so beaten up, she'd thought that track had started back with high school and the girl she'd been then. Hardworking, studious and so worried about becoming her mother that she'd never even gone out on a date.

She'd obviously gone wrong somewhere, so why not start where everything had been good?

But she was realizing now that everything hadn't been good. In fact, she'd spent all of high school scared to be herself.

Muttering a few choice curses, Charlie struggled out of the cardigan, holding the steering wheel with her knees as she yanked off the sweater and tossed it into the backseat.

"Screw this shit," she said triumphantly as she pulled up to the resort.

Five minutes later she was back in the car in the

clothes she'd worn back in Nevada. Tight jeans and heeled boots and a pretty little striped T-shirt.

Today she was going to get her groove back, damn it, and the clothes were only the first tiny step.

Charlie turned on some music and drove into town with the windows down. The breeze was too cold, but she didn't mind. It was the first time her nipples had been hard in months. She had to take her thrills where she could get them.

When she pulled up to the address Nate had given her, she saw that the apartment building was right next to the Crooked R Saloon. Her cousin greeted her from the sidewalk with a wave.

Thank God for Nate. Charlie had a brother in town, but he never offered any help unless it could benefit him, too. Nate, on the other hand…

Charlie jumped out of her car and threw her arms around his neck to squeeze him tight. "Thank you, thank you!"

"Hey, calm down. It's no big deal. I'm sorry the place at the resort fell through."

"Well, you know…" She let him go and crossed her arms to hide the nervous flutter of her hands. She didn't want to lie to him, but she didn't know how to explain. "Construction on the hotel is behind schedule. Naturally, the last big push goes into the rooms people are actually paying for. Hopefully my apartment will be ready in a few months."

"I think Rayleen wants to rent this place out through the winter. Six months, Jenny said."

"Sure, I understand. Of course. I have no problem with that. It was so great of you to arrange this for me."

"Walker was actually the one who pulled it off."

Charlie shook her head in shock. "Walker *Pearce?*"

"Yeah, you remember him?"

"Of course I remember him! He's still around?"

"Living right here at the Stud Farm, actually."

Well, that made sense. Walker had been a hell of a stud in high school. She'd had a serious crush on him, though she'd been careful not to let him know. Half the girls in the school had had a crush on him. Any time she'd tutored him in the library during lunch, girls had made a point of sauntering by like a rotating show of blondes and brunettes and redheads. All the prettiest girls in the school. The cheerleaders and the rodeo queens. And Walker had made a point of smiling at each and every one.

Charlie followed Nate into the apartment building and up the stairs to the second floor. The two-story entryway was clean and bright, sunlight shining through the old farmhouse windows that flanked the front door.

"Here's your key. You'll need to go by the saloon to pick up the lease agreement."

"Cool."

"Just a warning. If Rayleen Kisler is there, you might want to lay low. You know Rayleen?"

"I know of her."

"Walker talked her into letting you rent the place, but she'd much rather have had someone…" He stopped at the door to apartment C and shook his head. "Bigger and hairier."

Charlie grinned. "She hasn't given up her hobby, then, I guess?"

"Nope. She still likes to ogle. But she made an exception for you. Although there's another woman living in the apartment below yours. Merry Kade. So it was a damn miracle that Walker managed to get you in here."

"I'll have to find a way to thank him."

"Won't be hard. He lives right there." Nate tilted his head toward the apartment on the other side of the small upstairs landing.

She shot a surprised look at the other door before unlocking her own. Walker lived right there? That would be interesting. Or just irritating, if the parade of beautiful women was still marching after all these years. Maybe she could sit on the landing with a book and wave to each one. Recapture some of the fun of her youth.

Charlie let herself into the apartment and took in the simple white walls and the gorgeous shine on the wood floors. It was nothing like her studio at the resort. There were no fancy appliances in the kitchen or stained timber details. There was no hand-hewn rock fireplace. It was modest and empty and it was *private*.

She breathed a sigh of relief. "I've got a few things in storage. I'll pull them out as soon as I've signed the lease."

"Let me know," Nate said. "I'll help you move what you need."

"You don't have to do that."

"Come on. I know you're a kick-ass security specialist, but you're not that strong."

She punched him solidly on the shoulder, but he didn't even wince. Yeah, she wasn't that strong. Or kick-ass. Her specialty was really observation. Surveillance. Intelligence. Or it had been. Before.

Feeling her smile go stiff and strange, Charlie turned away from her cousin, pretending to check out the apartment a little more closely. "Okay, I'll call you when I need a hand."

"Perfect. You've got the key. Don't forget to go see Jenny for the lease."

"Oh, the new girlfriend, huh?"

Her cousin's cheeks actually went a little pink. "Not so new, actually. We've been together since February."

Charlie grinned. "Wow. Your mother must be over the moon. I can't wait to meet this woman."

"Want to come over to the saloon with me right now?"

Aw, he was so cute. It must be nice to be one of those people who believed in love. "Give me a few minutes and I'll meet you there."

As soon as Nate left, Charlie let her smile vanish and moved purposefully through the apartment. Though their entrances were separated by the landing, she noticed that she and Walker would be sharing a wall along the living room, bathroom and bedroom. She hoped the walls were thick. The Walker she'd known hadn't looked like a boy who'd inspired silence in the bedroom.

Chuckling at the thought, Charlie checked off a mental list of things she'd need to make this place comfortable. Her boots knocked against the wood floors and echoed off the ceiling, reminding her of exactly how empty the rooms were.

Her studio at the resort was fully furnished, so everything except her clothing and some knickknacks was in storage, but she had plenty of nice furniture from her old place in Tahoe. Some of it she could even move without help. She could rent a truck and have all her kitchen stuff by tonight, plus a table and chairs. Her lamps. Maybe even her bed. Hell, she'd sleep on the floor if she couldn't move the bed. The resort was unbearable. Just the idea of spending another night there made her break out in goose bumps.

Bad enough she had to work in that place. Bad enough that she couldn't quit.

Charlie shut off the lights she'd turned on and locked the apartment behind her. She wanted to get this part over with. Lying to her cousin made her stomach hurt, but she didn't have any choice. She wasn't going to admit another defeat. There'd been so many this year.

Charlie blinked back the tears of frustration that sprang to her eyes. The worst was behind her. There was no question of that.

All those years of living in Vegas and Tahoe, those years of building a career and a reputation, and it was all trashed, but it was going to be different now. She wasn't going backward. Not back to who she'd been in Tahoe, and not back to high school, either. No, she was going forward.

Charlie walked down the stairs of the Stud Farm, opened the front door and pasted a big smile on her face. If she wanted to be a new woman, it was time for the debut.

CHAPTER TWO

"I HATE HER," Rayleen groused to no one in particular from her corner table. Somehow, Walker knew he was the one being addressed.

He looked to Jenny, who rolled her eyes. "Charlie was in to sign the lease today," she explained.

Rayleen huffed. "She came in wearing skinny jeans and a big ol' shit-eating grin. I thought you said she was a nice girl, Walker."

"What?" he asked in honest confusion. "Nice girls don't wear skinny jeans?" In his opinion, the very nicest girls graced the world with skinny jeans. Tight denim was a gift to all.

"No, they do not. And they certainly don't walk in here like they own the place."

"Rayleen," Jenny sighed. "Charlie was perfectly kind. You just didn't like that she didn't take your bait."

"What bait?" the old lady snapped.

"Oh, I don't know. What about when you said you'd prefer a Charlie that damn well fit his name, and she just winked and said she'd take a cowboy over her own self any day, too?"

"Impertinent."

"Kind of like you?" Jenny said.

Walker tipped up his hat. "I like a lively lady my-self. Why else would I be hanging out in your saloon all the time, Rayleen?"

"Maybe because it's right next door to your place and you don't have a damn job!"

"Hey, now. I'm picking up work and I've got plenty lined up for roundup."

Rayleen dismissed him with a wave of her hand. "You're the one who got me into this. I'm not speaking to you."

"Are you just trying to get me to turn around so you can look at my behind, Miss Rayleen?"

"That's a perfect idea. Gives me a nice view and I don't have to talk to your lying self. Go on. Turn around now."

"Only 'cause you asked nice." He turned his back on her and raised his eyebrows to Jenny, who leaned closer.

"Charlie was great. Rayleen just wanted her to be intimidated, and Charlie met every one of her barbs with a smile and a wink. Sort of like you. Only without the big cowboy part."

"Which big cowboy part?" Walker asked.

"You're awful."

"Come on, now. That's not what you've heard."

Jenny threw her head back and laughed. "You really are incorrigible, Walker."

"That I'll admit to. Is Charlie all settled in? I haven't seen her yet."

"Nate gave her the key a couple of hours ago, and she took the lease to read over. Which Rayleen also didn't like. She likes you cowboys who just sign the thing without even glancing at it."

"We are adventurers at heart."

"Or romantic fools."

"That, too."

She winked. "Want a beer?"

"No, I was just checking in on the new tenant. I heard about some winter work up near Yellowstone, so I'm gonna head up there and check it out. I'm fine through fall, but I'm hoping to find enough work to get me through to spring."

"You'll find something, Walker. People like your face."

"Ha. That they do." People did like his face, thank God. It was one of the few things he had going for him. Otherwise, he was just another cowboy among thousands. A good one, granted. Good with his hands. Good with horses. Willing to endure heat and cold and snow and rain, not to mention low pay and physically punishing work for fifty years, give or take a dozen.

But people liked his face, so he'd been able to get jobs at dude ranches, which offered work that paid a little more and hurt a little less, as long as you didn't mind working with tourists. He didn't. But this damn sure wasn't dude ranch season.

He tipped his hat. "I'll see you later, Jenny. Have a good day, Miss Rayleen."

Rayleen shooed him away without looking up.

She'd get over it, and Charlie had a place to stay. His good deed was done, and he was wrapped up in his own troubles before he even stepped outside.

Finding work wasn't really a problem. He'd already gotten plenty of jobs at an old dude ranch he'd worked for years before, and they'd likely hire him on permanently in the spring. He had enough savings to get through winter. Things should be fine.

But if stories were circulating about him and the boss's wife... Shit. He'd really fucked up. Every boss had a wife. And none of them wanted their women sleeping with the hired hands.

Still, something more than that was tugging at his brain. Maybe—

His thoughts were sliced in two when he glanced up and saw a woman struggling to get a big round table up the front steps of the Stud Farm.

"Charlie?" he called, rushing forward to take the table from her hands.

She looked up, her brown hair sliding over her shoulders as she turned. Her light gray eyes went wide. "Oh, my God! Walker, is that you behind that beard?"

"It's me," he said with a grin that widened the longer he looked down at her. She was still damn cute. Actually, she'd gone from cute to pretty at some point in the past ten years. "It's good to see you, Charlie. Can I take this somewhere for you?" He lifted the table a few inches.

She shot his hands a look of irritation. "I can't believe you can just tote that thing around like it's nothing. I had to roll it like a barrel just to get it across the lawn."

"I see that." He plucked a few clumps of dirt and grass off the table and lifted it up to his shoulder. "Come on. I'll take it upstairs."

"Thanks."

"After you," he insisted. She held the door open for him, then started up the stairs to the landing above.

Walker followed right behind, noticing that she was obviously still an athlete. Still slim and tight and strong. But not quite as slim as she'd been in high school. No, now there were hips. And an ass. And black leather boots that hugged her calves. And most of all, there were those awesome skinny jeans showing off all the changes.

Yeah, Charlie was obviously just as nice as she'd always been. But maybe sweeter than ever before.

He glanced at his apartment door as he passed.

She was certainly much closer.

Shit. Maybe this good deed wouldn't go unpunished, after all.

"SWEET MOTHER OF everything hot," Charlie muttered under her breath as she watched Walker Pearce's biceps flex and bunch as he maneuvered her pine table through the doorway of her apartment. He wore a beat-up gray T-shirt with a Stetson logo on it, tight jeans, ancient boots and a black cowboy hat that threw a shadow over his blue eyes. But that was fine. She didn't need to see his smiling eyes right now. She was too busy taking in his body.

His shoulders hadn't been that wide in high school. His arms hadn't been so thick. And he hadn't been quite that tall. Jesus, he must be six-four now.

All in all, he looked like a dangerous, forbidden, older-brother version of the Walker she'd once had a crush on. Every butterfly she'd ever felt for him swarmed back to life in an instant, only now their restless wings brushed more sensitive areas. There was no reason for her stomach to feel nervous. After all, that wasn't the part of her body she wanted Walker to touch.

He set the table down close to the breakfast bar in the kitchen. "Is this good?"

"Oh, that's definitely good." She glanced at his left hand to be sure there was no ring. Not that she could imagine Walker married. He'd be a terrible husband. Carefree and aimless and throwing off pheromonal invitations to every ovary in town.

She was still trying to take all of him in when his chest suddenly filled her vision and he swept her up into a hug. "How the hell are you, Charlie?"

He squeezed her so tight the air rushed out of her lungs. When he set her back down, she inhaled nothing but the scent of him. Leather and hay and clean sky and something so deliciously spicy that her mouth watered.

"You look good," he said, holding her at arm's length and giving her a once-over. "City life has been good to you."

She wanted to say something witty. Something sexy.

But for the first time in a decade she was that high school girl again, too shy and uncertain to flirt with Walker Pearce. "Thanks."

"What else can I do for you, darlin'? You got a bed?"

"What?" Her cheeks flamed as if her body didn't want him to know what she'd been thinking. Stupid, brainless body. "A bed?" *Yes, please, a bed!*

"Surely you didn't haul a mattress up by yourself?"

"Oh, a bed!" She laughed nervously while her brain screamed for this retro Charlie to get her shit together. *You are not a sixteen-year-old virgin. You are an experienced woman who likes sex. Lots of sex.*

Retro Charlie won out with a tiny giggle. "Thanks, Walker. It's down in the rental truck. I'll help."

"Nah, you stay here and start unpacking those boxes. I'll have your bed set up in no time."

This was her chance. Crack a joke about hanging around after to test it out. Not that she'd jump into bed with him within minutes of their reunion, but just to let him know it might be a possibility. Just to plant the seed. But no. In the end, she only watched his ass as he walked away. It was a good ass. Strong. Muscular.

Ah. This was just like high school. Always watching him from afar even when he was so close.

"Shit," she muttered, kicking the box closest to her foot. When she heard the rattle of dishes, she winced and told herself to cut it out. This wasn't high school, and she'd lived a lot since then. Walker Pearce was no longer too much man for her. And hell, if he was, that'd be her dream come true. A big ol' cowboy to ride into the sunset. But only into the sunset. Best to keep the mornings a clean slate, especially with a roving boy like Walker.

Cheered by the thought, Charlie picked up the box she'd kicked and hauled it onto the kitchen counter. When she pried open the flaps and saw the familiar bright yellow of her dinner plates, a weight lifted from her shoulders as if a vulture had just left its vigil. She'd barely moved in and this place already felt more like home than the resort had after three weeks.

She'd been thrilled with the gorgeous studio apartment set aside for her. It wasn't normal procedure, but Charlie hadn't questioned her good luck. She'd just figured that being friends with Dawn, the executive manager of the resort and the wife of the owner, had come with its own perks. Dawn had explained that they wanted a permanent security presence at the resort and left it at that.

The offer had been a relief. Now Charlie realized that beautiful apartment had been nothing more than a cage.

Charlie unwrapped her yellow plates and put them precisely in the middle of the lowest shelf next to the stove. "Perfect." When her brain reminded her she had to be back at the resort by 8:00 a.m., she frowned and dug back into the box. It was just a job.

At the sound of boots on the stairs, she looked up to see Walker heading toward her door, her bed frame under one arm and her headboard slung over his other shoulder. He eased his haul through her doorway, then headed for the bedroom.

Her own personal mover.

She followed him in to watch as he propped the slatted wood headboard against the wall, and then she reached to help with the first part of the frame as he fitted it to the wood. "You don't have to do this, Walker. I can take care of the bed."

"You've been living in Nevada too long if you think a nice Wyoming boy is going to let a woman haul furniture on her own."

She grinned. "I guess you're right. I'll have to get used to Wyoming again. More chivalry, less gambling and legalized prostitution."

"There are subtle differences, but they're there if you look."

"Thanks for the advice. I'll put away my poker chips and platform heels and try to fit in."

He winked as he crossed to the other side of the bed and fit a new frame piece onto that side. "There's no need for anything that drastic, darlin'. Just be yourself. Let it all hang out."

She snorted at his ridiculous flirting, just as she always had. There was no way to take it seriously. He flirted with everyone, young and old. She'd always been smart enough to see that. But she was finally ready to flirt back.

"You have any beer in the fridge next door, Walker? There's no need for this to be all work and no fun."

He didn't seem to notice her inviting smile. "Oh,

I've always got beer, but I've got to head up toward Yellowstone for a couple of hours. I'll grab a couple bottles for you if you want, though."

"No, I'm good. If you need to get going, you should go. I'm fine."

"Girl, didn't you hear what I said about us nice Wyoming boys? I'll have the rest of your bed up here in five minutes."

Girl. Just like in high school. Charlie drew herself up, a tingle of anticipation zinging down her spine and tightening her nipples. She wasn't a girl anymore. And she wasn't his pal or his tutor or his favorite tomboy track star. He couldn't see that yet, but he would.

She'd always liked a challenge. "Then go get my bed, Wyoming boy. I'll buy you a beer tonight at the Crooked R if I see you around."

"That's a deal." He stepped past her, then surprised her by reaching out to ruffle her hair as he passed.

He *ruffled* her *hair*.

Unbelievable. That decided it. This boy was going down. Hard. And frequently, if she had anything to say about it. She was finally going to get a taste of Walker Pearce. And from what she'd heard, he'd taste damn good.

She hadn't gotten laid in months, and working at a resort that hadn't even opened yet hadn't exposed her to many opportunities. But opportunity had knocked now. And it lived right next door.

CHAPTER THREE

THERE'D BEEN NO room for Walker at the inn. Literally. All the bunks at the Blue Sleigh Inn and Ranch were full for the winter, which wasn't much of a surprise. Most of the cowboys who worked there during the summer stayed on, and there wasn't nearly as much work during the winter. But he'd been invited to stop by again in the spring, for what that was worth.

Muttering a curse, he stepped out of his truck into the icy night. The sun had set two hours ago, and he was already dead tired, stressed from dodging migrating elk on the highway and trying too hard to read the face of that ranch manager. She'd seemed sincere. She hadn't sneered at him. She hadn't flirted, either, or dropped any hints about rumors she'd heard. He was being paranoid, probably, thinking the word was out that he couldn't be trusted.

At least tonight he was too damn tired to lie in bed worrying about it. He wasn't cut out for this crap. His life was simple. He took care of horses. He taught folks how to ride. He roped and herded and branded cattle. It wasn't that hard and he wasn't that deep. Anxiety was for city folks and people a lot smarter than he was. He just wanted to work and hang with friends and occasionally have a little fun with a hot woman. Clearly, he should've been more careful about mixing all those up at the same time.

His legs felt weighted with lead as he trudged up the front steps of the Stud Farm. He grunted in surprise when the door opened before he could reach for it.

"Hey, Walker!" Merry Kade called as she bounced outside.

He automatically tipped his hat and grabbed the door to hold it open for her. "Evening, Merry."

"Your friend is so much fun!"

"My friend?"

She bounced her hip against his leg as she passed. "Charlie, silly. She's hilarious. You're coming over, right?"

He glanced over to the saloon, feeling not the least bit tempted. "No, I'm beat. I'll catch up another time."

Merry spun around at the bottom of the steps. "No, you have to come, Walker! Just for a little while. Charlie said to think of it as her homecoming party. Look, she made me go put on my heels." Merry lifted her foot and angled it so he could see the black heels she wore.

"I'd better not," he said with a wink. "I left my last pair of heels at the ranch anyway."

Merry snorted with laughter, but she didn't give up. "Even Rayleen's having fun."

That made him pause. And then Merry pushed the button that was hardest for him to ignore.

"Come on, Walker. I can barely walk in these things. Be a gentleman and let me hold your arm."

Well, shit. He wouldn't say no to that, and she knew it. Her smile tipped into triumph. Walker gave in with a sigh. "Fine, I'll walk you over to the saloon, and then I'm leaving."

"We'll see."

She took his arm even though he highly suspected she didn't need any help. Then again, he hadn't often seen Merry in heels. She was more a jeans and Converse kind of girl. "Where's Shane? I like it when he gets all riled up about you."

She grinned. "Me, too. But I don't think he's home yet."

"Aw, that's too bad. I was going to dance you around the saloon porch a little, just to rub it in."

"I don't dance in heels. I just sit on a bar stool and look stunning."

"Same as without heels, then?"

She elbowed him and snorted. "You're such a dork."

This was what he loved about Merry. No one ever called him a dork. And he was damn sure no one had ever called Shane Harcourt a dork, either, but Walker had heard Merry say the same to him. No wonder Shane was hooked. Merry was sweet and smart as hell. Unfortunately, that kind of woman didn't go for Walker. Not for the long term anyway.

He escorted Merry up the steps to the saloon porch, then hesitated at the door. He normally loved a good night out, but he wasn't in the mood quite as often lately.

Merry tugged him forward. "You can drop me off at the bar."

"In case you think I don't know I'm being played, I know I'm being played," he muttered, but he opened the door and waved her in.

Country music thumped through the air, and his heart immediately reset itself to the rhythm. Maybe this wouldn't be so bad. Maybe he could stay for a few minutes to be polite. He let Merry lead him toward the bar. She'd apparently dropped any pretense that she needed a steady arm to support her, but Walker couldn't resent it. He'd spotted a hot female ass in tight jeans and Merry was taking him straight toward it.

"Look who I found!" she called to the crowd at the bar.

Several faces turned toward him, but Walker was busy raising his eyes up the woman's spine and over long brown hair to see Charlie smiling over her shoulder at him. He blinked, surprised yet again that she was all grown-up and working a gorgeous ass. His eyes slipped down again, over her long, long legs to the bright red spike heels she wore. Damn.

"Hey, Walker," she purred when he drew near.

Wait, he thought as he leaned down to return her hug. *Charlie Allington purring?* He must've heard that wrong.

"You ready for that payment I promised?" Her

breath whispered over his ear, the words sneaking in-side him.

He pulled back quickly. "A beer, right?"

"Sure, unless you want a pomegranate martini." She pointed at the drink she held, which was such a bright red the reflection tinged the underside of her chin pink.

"You think I won't drink a pomegranate martini?" He lifted his chin toward Jenny and gestured to Char-lie's drink. "I'll take one of these," he called.

Jenny rolled her eyes, but she grabbed the martini shaker.

Charlie looked up at his hat, then down to his boots, but she stayed silent until he reached over to the bar and snagged the drink.

"Thanks," he said, raising the glass toward her be-fore he took a sip. "Perfect."

"You're pretty damn adorable," she said. "A big old cowboy drinking a pretty little cocktail."

"Yeah?" He leaned a little closer out of flirtatious habit.

"Yeah. Those rough fingers curved around that deli-cate glass? It's…promising."

His blood heated by a few degrees. She liked see-ing his fingers on something delicate, did she? She'd moved closer, too, and he could smell her hair. He could also see straight down the front of her red shirt, and the rise of her breasts were faint curves that ended at a silky black bra. "You look awfully promising your-self, Charlie."

The shape of her name in his mouth stopped the

rush of his blood. He blinked and leaned back a little, reminding himself that this was his pal Charlie, but she just clinked her glass against his and smiled. "Thank you," she murmured softly before turning toward the man who'd appeared at her side.

"Hey, Nate!" she gushed before hugging her cousin.

Walker took the chance to enjoy the sight of her from a new angle. The long line of her side curving out to that perfect ass, then those ridiculous legs. He'd noticed those even in high school. How could he not? She'd been one of the tallest girls in school. Still about six inches shorter than him, but tonight the heels added a few more. Hell, he could kiss her for hours without getting a crick in his neck. He could even bend her over a table and—

His eyes skittered away from her ass as if they were horrified at where his imagination had gone. This was Charlie. Way too smart to date a guy like Walker, and way too sweet to be used to scratch an itch. But damn, it'd been easier to be friends with her before she'd grown into heels. And flirting. And shiny lip gloss that made her mouth look full and plump and—

He looked up to find Nate glaring at him above Charlie's head. Walker shrugged and gave an innocent grimace of confusion as if he had no idea what Nate could be upset about. Nate didn't look appeased. And he looked downright dour when Charlie reached back to lean her hip against Walker and loop her arm around his waist. She craned her neck up until Walker leaned his ear closer to her.

"Why's my cousin shooting you a death glare? Were you checking out my ass, Walker Pearce?"

"Uh." He cleared his throat. "That may be what he thought I was doing."

"You can look. I think it's pretty nice myself. What do you think?"

"I, uh…" He'd never once in his life gotten tongue-tied around a woman. If there was one skill he could rely on, it was the power of flirtation. He enjoyed it. Women liked it. No one got hurt. But the invitation to make a comment about Charlie Allington's ass had thrown him off his game.

"Aw." Her lower lip turned down in a pretty pout. "You don't like it? I think it's nice and round and firm."

Oh, fuck. What was she doing? Didn't she know the kind of image her words would conjure? Of her stripped out of jeans and panties, her naked ass taut under his grip as he positioned himself behind her and… "Damn it, Charlie."

"What?" she asked with a laugh that tickled his ear.

"Stop teasing me. You're not…" He stopped himself and took a deep breath.

"I'm not what?"

"You're not that kind of girl."

"What kind of girl is that?"

His face felt odd and hot. He reached up to adjust his hat so he could think a little more clearly. "You know. You were a smart girl. You never got into trouble with the rest of us. You—"

"I'm still smart," she said, talking so close now that

her lips brushed his ear. "But I'm not any kind of girl at all anymore. I'm a woman, all grown-up. Can't you tell?"

Yes, he could damn well tell. In fact, his cock was starting to swell as the tingle of her words raced down his neck and kept right on going. This definitely wasn't Charlie from high school. "It's gorgeous," he murmured.

"What?"

"Your ass. It's beautiful. But I can't give any opinion on whether it's firm. It might be. It might be the sweetest, tightest ass in the county, but that's not something I can tell just by looking."

Her face was angled slightly away from him now, but it wasn't hard to catch the way her mouth turned up in a wide grin. "You don't believe me?" she murmured. He watched her fingers slide over her own hip, spreading a little as if she meant to test the give of her flesh right there.

Walker didn't dare look up. There was no way Nate could've missed the way Charlie had snuggled so close. And Walker knew there was no hiding the heat in his gaze. And there wouldn't be any hiding his erection if this went on much longer. The hand at his waist had started tracing slow circles that made waves of pleasure radiate out over his body. And he was picturing that scene again. Of Charlie naked, her hand opening over her own hip as his fingers spread over her ass. She'd look back at him with that taunting little smile, just as she did now. *Do you like it?* she'd ask. And he'd answer by squeezing her ass hard and laying his cock against the plump mounds of her cheeks as he—

"Jesus," he cursed with a harsh laugh as he eased his hips back and shook his head. "You turned cruel while you were gone, Charlie. Good God."

She shrugged. "Maybe a little cruel. But I bet you can handle it. You're a big boy."

And getting bigger by the second, damn her. But Charlie didn't notice. The jukebox rang with the opening notes of a song from their school days, and she danced away from him.

"Miss Rayleen, do you allow two-stepping in here?" she called.

Rayleen plucked her cigarette from her mouth and pointed it toward the tables. "If you can find room for it, knock yourself out."

"Hmm." Charlie turned back to look him up and down, then shook her head. "I do believe this one is too big to be nimble."

Rayleen cackled. "You've got that right. That's a tool for blunt work."

"Hey!" he protested, but Rayleen laughed harder.

"Look at his face, poor thing!" the woman hooted.

Charlie shook her head in mock sympathy. "Too bad. I'll have to find another partner."

"I'm nimble as hell," he grouched. "I've never had any complaints."

He should have known by the thrilled smile on Rayleen's face that she was about to cause trouble, but he didn't move fast enough to stop it. "Naw," she drawled, "he comes with good reviews. Just like a nice hotel. With pictures online and everything."

Charlie's eyes lit up. "What?" she gasped.

"Damn it, Rayleen, that is not true!" He took off his hat and scrubbed a hand through his hair. He couldn't believe they were having this conversation again. And this time it was in front of *Charlie*.

But Rayleen was relentless. "You know when men sometimes take pictures of their—"

"That is not what happened!" He cringed at the volume of his own voice and muttered, "Pardon me, ma'am," but Rayleen was howling and slapping the table while Charlie looked from her to Walker, her jaw dropped open in a wide smile.

"Seriously?" she gasped.

"No! Not seriously! There is no picture of my…" He glanced at Rayleen, self-conscious about his language even if she did have the mouth of an old sailor. "…manhood online. Or anywhere else. As far as I know."

"Ah. Cell phone cameras are tricky beasts, aren't they?" Charlie tried to make her words sound sympathetic. It didn't work. She broke down in laughter.

No, there were no cock shots of him anywhere, but there was one small problem that—

Rayleen cupped her hand around her mouth as if she were going to whisper a secret. "Someone posted a picture of his naked ass on Facebook."

"Rayleen," he groaned.

"Took me a few days to find it, but it was worth the work."

Walker closed his eyes against the sight of Charlie's horrified delight. He shook his head. "Why do you have to tell everyone? It's just a picture of an ass, for God's sake."

"Just a picture of *your* ass while you were sleeping naked on some girl's bed."

Not for the first time, he said a quick prayer of thanks that he was a stomach sleeper. He should've known that woman would be trouble. She'd started texting her friends five seconds after orgasm.

"Oh, Walker," Charlie said, her voice closer than it had been. But he didn't open his eyes, even when her hand patted his cheek. "You haven't changed at all."

Much as he'd like to, there was no denying the truth. When he'd woken this morning, he'd greeted the day with exactly as much to his name as he'd had when Charlie had left town for college: a big truck, a strong back, good hands and some almost-promising ranch work lined up. The only thing he'd managed to add were a few aches and pains, a small savings and a little regret.

He suddenly remembered that he'd been too tired to hang out tonight.

When he opened his eyes he found that everyone had moved on. Rayleen was reabsorbed in her game of solitaire. Nate and Merry were propped on bar stools, laughing with Jenny, and Charlie…Charlie had cleared a small space near the jukebox and pulled some cowboy into her arms to two-step.

"You were right about her," Rayleen said without looking up. "She's all right. Bought me a drink and everything. In my own bar. My best Scotch."

"I'm glad to hear it."

Rayleen nodded. "Yep. You were right. I like that girl."

Yeah. Unfortunately for his pride, so did he.

CHAPTER FOUR

CHARLIE STARED DOWN her hangover in the mirror. Unless Rayleen had installed fluorescent bulbs in the bathroom, her face was a damn unattractive color this morning. She looked closer, scowling down her own bad mood and daring her stomach to rebel.

It'd been years since she had a hangover. A few unwise nights during her first year in Las Vegas had taught her about pacing.

But the hangover hardly mattered. She dreaded going to work anyway. No point wasting good health on it. It would be a bad day with or without a shifty stomach and a headache. At least she'd had fun flirting with Walker last night.

Resigned to her miserable day, she forced herself to drink a full glass of water, then showered and shaved her legs and put on enough makeup to hide the green before slouching to her car. She already had antacids in the glove compartment. This wasn't the first stomachache the Meridian Resort had given her. She was prepared.

She'd thought this job was her saving grace. She'd thought Dawn was swooping in to save her like an old friend riding in on a white horse. Now Charlie was tied to the railroad tracks and trying to figure out what the hell had happened.

Then again, it wasn't really something that had *happened*. She'd done it to herself. Not deliberately, just…stupidly. And she'd always thought she was so smart. She'd spent a blissful twenty-nine years believing she wasn't an idiot, and then she'd been arrested for criminal conspiracy. Lesson learned.

The drive to Teton Village was over in a flash, fifteen minutes accelerated to mere seconds by her dread. The scattered resorts and gigantic lodges were beautiful. There were miles of exquisite architecture and landscaping designed to look perfect amid the snowdrifts and icicles. But to her, the whole village looked like so much trash washed up on the shore of these mountains. She wove her way through the maze and headed toward the Meridian Resort halfway up the hill.

Three weeks ago, she'd been grinning through this whole drive, so thrilled and excited to have an opportunity. Any opportunity.

Clenching her jaw, she waited for the gate to the employee parking garage to open, staring straight ahead so she wouldn't glare at the tiny camera lens to her left. Her stomach turned. She ignored it and pulled into her numbered spot. Another little camera lens watched as she got out of her car and headed toward the utilitarian steel door set in the cement wall. On the guest level, the cement walls were painted a homey beige, and the fire doors were paneled with wood. But the employee floor had all the appeal of a prison. Appropriate.

She took the stairs up one level and headed for the basement offices of the security department.

Dawn's office was two floors up, with a lovely view and high ceilings, but Charlie wasn't the least bit surprised to see Dawn sitting on one of the metal chairs outside Charlie's door.

Dawn leaned back in her chair with a smile. "This is quite the walk of shame, Charlotte."

"What are you talking about?" Charlie asked with a sigh. She unlocked her door, aware that she was an idiot to bother with locking it in the first place. Dawn had keys to everything, after all, and she used them.

"You haven't been in your apartment since yesterday. Already out making new friends, I guess."

Charlie hid her grimace of frustration before rounding her small desk. "What I do when I'm off the clock is none of your business."

"As long as you're not sleeping with other employees of the resort, you mean. Or anyone in management." Her tone was always sweet, always helpful, which only made her words so much creepier.

"I'm not."

"With your history, we can never be too careful, can we?"

Charlie squeezed her eyes shut for a moment, just so she wouldn't have to look at that cute cherubic face. "I already explained about the facilities manager. Twice. And your husband—"

"Oh, I'm not worried about my husband, Charlotte. He likes nice girls. Like me. He wouldn't risk everything he's built just for a few moments of sordid… What's the word I'm looking for?"

"Pleasure?" Charlie muttered, thinking Dawn must be a real treat in bed, with her stiff neck and her inability to even say something dirty, much less do it.

"No," she snapped. "Depravity. Or plain old sluttiness."

"You should try it sometime. You might like it."

Her face wasn't looking so cherubic anymore. Her perfectly rouged cheeks went red. "I pushed for you for this job in spite of your reputation. Nobody else wanted you. You should remember that."

As if she could forget. As if she'd still be sitting here for any other reason. "Why?" she asked.

"Because if you don't remind yourself of that, you're going to—"

"No, I mean, why did you want to hire me?"

Dawn drew in a breath and smoothed down her blond bob. Her smile reappeared. "Because we're friends. And I'm not the kind of person who'd turn her back on a friend in need."

She was insane. That was the only explanation for it. Dawn had lost her mind sometime after high school. Sure, she might have been a little uptight and judgmental, but she'd been *normal*. But this? This wasn't normal.

"Nobody else would've hired you, Charlotte."

"Yes, so you've reminded me." It was true. She'd

sent out dozens of résumés. With her education and experience, she should've been an automatic interview. She hadn't received one phone call. Until Dawn.

"And nobody will ever hire you again if you leave here under bad circumstances."

She knew that, too. She had to stick this out. Just for a little while. Just until the memory of what had happened in Tahoe began to fade from sight. If she could work here for a year or two, she could send out some quiet feelers. Maybe somewhere farther east.

"You need to make this work, Charlotte. And I'm happy to help you, but I expect a little more cooperation on your part. You're being nasty today. I'm not sure what's gotten into you…." She swept a hand down to indicate the sexy black pencil skirt Charlie had dared to wear. "But you need to watch your attitude."

Charlie took a deep breath. She did need to watch it. Dawn was her boss whether Charlie liked it or not.

"And stop fraternizing with male management."

"That drink with your husband was just a drink. He was reviewing the restaurant menu, and—"

"Of course it was just a drink," Dawn snapped.

Charlie wanted to scream with frustration. She was at a complete loss here. What could she do but scream? She breathed deeply, trying to let the feeling go. Finally she opened the laptop on her desk. "I need to get to work."

"You do. Is everything going to be ready?"

Charlie nodded. The resort's grand opening was in three weeks. Charlie had been so determined to make a good impression that she was ahead of schedule, but she wouldn't slack off now. For one thing, staying busy kept her mind off her desire to drop everything and race out the front doors.

"All right, I'll be back to check on you later."

"I know," Charlie said under her breath. Dawn checked on her several times a day. And probably had several times a night, too, before Charlie had moved out of the resort apartment.

"I'll leave your door open," Dawn said breezily as she walked out on her five-hundred-dollar heels. Charlie couldn't help being jealous of the gorgeous shoes. She was going to don heels as soon as she got home.

Her hangover was starting to fade, at least. Probably the rush of adrenaline from wanting to strangle Dawn. She grabbed herself a cup of coffee, poured in tons of cream and sugar and sat down with her simplest task: background checks of every employee that would be hired before opening day. She'd tweaked nearly every camera in the resort, though a few were still waiting to be installed, and there wasn't much monitoring to be done at this point. But the background checks were piling higher every day.

The last thing any hotel manager needed was a maintenance man or bellboy with a history of theft or sexual assault. A high-end place like this was hyper-vigilant about reputation. Charlie was more concerned with actual safety, but luckily, those two concerns coincided.

She'd insisted on installing more cameras in the employee areas than had originally been planned. That had been commonplace at gambling resorts where management considered employee theft an important target, but Charlie had found that just as often those tapes could be used to weed out gross managers who harassed their female employees. There were few things more satisfying than showing incriminating video to some asshole who thought he could act with impunity because his employees were women who barely spoke English. The back rooms of hotels were called the heart of the place, and she liked to do her part to stick to the spirit of that term.

But for now, with the employee halls mostly empty, it was time for the mind-numbing task of background checks.

An hour later, her mind was sufficiently numbed. Her headache had vanished and the three cups of coffee had cleared the haze. Charlie set aside the two applicants whose checks had set off alarm bells. She'd press a little harder on those after lunch, but first she had a more personal investigation to pursue.

The surveillance room was a vivid cave of darkened lights and bright video feeds that would have devastated her sore head an hour before, but she was ready for it now. Eli, one of the security guards, was stationed in the room but he was working a crossword puzzle. If the resort were up and running, Charlie would've read him the riot act, but right now he was a bit superfluous.

"Hey, Eli. Why don't you get out of here? Make the

rounds of all the current construction areas just so they know you're around."

"Got it," he said, giving her a quick nod of deference. Sometimes security guys could get shitty and macho about working for a young woman, but she'd managed to assemble a good team so far. She didn't know how long that would last, though. Dawn's disrespect would start filtering down. Charlie had to figure out what was going on with that woman and stop it before it spread.

Once Eli was gone, Charlie called up the video feed for the corridor that led to her studio on the first floor. Her place was near the elevators for easy access, so the camera was only a few yards from her door.

She fast-forwarded, flying through hours of video. When the tape showed 11:05 p.m., Dawn appeared in the hallway, and Charlie slowed the tape. She wasn't the least bit surprised to see Dawn knock on her door, then knock again. She was surprised to see her try the doorknob, as if Charlie would leave her place unlocked, or, more importantly, that she'd be okay with her boss opening her door uninvited.

When the door didn't budge, Dawn stared down at the knob for a long while. She glared at it, then turned to look directly up at the camera.

The skin on Charlie's arms drew tight as goose bumps sprang to life.

On the video, Dawn frowned and then walked away. Charlie backed up the tape and paused it.

This wasn't the kind of video they used at the local

convenience store. This was crisp and digital. She could clearly see the tightness around Dawn's eyes. The furtive line of her mouth.

Charlie stared her down.

People were always surprised that Charlie was in security, but these days it wasn't about big, burly guys with concealed handguns. Well, it wasn't *only* about them, though they certainly had their place in the ecosystem. These days it was more about prevention than enforcement. Charlie could read people. She could anticipate. She could pick up on interference that disturbed the flow of normal traffic. On small tells that revealed intentions.

She'd lost a little confidence in her own intuition after the setup in Tahoe, but it didn't take much skill to read Dawn's thoughts. That glance was irritation and arrogance, not with Charlie, but with the camera. She was clearly thinking, *If only that stupid camera wasn't there, I could use my master key to get inside.*

What Charlie couldn't see on Dawn's face was why. *Why?* Yes, Charlie had met Dawn's husband for drinks one evening, but if Dawn was going to be that paranoid about Charlie being a femme fatale, why had she recruited her for the job? It made no sense. None of it did.

They'd been close in high school, despite their different interests. Charlie had filled her time with volleyball and track and tutoring, and Dawn had been student council president and head of the honor society and in charge of half the student volunteer organizations. But they'd had something in common, she and Dawn and

Sandra and a few other overachievers: none of them had been popular with boys. While other girls had been out drinking beer around bonfires with horny teenage cowboys, Dawn and Charlie and their group had usually been at school. They'd shared running jokes about saving themselves for marriage. They'd assured each other that those party girls were going nowhere fast. They'd shaken their heads at the bad judgment.

But they'd also secretly yearned. Charlie had, at least. She'd tutored those boys in the library after school. Sometimes she'd even gone to their houses to sit in their rooms with them. But she'd never been in danger of being led astray. She was just Charlie. One of the guys. Another runner on the track team. Taller than most of them and flatter-chested, too. They'd hung out with her. They'd asked if they could copy her homework. They'd shoved her on the shoulder when they joked. And then they'd sidled away to flirt with the fun girls.

So she'd claimed not to want anything to do with them and their restless hands and crude mouths, but boy, had she imagined!

Luckily, when she'd gotten to college, she'd found a new role. A new group of friends. She'd assumed Dawn had, too. But all Dawn seemed to have gotten was more uptight.

Charlie shook her head and unpaused the video. Shoulders tight, she scanned the remaining hours, but nothing else happened. Tears sprang to her eyes.

Her instincts had failed her in Tahoe, but she wasn't

going to let them fail her here. Dawn was jealous, that was all. Maybe Dawn's husband had made a stupid comment about Charlie's ass or something. Maybe Dawn had just expected Charlie to be the same harmless tomboy she'd known in high school. Whatever the reason, it was Dawn's issue. Charlie wasn't going to get sucked into it. Dawn had started spying on her, commenting on Charlie's comings and goings, implying she was a man-stealing slut, so Charlie had moved out. End of story.

She wouldn't be paranoid and scared. She wouldn't turn into one of those people who was carried along by life, tumbled over and knocked around every time the current got too fast. Like her mother, who could never grab on to anything, could never find a handhold.

No. Charlie would work hard. She'd let the scandal in Tahoe die down. She'd pay off her legal bills. And then she'd find a job somewhere else. Anywhere else. Just not at the Meridian Resort.

But for today, just having her apartment at the Stud Farm was enough. She felt a little stronger. A little more herself. She'd hit rock bottom, but she was on her way back up now, and she'd be damned if she'd leave the best parts of herself behind.

CHAPTER FIVE

"GODDAMN IT!" the ranch foreman yelled. "Pull!"

Walker wrapped the rope more tightly around his wrist, took it in both hands and hauled as hard as he could as the heifer struggled and fought against the mud. The slick goo must have felt like a predator's mouth tugging her deeper in, and her eyes rolled in wild panic. Walker pulled harder, urging the other men on when they wanted to stop. The poor girl was going to freeze to death if they didn't get her out. Granted, she was destined for the packing plant in a year or two, but there was no reason for her to go like this, cold and shaking and scared.

"Fuck this," the hand next to him muttered.

"She's almost there," Walker said, getting a new grip on the rope. Actually, she seemed to be slipping deeper, but he wasn't going to give up. "Come on. One more good haul should get her." In the end, it took three more hauls, but they pulled her free. She stumbled a few feet, then went to her knees.

There wasn't anything out here to clean her off with, and the ranch was a mile away, so Walker swept his gloved hand down her flank, over and over, sluicing off the thick mud. Her big body shook under his hands, but her panicked lowing had stopped. By the time he stood and went to his horse to grab a blanket, she was breathing almost normally. She struggled to her feet and took a few steps toward him.

"Well, look at that," one of the cowboys crowed. "You really do have a way with the ladies."

The younger one laughed. "I've heard they follow you around like cats in heat, but damn, I'd never heard anything about heifers."

Walker laughed off the jokes and took the blanket over to scrub some warmth into the cow. It only took a few moments before she was alert enough to jerk away from his ministrations and trot back to the herd. Hopefully she'd stick close to the others and the collective body heat would do the rest.

"All right," the foreman snapped. "Move 'em on the last mile, and come collect your pay." He trotted off without a word of thanks.

They remounted and spread out to move the herd on. Once they got them going, the older cowboy rode closer. "Mr. Kingham is a real asshole, but the trail work with the guests is okay if you can get hired on at the lodge. Heard you was looking for work."

Walker glanced at the guy. His name was Tom, but Walker didn't know more about him than that. "Where'd you hear that?"

"Well, you're here, aren't you?" He tipped his chin toward the foreman. "He asked me to keep an eye on you, see how you did. Too many years at one of these dude ranches can make for a soft cowboy."

"You think?"

Tom shrugged. "Teaching pretty ladies how to ride?" He shot Walker an arch look, but he smiled and shook his head when Walker met it with a straight face. "Hey, I'm not saying there's anything wrong with it. Just saying if you're used to having a warm woman at hand, it might make it harder to face a cold night on the range."

"Yeah, well. They bring their own sets of problems."

"Don't I know it? Anyway, the back end of the operation is pretty quiet. No guests out here. Obviously Kingham's not 'customer service oriented.'"

"Yeah, I worked here ten years ago. Kingham wasn't here, but I know they only use a few dozen head of cattle in the guest areas and keeps the rest of the work behind the scenes."

"Well, you don't seem soft. I'll put in a good word."

"Thanks." Walker was thankful, but not as thrilled as he should've been at the prospect of a permanent job. Maybe Tom was right. Maybe he had gotten soft. He looked toward the distant buildings of the guest ranch almost hidden in the long evening shadows cast by the hills. But they weren't headed there. The working side of the ranch had its own outbuildings and trailers. The guest ranch was only an attractive outbranch of an operation that ran two thousand head of cattle every year.

It'd be good work, but Walker's heart fell. He'd gotten used to being around people. Ten or fifteen cowhands, the whole staff of the lodge, the clients: moms and dads and lots of kids. And yes, the occasionally group of raucous ladies looking for a mountain adventure.

Working at a dude ranch was a hell of a lot of fun.

This assignment, on the other hand… Well, shit. At least he could go back to his own place every night. That, and the steady income was probably the best he could say about it.

Freezing rain hit his hat in a slow patter before it picked up to a steady drizzle. The rain left him feeling even more defeated. Apparently he could've just left the damn heifer wet and muddy, because she was about to get that way again.

Turning his collar up, he concentrated on edging in a few cattle who were trying to break off from the herd. Soon enough, he was tracking mud and water into his truck and leaving for home, his pay for the day's work stuffed into his pocket. He'd earn another few bucks tomorrow. It wasn't comfortable, but it was something. He'd rather not dip into his savings any more than he had to.

Body aching from the cold, Walker cranked up the heat in the truck, then cranked up his favorite George Strait album, as well. No point dwelling on his problems. If he'd wanted stability, he'd chosen the wrong career. At least it came with damn good music.

He was just settling into a good fantasy about the scalding shower he was about to take when his cell phone rang, and his fantasy morphed to something else.

Maybe what he needed was a shower and a beer and a woman in his bed. He pulled the phone from his pocket, already wondering which old friend it could be. Granted, in the past few years, most of his lovers had been brief hookups with ranch visitors, but there were always a few—

His fantasy of a quiet night of good sex died when he saw the display.

Nicole.

Apparently she'd let go of her anger. But Walker hadn't let go of his, if that's what it was. Anger at her, maybe, or just at himself. He'd been stupid enough to mess around with another man's wife. That didn't mean he had to make it worse.

He declined the call and slipped the phone back into his pocket. A shower and a beer and his hand, then. Good enough. And a hell of a lot smarter than a bad-news woman.

He was so tired by the time he pulled up to the apartment, his hand would've been the only good choice, regardless. He'd never been the kind of guy to get off and go straight to sleep. Taking care of a woman the right way was hard work, and he didn't have it in him tonight.

He took a deep breath and closed his eyes for a moment. Normally, he'd never have gotten into his truck covered in mud, but there'd been no bunkhouse washroom to clean up in. And he couldn't face cleaning off his floor mats tonight. Or the seat. And tomorrow would likely be just as muddy. He'd take care of it when the job was done.

A knock on the window startled him out of his stupor. He rolled down the window and was surprised to see Charlie's face a few inches from his.

"Hey, cowboy!" She held both hands over her head as if to shield herself from the few raindrops still falling.

A smile stole immediately over his mouth. "Hey, Charlie. What are you doing out?"

"Heading to the saloon. Are you coming over?"

His gaze slipped to the porch of the saloon as he reached for the door. Charlie hopped back as he eased the door open and got out. He stretched his back. Yet again, he found himself turning down a good time. "I'm sorry. I'm beat. I need a shower as soon as possible. And then bed." He cleared his throat, knowing what he meant by bed and telling himself she couldn't have any idea.

Her eyes swept down his body. "You are kind of a mess. You look like..."

"I've been wrestling cattle in the mud?"

"Something like that." Her eyes lingered on the mud smeared across his shirt. "So shower and then come play."

Come play. Jesus, did she say that kind of thing on purpose? "I wish I could."

"Aw. Are you really too tired?" Her little smirk was a challenge. He wanted to accept it.

He found himself leaning a little closer before remembering that he smelled like horse and mud and sweat. "I'd love to. But after I take a shower, I won't be able to talk myself into going back out in the cold."

"Well, I can't fault that, I guess. But I won't lie. After the day I had, I'd be willing to dare a lot of discomfort for a drink."

"Trouble in paradise?" he asked.

Charlie opened her mouth; then her eyes swept down his body again and she shook her head. "All right. I wasn't exactly wrestling cattle in the mud. I suppose I'll recover from the office politics."

"Hell, Charlie. Any redneck can wrestle a cow. Put me in a room with computers and the kind of work you do, and I'd look like a trapped bear."

A wide smile spread slowly over her face. "I admit, I can't imagine you dressed in creased pants and sitting at a computer."

"Aw, shit, darlin'. Nobody can. That's why I'll never be anything but a dirty cowboy."

"Nothing wrong with that," she purred. "Hard work is a beautiful thing, Walker Pearce. It really is."

"Jesus, Charlie," he said, huffing out a shocked laugh.

"Go on and take your shower. Get cleaned up and maybe I'll take pity on you and bring you a beer later."

"Ha. I'll be sure not to still be in a towel, then."

"Don't get all dressed up on my account." With that, she sauntered off toward the saloon, her ass a sweet, swinging demand for attention.

Suddenly, Walker wasn't half so tired. In fact, he felt

like a man who'd just gotten home from a two-week vacation. Or so he assumed. He'd never had more than a few days off at a time, but one thing he'd learned was how to jam a hell of a lot of good time into a quick moment. Maybe he could put that skill to use tonight.

He forgot all about his muddy truck and headed inside.

CHAPTER SIX

THIS DEFINITELY WASN'T the Charlie he'd known in high school. That Charlie had been comfortable and low-key and studious. This Charlie was sitting on a man's lap at the bar, leading the whole damn room in a sing-along of "I've Got Friends in Low Places."

Walker shook his head in shock, but he was smiling when he headed toward the bar. He tipped his hat when she looked up.

"Oh, my God! Walker!" She hopped off the stranger's lap and hurried over to hug Walker. He couldn't say he minded. "I thought you were too tired to come down?"

"I decided I didn't want to miss the fun."

"We're just getting started."

He raised an eyebrow. "This is you just getting started?"

"Oh, sure. I've got *hours* of fun left in me, Walker. I could go all night."

Yeah, she was definitely doing this on purpose. And now that he was clean and scrubbed, he could lean as close as he wanted. "When did you turn into such a flirt, Ms. Allington?"

"I've always been a flirt."

"Liar. You never flirted with me. I would've noticed."

She threw back her head and laughed, drawing his gaze to the long curve of her neck. "You wouldn't have noticed in a million years, Walker."

"I would have. You smart girls didn't flirt with me, so it would have been memorable."

"I guess we were too smart to get pulled into trouble with boys like you."

"Exactly. So what happened?"

Her hand curled around his arm as she edged close enough to speak into his ear. "Now we're smart enough to know exactly the kind of trouble we want."

He couldn't sleep with her. He couldn't. And she was just flirting anyway. It meant nothing more to her than sitting on that other guy's lap had. But, God, his heartbeat picked up at the thought. Charlie. Sweet, smart Charlie, filling his head with images of sex. It was wrong. And more than a little intimidating.

She was way smarter than he was. Always had been and always would be. She'd been a great tutor, but his skin still prickled in fear at the memory of having to write in front of her, concentrating so hard at shaping the letters the right way and spelling everything correctly. Damn embarrassing that the only girl he'd had to do schoolwork in front of had also been the smartest girl he'd known.

He'd hated every moment of it, but her kindness had made it easier to make a fool of himself in front of her.

Despite all that, she still seemed to like him. And he'd never have to do homework in front of her again.

Charlie pressed a beer into his hand.

He tried to give it back. "I'm not drinking your beer."

"I've got a whole pitcher. I'm a big girl, but I can't drink that much on my own."

"I suppose. You are tall, but not as tall as you used to be."

"That's because you kept getting bigger and bigger. I like that. Have you ever stopped growing, Walker?"

This time, when she pressed the beer into his hand, he took it. And downed it in two gulps. He could handle this. He could. It was just good-hearted fun, like flirting with any other woman.

"Come on." She took his hand and tugged him toward the corner of the bar. "Rayleen's having trouble getting a clear view of your ass and she's giving me the evil eye."

Sure enough, when he turned around, Rayleen gave him an irritated wave, urging him closer.

"Hey, Rayleen," he said when he got within earshot. And eyeshot.

"Hey, nothing. Ain't that your dirty little piece over there?"

"What?" He looked down for a moment, then over at Charlie, but she shrugged.

"No, there," Rayleen said, pointing toward the pool table area.

When Walker's eyes focused on the far side of the

saloon, he was hit with a rush of alarm. Several waves of panic fell on him at once, flooding his body with adrenaline.

First, that Nicole was here. Second, that she was glaring at him. And third, that someone who shouldn't know anything about her knew more than enough.

He spun back to stare wide-eyed at Rayleen, but the old woman just shrugged. "A dog shouldn't shit where it sleeps," she offered. Nice imagery, but not exactly helpful.

Charlie's head turned from Rayleen to him and he winced.

"Romantic troubles?" she asked.

No. Not romantic. "Fuck," he cursed, inadvertently correcting Charlie's words as he scrubbed a hand over his beard.

Charlie rolled her eyes. "Oh, is that all?"

When she laughed, he shot her a pained smile. She wasn't offended. But she would be if she found out the details. "Pardon me," he said, hesitating for only one second before he turned away.

For a moment, he was disoriented, looking for Nicole and not finding her. Maybe she'd gone. His gaze dropped. Or maybe she was standing right in front of him, her arms crossed over her admittedly nice chest.

He cleared his throat and slid his eyes toward the door. "What are you doing here?"

"Having a drink," she snapped, tossing her straight blond hair with a twitch of her head.

"Right." He stepped forward, edging her away from

Charlie and the rest of his friends. "But there's plenty to drink at the ranch."

"But no good company these days."

"Slow season," he said.

"That's not what I mean and you know it." Her eyes shifted. "Who's that?" she bit out, tipping her chin toward the bar. He didn't have to ask who she meant. "Your new bed warmer?"

"Nicole." He sighed. "I don't want to argue about that. You're married."

"Right. That didn't stop you from kissing or touching but now it's your excuse for ignoring me?"

Shit. He tried to sneak a look over his shoulder toward Charlie. She caught his eye and offered a sympathetic wince. "I'm sorry. Really. I've been busy. I'm scrambling for work."

"Maybe I could help get you hired on somewhere. If—"

"I don't think that's a good idea," he interrupted. "It's already complicated enough." He glanced around the room and saw enough eyes on them to make him squirm. "As a matter of fact, why don't we talk outside?"

"Don't want to be seen with me?"

"Jesus, Nicole. You have a husband!"

She shrugged. "As if he cares."

"He cared enough to fire me, apparently."

Mouth tight with anger, she finally said, "Fine," and headed toward the door. Walker followed, wondering if the back of his neck was as red as it felt. Thankfully he still hadn't gotten that haircut.

Why the hell had she come here and drawn attention to both of them? At least he didn't have to wonder what the town knew anymore. Everybody suspected. If they hadn't before, they certainly would now.

He almost started down the sidewalk to take her to his apartment, but the idiocy of that struck him before he hit the first step. The porch of the Crooked R wasn't exactly private, but twilight had settled in and it was cold enough that no one else had taken a seat on any of the ancient bar stools.

She bumped into him when he changed directions and headed for one end of the porch. "Don't you live right there?"

"I do," he said, and left it at that.

For a moment, he thought she was going to explode. Her jaw clenched, her eyes narrowed and she drew in a deep breath. Walker braced himself for some of the cursing he'd heard her aim at her husband during fights. But in the end, she let the breath out slowly and paced to the railing to look out at the street.

"You're treating me like shit, you know. I know I'm not your girlfriend, and I know I'm married, but how can you just walk away from me like I'm nothing?"

"I'm sorry," he said, and meant it. "I don't want to make you feel bad. I just…"

"I'm lonely, Walker. My husband and I aren't talking, and you're the only one who ever treated me as more than the owner's wife. It's a hundred times worse now. People don't know if they should even be nice to me."

"We shouldn't have done what we did. What we were thinking about doing. If he thinks we—"

"Oh, please. Like he doesn't cheat? Everyone knows that black-haired bimbo who stays in the Settler's Cabin every July isn't there to get in touch with nature. Jesus Christ, last summer she didn't even bother with one trail ride. Do you all think I'm an idiot?"

"Ah." Walker swallowed hard, glad she was facing away from him. Yeah, they'd all known. It was part of the justification he'd given himself for messing with her in the first place. "So why don't you just get divorced?"

Her back stiffened. "Why don't I get divorced? Really? I like how you say that as if it never would've occurred to me."

He shrugged. "Well?"

"You want the truth? My husband wants me around to raise his kids and I stay because of the prenup. Lovely, isn't it?"

He didn't understand rich folks. Wouldn't she rather be free and a little poorer? "You can leave, Nicole. Just move on. I'm sure you love your stepkids, but they have a mom. You could start over."

She turned to face him. "I don't want to start over. I just want what I had. A nice house. A pretty life. And you, Walker. You were always around when I needed you." She smiled. That sweet little smile she used when she wanted something. "It would be good between us. You know it would."

Well, hell. Yes, it'd be good, but he couldn't say he'd ever had *bad* sex, per se. You got what you put in, as far as he could tell, like most things in life. "Yes, it'd be good, but… It's not right. I'm sorry. I don't mean to treat you badly. I thought it was just about convenience for you. You were bored. I was there. But if your husband suspects…" *If everyone suspects…* "It's silly, I guess, but a man has to have some standards."

"Some standards, huh? Real nice, Walker."

"I'm not talking about you! I'm not one of those guys. We were both there, together, doing the same thing. I'm just talking about myself. For whatever reason, it seemed harmless for a while, a few kisses, some fantasies…but I don't want to take it further."

"You damn sure did that night in the tack room."

Walker took off his hat and ran a hand through his hair, trying to scrub away the panic that raced through his head at the memory. Yeah. He'd already shoved up her skirt and unzipped his pants when someone had walked past the tack room door. He'd thought his heart was going to jump out of his chest in that moment, waiting for whoever it was to open that unlocked door and expose them. It had only taken him a few seconds to zip back up and straighten her clothes and then feel damn grateful they'd been interrupted. Nicole hadn't been so thankful.

She crossed her arms, her hands gripping her own elbows as if she was trying to find a little security. "I miss you," she whispered.

Oh, God. What was he supposed to say to that? He

couldn't be cruel. "You're lonely, Nicole. You should leave the ranch. Find something else."

"No." Her hands squeezed harder.

"Well, I can't be your big distraction from your life."

Her hands still squeezed her elbows, but she tried that sweet smile again. "Why not? You're so good at it, Walker. You're fun."

Yeah, he was fun, all right. A lot of fun. "I know. But that fun got me fired and it's making it hard to find new work."

She finally let herself go and moved closer to touch his arm. "I'm sorry. Really. Let me help. Maybe… maybe I can get you hired on back at the ranch."

"No way. I can't work there now, knowing what everyone's thinking."

"No one knows anything! It will be fine, and I'll get to see you every day. I'll talk to—"

Walker cut her off. "I can't."

She nodded, but her face went tight and there was no missing the way her eyes glistened. "So you just never want to see me again?"

"Come on. I didn't say that. And you can call anytime you want to talk."

"Talking isn't really what this is about. I don't want to *talk*."

Right. That wasn't what she wanted from him. It wasn't what anyone wanted. "Thanks for being honest."

She rolled her eyes. "Why do you have to be this way? When we're alone, everything is fine. As soon as I leave, you start regretting what we both want. Just take me to your place and fuck me, Walker. You told me you didn't want to do it because you worked for my husband. Because it was his house and his ranch. But none of that applies anymore and I want you."

A tiny part of his brain was telling him it didn't matter. He might as well. Everyone suspected they'd been fooling around already. Hell, even Charlie knew now. She was probably getting an earful at this very second. So what did it matter?

A bigger part of his brain told him to sit down and shut up. "I can't. I'm sorry," he said softly.

"You'll regret this. You'll miss me. Give it another week." She turned away, her hair flying out in a bright arc when she spun to stalk off the porch. Walker let her go, relieved that the conversation was done. He should have been up front in the first place, instead of trying to avoid her. But hell, he'd assumed their friendship would just die its natural death. Done. Over. He hadn't expected her to demand her due.

He'd liked Nicole at first. He'd been flattered by her attention. He'd gotten caught up in the thrill of flirting with the boss's hot wife.

Damn it.

He collapsed onto one of the outdoor bar stools and set his hat on another. For a moment, he stayed like that, head in hands, lost in indecision.

He shouldn't have come to the saloon and he damn sure didn't want to be there now, but he had to go back in. Otherwise, the story would end with him leaving the bar with Nicole and not returning.

Suddenly he was a hundred times more tired than he'd been an hour earlier. A thousand times.

But he stood, put on his hat, pasted a smile on his face and walked back into the saloon.

"You came back!" Charlie said as soon as he was in earshot.

"I never left."

Rayleen watched him with sharp eyes, but for once she didn't say a word.

He grabbed a beer but only drank half of it before he shook his head. "Listen, I'm exhausted. I'm gonna go fall into bed."

Charlie cocked her head and studied him for a moment. "All right. Walk me home? I'm tired, too."

Was she trying to catch him in a lie? Did she think Nicole was waiting at his apartment? "A few minutes ago, you were leading the whole crowd in a song. You said you could go for hours."

"I guess I was wrong. That level of awesomeness apparently wears a girl out."

He could hardly say no to walking a woman home after dark, even if it was only across the parking lot. She had him roped with that one. "I'd be happy to walk you home, Charlie."

"Let's go."

Before they took two steps, Rayleen called, "Where are you going, Ms. Thang?"

"Beauty sleep!" Charlie shouted back. "And I have to rest up for the weekend. I've got men to hunt."

Rayleen howled with laughter. "Keep me in the loop. I'll help you tag 'em."

Walker couldn't believe it. "That woman doesn't like anyone, not even her own flesh and blood."

"Aw. Everyone likes me, Walker. After all, what's not to like?"

His eyes fell to the dip of her collar and the faint rise of her cleavage. "Not a lot."

"Are you calling me flat-chested?"

His gaze flew up to meet hers as he pushed open the saloon door. "No! What?"

She didn't bother answering, she just swept by him with a gorgeous laugh, the scent of something crisp and flowery trailing behind her.

"Who was that woman?" she asked as she stepped off the porch stairs and headed toward the street.

"A friend."

"Oh, playing coy. Is she a girlfriend?"

"No."

"Is there someone else?"

"Nope."

"Walker Pearce with no woman? That's rare. I should make a move quick."

She was teasing again. Pressing him. He should call her on it to scare her off. But in his current mood, he didn't want to scare her off.

He'd been caught up in the idea that she wasn't the same girl she'd been in high school. It had so confused him that he hadn't put time into figuring out who she was now.

She wasn't that sweet, studious girl, obviously. Now she was a successful businesswoman, bold and beautiful and wild. Exactly the kind of woman he was attracted to. And exactly the kind who saw him for what he was: a big, dumb ride to adventure.

He felt a little calmer now. A little less worried or maybe only worn-out from his conversation with Nicole. But he was also kind of pissed, and there was just enough adrenaline left in his veins to make him horny. And just enough regret to make him want to forget his mistakes.

Walker didn't know what to do with a sweet, innocent girl, but this new Charlie? Yeah, he could deal with that.

"Are you okay?" she asked, her arm nudging his as they turned and headed up the walk to the Stud Farm. "You still look tense. Did she give you trouble?"

"Not too much."

"I guess you're used to it."

He tightened his jaw. "Mm."

"Even in school, some girl was always mad at you. You sure do cause trouble, Walker."

"Yeah." He shot her a dark look as he opened the door of the building. "You looking for trouble, Charlie?"

Her small smile bloomed into a wicked grin. "You sound like you don't quite believe I am."

"I guess you've changed."

"I have changed," she said as he followed her up the stairs. "I hope you're not disappointed. You might have liked that innocent, careful girl, but I can tell you from experience that being innocent gets a little lonely. And being careful doesn't actually... Well. Never mind. You, on the other hand..."

He couldn't tell if she was deliberately putting more swing into her hips or if that exaggerated sway was the result of her ass rising to eye level as she took the stairs. All he knew was that in that moment, her heels and tight jeans and sleek curves conspired to melt his brain into a pile of horny mush. Goddamn, he wanted to see that ass naked.

She stopped on the landing and turned to face him. "You were never, ever lonely, were you?"

Walker took the last step and looked down at Charlie. "I'm lonely tonight."

Her eyes went wide in a brief moment of shock. He waited for her to laugh then. Waited for her to change her mind and say *Oh, Walker, I could never do that with you. Not like this. We're friends.*

But she didn't say that. Instead her gray eyes sparkled. Her lips parted so she could draw a shallow breath. "Are you?" she whispered.

"Don't I look lonely?" He stepped forward. Charlie stepped back. They played it out a few more times until she was against the wall and he was standing over her.

Now all of her breaths were shallow. She looked up at him with the faintest little smile on her parted lips. Her hands rose to rest on his chest, and the touch spread hot zings of awareness through his shirt.

"You don't have to be lonely, Walker," she whispered, tipping her mouth up so her words chased over his jaw. "I'm right…" She rose on her toes, and her hips brushed against his. "Here."

He dipped his head and caught her mouth and he forgot to be mad about being a big, dumb ride. He'd be that for Charlie all damn night if she wanted.

THIS WAS A moment she'd considered many, many times in her youth. Walker Pearce leaning slowly down, his hands drifting to her hips to hold her steady, his mouth brushing faintly over hers. In her imagination, her heart had pounded just like this. Her nipples had tightened the same way they did now. But other than that, every-thing was different.

It wasn't the sweet, tentative kiss her teenage mind had painted, some gentle version of romance that had never existed for the boys. Walker's mouth was hot against hers and his beard brushed soft against her skin. His lips pressed hers until they opened, and then his tongue stroked her. He tasted…right.

His hands were on her hips, yes, but they were so much bigger than she'd imagined, the strength of them holding her in a steady grip that pressed her to the wall.

The brim of his hat drew sunset around them. They might have been in the stairway of the building, but it felt like complete privacy as she licked at his tongue and sighed at the feeling of him pressing his body to hers.

It didn't matter that they were in public. Her eyes were closed, the lights had dimmed and Walker

Pearce's cock was hard and pressed to her. Just like that, she wasn't his buddy anymore. She was a body he wanted to be inside. Strange to find herself fighting for that. To be objectified. Seen as someone worth using. But it was honest, at least. She could trust what Walker wanted from her.

She tilted her hips toward him and took his tongue deeper, twining her fingers behind his neck to pull him down. He was so big, tall and solid and curved above her. For the first time in her life, Charlie felt small. It made her want to whimper and go to her knees for him. Or maybe that was just her reaction to his taste.

"Mmm," she hummed against his mouth. He answered by sliding his hands up her sides, then back down again. His fingers pressed briefly into the curve of her hips, as if he liked the shape of her.

Then he reached up, drew off his hat and tossed it in the general direction of his door. She was suddenly plunged back into the exposure of being on the bright upstairs landing. But Walker ducked his head and put his mouth to her neck and she didn't care.

Oh, God, that felt sweet. His hot mouth and hard teeth and the soft warmth of his beard on her skin. Charlie tipped her head back and let him have his way with the sensitive skin of her throat.

"That feels so good," she moaned. He pressed his hips harder to her. "Oh, that, too."

He chuckled against her neck, sparking waves of delicious vibrations that twined through her body. She felt suddenly aware of her hard nipples and the pleasure drawing the nerves between her legs tight. She felt her pulse beating through her entire body. She felt it speeding for Walker.

Unable to control herself, she slid her hands over his shoulders, his arms, down his chest…and everywhere she touched he was solid, hard man. Nothing soft about him. Nothing yielding. She plucked at the top button of his shirt, then the next, and now her fingers were touching warm curls of dark hair. When his teeth scraped over her neck, Charlie moaned, already overwhelmed by so many lovely sensations.

She unfastened the next button, and the one after that. Then she pulled his shirt free of his jeans and spread it open so she could glide her hands over his hairy chest.

He eased back so he could look down and watch as her fingers explored every muscle on his chest. "God," he growled. "Maybe…" He gave his head a slow shake, then tried again. "Maybe we should go inside?"

She nodded, but the spicy scent of him was too much to resist. She pressed her open mouth to his collarbone and tasted his skin. Every cell inside her seemed to sigh with relief, as if she'd been craving this taste her whole life. It was just so damn *right*. His skin and hair and soap and the faint, delicious tang of sweat. This was the chemistry that had driven her to those slightly blurry, not-quite-dirty fantasies about him in high school. She didn't know if it was the same for him, but she could package the smell of him and live on it for weeks.

"Charlie," he groaned, throwing his head back as

she slipped her open mouth up his throat. "Let's go inside." But his hands roamed restlessly over her back as he pulled her tight against his erection.

Oh, man. That was something she wanted to taste. But…

"We can't have sex," she whispered.

"Yeah. Absolutely. Let's just… What?"

She smiled against his neck. "Well, we *can*. And quite easily, judging by how wet I am right now." His throat clenched beneath her mouth as he choked on her words. "But we won't. Not this time."

"What?" he repeated, the word still a syllable of drowsy confusion.

She finally leaned back a little to look up at him. "I want to savor you, Walker. Don't you think you deserve to be savored?"

"I… No? Or maybe. I don't know what you mean."

"Come on." She tugged him toward his door. "I've waited a long time for this. I don't want it all over in just a few minutes."

"Hey, that's not how it'll be."

She giggled and grabbed his hat off the floor. His door wasn't locked, so she just led him through and tugged him over to the couch. "Come on. Let's make out."

Confused as he might be, he was delightfully cooperative. He dropped right onto the couch and reached for her. Charlie plopped his hat onto her head and straddled him.

"Make out, huh?" he murmured.

"Sure." Her words got caught in her throat when his hands cupped her breasts, but she soldiered on. "When was the last time you just had some nice, innocent fun with a girl? Don't you think it would be good?"

He smiled and thumbed her nipples. "Innocent? I'm not sure I can remember."

"Mmm." Eyes closed, she arched into his hands, loving the way her nipples got harder under his attention, as though her body wanted him to know it approved. As if they were showing off to reward him. She was actually glad now that they hadn't done this in high school. Back then, she'd felt overwhelmingly inadequate about her body. Embarrassed by her lack of curves and her A-cup breasts. But now as he eased her shirt up, she helped take it off. His hat tumbled off her head. She hardly noticed.

Charlie didn't try to hide behind her hands when he unclasped her bra. No. Now she opened her eyes and watched his face as her bra slid down her arms.

Yes, one thing she'd learned was that men liked breasts. Big or small, it didn't matter to most. They just liked the round shape of them, and the hard, flushed nipples, and they liked to— "Oh," she gasped as his mouth closed over one nipple and sucked. Yes, they liked that most of all. Sucking and licking and biting.

She groaned his name, egging him on, and he responded in the exact right way, sucking harder. His mouth drew pleasure through her body, pulling everything tight. He'd feel so good inside her right now.

He'd feel so good she could barely comprehend that she wasn't going to let him fill her up.

But she had a first-night rule. Not because she hesitated to put out. Not because she worried about her reputation. But because she'd found a night of making out was a good judge of a man's skill in bed. Weeding them out before penetration kept her numbers low. Or lowish. She didn't need love or even commitment to enjoy sex, but she did need a halfway decent chance that she'd leave satisfied. That was just logical.

Still working her with his mouth, Walker gripped her hips and pressed her down so she was snug against his cock. They both grunted slightly at the shock of pleasure.

"You really don't want to have sex?" he asked, pressing his hips up.

She shivered at the way his words cooled her wet nipple. When he pressed his hips up again, she groaned. He was so hard for her. "No sex. But I do want to have a little fun."

"Seems like a halfway decent time so far, but maybe I'm being led astray by the breasts." He pressed a soft kiss to each one.

"Mm. Let's make it even more fun." She eased away, sliding backward to rest her weight on his knees. He didn't try to stop her, he just watched, with what seemed like fascination, as she unbuckled his belt.

She got the first two buttons of his jeans open, then paused for a moment to enjoy the image of him with his dark blue shirt spread wide and his pants only half-fastened. His nearly black chest hair tapered down into a tantalizing trail that dipped beneath his briefs. "You are a fucking treat, Walker."

"You're not so bad yourself." He thumbed one of her nipples, making her suck in a breath. The slightest touch from him was enough to make her swoon. This was going to be fun.

She eased his shirt off his shoulders. When she opened the rest of the buttons of his jeans, she brushed her knuckles against the erection that strained at his dark gray briefs. "Mm. That's nice."

A dark laugh huffed from his throat. "Thanks."

"You seem a little tense, though."

"I am."

"Would this help?" She snuck beneath the band of his underwear and wrapped her fist around his cock. When she realized he was exactly as thick as he seemed, adrenaline burst into her blood like fireworks.

"Fuck. Yes. That helps."

Wanting to see exactly what she was handling, she tugged at his jeans and he helped by raising his hips enough for her to slide all that annoying material down a few inches. When his cock sprang free from his underwear, Charlie had to close her eyes for a few moments and breathe. Once she'd steeled herself, she opened her eyes and looked again.

"Jesus Christ, Walker. That is one beautiful cock."

"You like it?"

She could tell by his voice that he was smiling, so she wrapped her hand around it and gave it a careful squeeze. His cock jumped in her hand and his gasp made clear he wasn't aiming an arrogant smile at her anymore. Not that he didn't have the right. He was a work of art, long and thick and straight.

Regret stabbed her in the chest. If she'd just kept her mouth shut about not having sex, she could ride this cowboy until her ass muscles cramped. But now she'd be damned if she'd let him think he'd talked her into anything.

She had to be strong. She had to resist its lure. But saying no to this man's penis was damn difficult.

She stroked him and felt his muscles shudder under her. "Why don't you tell me what *you* like? Does that feel good?"

"Yes," he said as she stroked. Now he was the one who had to close his eyes.

"Like this?" She slid her hand all the way up, then back down again. "Or faster, like this?" Shortening her strokes, she watched his head fall back on the couch.

"Oh, God. Like that. What you're doing now. Just…"

She did as he asked, watching his face when she wasn't staring at his cock. Her hand looked pale and small against the flushed, dusky skin.

Smiling, she looked up to see that he'd recovered enough to watch now, and he seemed transfixed by the sight of her jerking him off. He spread his fingers over her thighs, and they pressed into her flesh every time her fist stroked toward the base of his cock.

"God, that feels good. Charlie…." He looked up then and met her gaze, and there was none of the old playful Walker left. His blue eyes glowed with lust, the skin over his cheekbones was tight and flushed. "Keep going," he said when she started to slow. "Just like that. Don't stop."

Her smile fell away and she nodded, still locked with his gaze as she stroked him.

"Don't stop."

"You want to come like this?" she whispered. "You want to come for me?"

His jaw clenched. His eyelids fluttered for just a moment and she saw his gaze fall to her bare breasts. "Yes. Fuck yes." His big hand slid up to her breast and he pinched her nipple and rolled it carefully between his thumb and finger.

Charlie gasped and faltered for a moment, but his other hand covered hers and he set her back on the rhythm he wanted, not letting go until she had it right. It was harder to concentrate now, with his fingers rolling pleasure into her, but she frowned and tried her best.

His breath sounded shaky now, and precome leaked beneath her fingers, so she squeezed him a little harder, ignoring the way her tired muscles whimpered. She was rewarded with a shuddering gasp. His hips pressed up.

She wanted to take him into her mouth. She wanted to strip off her pants and mount him. She couldn't do just this. She needed to feel that cock inside her. Her rules didn't matter. And her pride was idiotic. She—

"Oh, fuck," he ground out past clenched teeth.

"Charlie…" And then he was pulsing in her hand, his come shooting out onto his belly with every jerk of his cock.

Charlie was breathing almost as hard as he was. Excitement and joy and frustration tangling up inside her and making her pussy feel all the more empty.

"Holy hell," he gasped as his body settled from shuddering to shivers. "I… Man, I don't think I've done that since…"

"High school?" she suggested.

He nodded and his head fell back again. She held him like that for a moment. Just taking in the gorgeously pornographic sight of Walker half-undressed and fully sated. His dark beard and strong neck and wide shoulders and that gorgeous chest, all leading down to the flat belly splashed with his come.

Charlie slowly loosened her grip before leaning past him to grab the Kleenex box. "You've made quite a mess, Walker Pearce."

His smile was decidedly lazy as he reached for the tissues and cleaned himself up. "I think you're the one who has to take the blame for that."

"Me? I was only doing what you told me."

His big, deep laugh filled the room and made her heart thump. "Well, if you're so good at following directions…" His hands spread over her back and he swung her around. "Then lie down." She found herself suddenly staring at the ceiling, her jeans being stripped down her legs.

"No sex!" she shrieked, laughing almost too hard

to form words. She covered herself with her hands in an attempt to keep her panties in place.

"Darlin', if you think I'm capable of sex right now, I'm truly flattered, but you are very, very mistaken." As if to make the point, he tugged up his briefs and jeans.

"I just mean, no…you know."

His dark eyebrows rose. "You don't want my mouth on you?"

She tried not to groan but couldn't stop the tortured sound. Oh, she wanted his mouth on her. *Everywhere* on her.

When he braced himself above her on the couch, his shoulders filled every inch of her vision. "I got it, Charlie. Don't worry. I'll be good."

Was this man made of sex? Everything he said was a dirty promise that ratcheted her up another notch. Yes, he'd be good. No matter what he did. Hell, at this point, he didn't even have to be better than average. She could get off just on the memory of him coming for her.

Walker kissed her, and when she closed her eyes, she was happy for his beard, because even with her vision dark, she knew who was kissing her. There was no question of it. Aside from the firm softness of his lips and the unmistakable taste of his mouth, there was his beard tracing over her skin. For a moment, the stark heat of his chest pressed against hers, but then he slid to the side, wedging himself next to her on the couch. She couldn't protest, though, because his hand was at her breast again, teasing and touching.

"Yes," she whispered against his mouth. Then "Yes," again when his hand slid lower.

The slide of his fingers down her belly recalled every second that she'd touched him. Every nerve that had fired its eagerness to take him. Her belly sucked in, and then his hand slipped beneath her panties and she gasped at the feel of his rough fingers sliding over her plump, wet flesh.

In that moment, she was so glad she'd kept up waxing. She loved this feeling, of a man's skin against her bare, sensitive lips. And for Walker, she was already soaking wet, so it felt wicked and delicious and perfect as he stroked her. He brushed her clit and she cried out.

"Oh, sweetheart," he murmured.

She wanted to protest that it wasn't that bad, that she didn't need him that much. But he stroked her again, and she was too busy whimpering like a needy animal. Her hips pushed toward him, urging him on when she was trying to order them to play coy. But they were far beyond coy. Her hips were trying to talk her into doing anything. Anything for Walker and his calloused fingers. Anything he ever wanted.

"Fuck," she cursed, trying to fight it.

"No. No fucking, Charlie. Just this."

"Oh, God," she groaned. She bit her lip, trying to hold back, but she needed to feel him inside her. "Please," she finally let herself say.

The fingers teasing her clit slipped lower, and then they were pushing inside her, thank God. "Yes."

Two of his wide fingers stretched her and she gasped her relief.

"Is that better?"

She nodded, clenching her teeth tight against another shameless moan.

"Good," he whispered against her cheek. He set a slow rhythm for a few strokes, then slid out to touch her again, his fingers hot from her body. This time he didn't tease. This time he stroked her clit with a steady rhythm that slowly, slowly increased. Charlie's breathing became shameless panting. Her hips rocked toward every circle of his fingertips.

When he slipped down to push inside her again, she cried out at the pleasure and grabbed his forearm. To make him stop or force him not to… She wasn't sure. All she knew was that it was torture to feel him inside her when she was so close.

"Shhh. That's good," he whispered. "That's so damn good, isn't it?"

"Yes," she panted. "Yes. Yes." His fingers filled her so thoroughly that, at that moment, she couldn't even imagine taking his thick cock inside her. Just this was all she could handle. She was overwhelmed with each push of his hand, everything too tight and full, her nerves stretched past tension into something like torture.

He shifted his body a bit farther from hers, changed the angle of his arm and then his thumb was rubbing her clit while he pushed his fingers deep into her, and that was all it took. A few circles of his thumb and her nerves gave up all that tension in a shock wave of pleasure. And then another, and another. She couldn't hold back her screams as she came harder than she had in years. Her world shuddered and shook. Her throat went hoarse.

From just a little foreplay.

Holy God, sex with Walker was going to be so good.

CHAPTER SEVEN

"WHERE WERE YOU last night?"

Charlie ignored Dawn and kept typing up the security procedures she wanted in place for guest emergencies. Her keyboard clicked in the silence.

"Charlotte," Dawn said more loudly, her voice grating over Charlie's eardrums. "I asked you a question."

"I was at my new apartment," she answered.

"Your *what?*"

Charlie kept typing. "My new apartment."

"What do you mean? We've provided you with an apartment here!"

"Yeah, well. I'm not required to stay here and I found it a little confining."

"No! You're supposed to be here, at the resort, so that you can be around for any emergencies."

"I'm sorry, Dawn, but that's not in my contract," Charlie countered, trying to keep her voice level. It wouldn't do to let Dawn hear the disdain and hate and impatience that were eating her alive.

"Oh, really? You know what *is* in your contract?" She paused long enough to make Charlie respond.

"What?" she finally growled.

"A morality clause."

Charlie rolled her eyes. "A what?" When she looked up, Dawn smirked.

"Oh, now you're paying attention. Clearly you're aware of what your weaknesses are."

"What do you mean a morality clause?"

"Look it up, Charlotte. You signed it."

She couldn't look it up, because her personal files were at her new apartment, safe from prying eyes. Then again, she didn't really need to look. The arrogant smile on Dawn's face made clear she was telling the truth.

"After the things you did in Tahoe, we had to protect ourselves."

"I was cleared of any wrongdoing," Charlie said, her voice still calm, but her heart was picking up speed.

"I know, sweetie. And we want to believe in you. We've known you for years. You're like family. That's why we gave you a chance. But that doesn't mean we have to bury our heads in the sand."

"I did not break the law in Tahoe and I won't break it here. Anything else I do with my life is none of your business."

"Oh, not *anything.*"

Charlie sighed. What she wanted to say was *I don't want your boring-ass husband, so you don't need to worry.* Instead she gritted her teeth and said, "Is there anything about the work I'm doing that concerns you?"

"Aside from the fact that you decided to abandon your post? No, not so far. But I'm having Eli train me on some of the video surveillance so I can understand what you do better."

Charlie blinked. "Excuse me?"

"I want to be the best executive manager I can be," Dawn added with a heavy layer of false cheer. "To do that, I need to understand everyone's work."

"You can't just play with the surveillance equipment! One wrong move and you might erase important files. Those videos might be needed in court if there's ever a crime committed here."

"I absolutely understand. That's why I want you to take over the training from Eli. Make sure I'm learning everything I need."

Charlie stared at her in disbelief. Dawn wanted Charlie to train her on the surveillance equipment. So that Dawn would be able to more thoroughly spy. On Charlie.

This was her life. Good God.

"Sure," she forced herself to say. "I'd love to train you." Dawn could spy away. She wasn't going to find anything.

"Great. We'll start now."

"I…I need a few minutes to wrap this up and answer some emails."

"I'll be back in thirty minutes."

Charlie held her breath as Dawn stood, smoothed down her perfectly pressed pink skirt and patted her hair. As soon as she stepped out of the office, Charlie hunched over her laptop and typed "morality clause" into the search engine.

A few clicks and she was pretty sure she could relax. Dawn couldn't control her with a morality clause. She couldn't be fired for just having sex or staying out all night, even if that offended Dawn's puritanical sensibilities. The morality clause could only be enacted if Charlie's behavior adversely affected the resort's ability to be successful. And hell, hotels made a big chunk of money turning a blind eye to people's sex lives. They really wouldn't want to take a stand against that.

Her relief didn't remove any of her determination. She quietly closed the door of her office and dialed her brother's cell phone number. She hadn't seen him since she'd returned to Jackson. She still didn't want to see him, but maybe he knew something about Dawn and her husband that would help make things clear.

"Hi, Brad. It's Charlie."

"Hey. What's up?" He sounded neither surprised nor pleased to hear from her.

"Do you have time to grab a bite tonight? I'd like to catch up."

"Sure. Sounds good." Again, no surprise or pleasure on his part. Just flatness. It was the story of their relationship.

"How are you?" she ventured, but he only responded with an impatient grunt, as if he had nothing to say to her.

Charlie gave up and they made arrangements to meet in town. She doubted he could help, but he was a commercial developer. He likely knew the Taggerts or had at least heard things about Dawn from other people in his circle.

As soon as she hung up, Charlie opened the site of her preferred background investigator. She'd done a quick background check on the Taggerts before she'd accepted the job, because she damn sure wasn't going to end up working for a criminal again. But Dawn's behavior called for more insight.

With a glance at her closed door, she typed in the information she knew about Dawn Taggert and ordered a more specialized report. Maybe signs of a personality disorder would turn up.

A thorough hundred-and-twenty-five-dollar report might solve this mystery. She should have done it days ago, when things had begun to feel fishy. But it felt like treason. Even though the receipt for the report wouldn't show the name of the person checked, Charlie still paid for it herself just to make sure the report wouldn't be discovered.

Despite her precaution, a chill ran down her spine. She felt she was being watched, but that was an old familiar paranoia. After all, she spent her days watching people. It only made sense that she'd live with that feeling herself.

Still, Charlie carefully closed the window, deleted all her search histories and caches and even destroyed the email receipt that popped into her in-box. A girl could never be too careful, after all.

CHAPTER EIGHT

"CHARLIE," HER BROTHER said as she gave him an obligatory hug. "You look good."

"Thanks. So do you." That was a bit of an exaggera-
tion. Brad looked tired, but that was hardly a surprise.
He was currently on his third divorce at age thirty-four
and losing a lot of hair.

Her older brother had never been good at relationships of any kind. He was as selfish as their father had
always been, but he lacked the charm that helped keep
people attached to arrogant bastards. Charlie couldn't
imagine why even one woman had agreed to marry
him in the first place, much less three different women.
Then again, she'd seen a lot during her time in Vegas
and Tahoe. It was amazing the kind of men women
would date for money. And sad just how little money
it took.

She and her brother made small talk as they looked
over the menu, pretending to care what each had been
up to since they'd seen each other three years before at
their dad's funeral. That had been an even more awkward visit, surrounded by family that neither of them
knew. Their father's other grown children, who offered

polite, distant smiles. Aunts and uncles and cousins Charlie and Brad should've known but didn't.

Their father had been their mom's first husband, and she'd quickly moved on to several more. There'd been way too many relatives in their childhood, and none of them permanent.

Once the small talk degenerated to a discussion of her brother's divorce, Charlie tuned him out. She didn't care about his latest wife's attempt to "rob him blind," and he looked equally impatient with her whitewashed version of the past year.

"So, how's the new job?" he finally asked.

Ah. The crux of the matter.

"It's interesting. I'm working for Dawn and Keith Taggert."

"Right. The new resort. It's gonna be a big deal."

She nodded as if she cared. "What do you hear about them?"

"You mean like divorce rumors?"

"No, not necessarily. It's just that Dawn has been surprisingly difficult to work for."

He shrugged, more interested in the fact that his burger had arrived.

Charlie pressed harder. "We were good friends in high school, but she seems sort of…odd now."

"Odd how?"

"Odd like she's watching me every second. She seems paranoid that I'm going to do something that will ruin her life."

He shrugged again. "Seems logical," he said past a mouthful of beef.

"What the hell? What do you mean it seems logical?"

"You helped your last employer embezzle money, right?"

Her jaw dropped. She couldn't believe this. Not from her own *brother*. "Are you kidding me, Brad? Is that what you think? I didn't do anything wrong. I was cleared in pretrial, for God's sake."

"Yeah, I get that. But everyone knows you turned a blind eye."

"I did not! Maybe I trusted the wrong people. Fine. I was an idiot. But I didn't do anything to help them, and I didn't ignore anything!"

Brad rolled his eyes. "Fine. I apologize, but you still can't blame Dawn for keeping a close eye."

"Oh, I can't?"

"You were screwing your married boss, right? And her husband is now your boss. Do you two get along?"

Charlie had been shocked at Dawn's animosity and paranoia, but these casual swipes from her brother nearly knocked her off her chair. She couldn't imagine how he could be so harsh about it.

"Where did you hear all this?"

"First of all, it involved a commercial development scandal in a state that a lot of people I know do business in. Some of them had ties to that company. They all wanted to find out what I knew about it."

Charlie blinked hard against a sudden burning in her eyes.

"Second, I've done business with Keith Taggert. We talked about him bringing you on."

Her mind was spinning. "You did?"

"Yes. I told him I'd talk to you about it if it came down to it, but you guys worked out an offer, so I stayed out of it."

"You knew they were offering me the job?"

He took another bite and shrugged. "Sure."

"Did you ask them to?"

"I told Keith I thought you'd do fine. I figured you'd probably learned your lesson, and you'd keep your head down and be a solid, loyal employee."

She nodded, thinking she should thank him for that, and hating that those were the most positive things he'd had to say about her. "I just... You should know that I didn't know my boss was married. I'd never have...I'd never have done that."

Brad shrugged again, that infuriating, dismissive movement that told her he couldn't care less what she did. "I guess you should be more careful who you sleep with. If you'd taken Mom's advice and settled down, none of this would've happened."

"Seriously?" she whispered. Then repeated it more loudly. "*Seriously?* You're telling me about settling down, Mr. Successful Marriages?"

"Hey, I'm willing to try instead of just living some party lifestyle."

"My party lifestyle doesn't hurt anyone! You, on the other hand, have treated three women like shit."

Another shrug. "I'm an asshole when they marry me and the same asshole when they leave. How is that my problem?"

"Oh, my God. You are so…just…"

"Get off your high horse. You slept with the boss and got a promotion. I don't have a problem with that. I'd do it if I could. But then the guy used you the way you used him. It happens."

Her vision went blurry for a moment as her blood pressure spiked. "I didn't get that job because I slept with him!"

"A twenty-eight-year-old woman in charge of security at a Tahoe resort? That just happens?"

"Are you kidding me? Could you be more of an asshole? How can you just talk about my problems like I'm some story you heard about at a dinner party? I'm your sister. Why can't you give me the benefit of the doubt? Why would you *assume* I didn't deserve what I worked for?"

"Charlie, it's no big deal. You screwed up and someone got caught while your pants were down. It happens. You asked why Dawn would be leery of you, and I gave you an answer. I'm sorry it wasn't the one you wanted."

She stared at him, still in utter shock. "Brad… Just… God, I just wanted to know if she was a psycho or not, because she's sure acting like one. And if I'm so damn awful, why did they hire me? Just to make my life hell?"

"Dawn Taggert is a woman. So yeah, I'm sure she's a little psycho. Aren't all of you?"

"Wow. You have really turned into a steaming pile of shit, you know that?"

For the first time, he looked irritated, but he still managed to pop another fry into his mouth.

"What? Aren't you going to ask if I'm PMSing now?"

He snorted in a way that let her know that was exactly what he was thinking.

Charlie glanced down at the Cobb salad she'd ordered. She'd been starving earlier, but now her stomach turned. What a tragedy. The salad looked so good. At that moment, she cared a lot more about the salad than her brother.

A waiter walked over when she met his gaze. "I'm so sorry, but can you box this up? I have to go."

"Come on," Brad said as the waiter whisked the bowl away. "I didn't mean to hurt your feelings."

"You didn't hurt my— Actually, yes, you did. You hurt my feelings, and I've had enough of that shit from strangers lately. There's no reason I need to sit here and hear it from my brother, too. I'm the only sister you've got. Someday all you're going to have is me and half a dozen ex-wives and none of us will want to talk to you or take you to the doctor for outpatient surgery. You should think about being nicer to me."

She stood up, started to reach into her purse for some cash, then changed her mind. Screw him. He probably didn't want her dirty money anyway.

"By the way, you know how you can be sure you're being an idiot, Brad? Because you're advising me to take relationship advice from our mother. Think about that, you asswipe." She took the box from the returning waiter and walked away. She'd go home and eat her salad in better company. By herself.

WALKER STARTLED WHEN he heard Charlie's keys in the hall at 8:00 p.m. He'd been nervous on the drive home, realizing he might run into her and sure that he had no idea what to say. Her windows had been dark when he'd pulled up, so he'd bought a little more time, but his brain hadn't offered any ideas in the past hour. No big surprise.

He turned down the volume on the television and waited. He didn't realize he'd been holding his breath until her door closed and he exhaled. That momentary possibility of seeing her had shaken him. *Charlie* had shaken him.

Last night, he'd been in a mood. A bad one. Pissed and frustrated by the latest turns of his life, he'd reacted by trying to distract himself and by jumping to conclusions about Charlie. She'd struck him, suddenly, as the same as every beautiful, successful woman who'd ever hit on him, so he'd run with it. Why not? The outcome would be sex, after all. A damn good distraction if he needed one. So if she'd wanted sex, he'd planned on giving it to her. His mood had made it that simple.

Thank God she'd put the brakes on. It seemed Charlie wasn't quite as fast as she pretended to be.

The smile that tugged at his mouth was impossible to stop. It was damn sweet that she'd only wanted to make out.

It had also been insanely hot that her version of making out had included sitting topless on his lap to jerk him off.

The twinge of lust that jolted him at the memory was nearly painful, but his moan sounded suspiciously like a laugh. Wild or sweet, that had been hotter than any dirty movie he'd ever seen.

"Damn," he muttered, shifting his erection to a more comfortable position in his jeans. It had been a long day on that horse being plagued by memories of what they'd done. He'd worked hard all day, pushing himself, trying to wear himself out so much that he'd be too tired to remember. It hadn't worked for more than a few minutes at a time. And now they were both home, only a few feet apart. He could hear the water run in the bathroom when she turned on a tap.

He had no idea what to do.

How should he treat this new Charlie? He'd always considered her a friend. He still did. But friends didn't jerk friends off. Did they?

No, he couldn't just treat her like a buddy now. He couldn't ruffle her hair and tease her and pretend he didn't want to strip her naked and bend her over his bed.

He shifted again, eyes darting toward the door. Should he go over? Take her a beer? Or maybe grab some flowers and...

"What the hell?" he muttered to himself. "Flowers?" He'd lost his mind. She'd left his apartment with a friendly "Thank you," as if he'd done her a service. And that's probably all it had been to her. He'd heard that same "Thank you" before. More times than he cared to count, actually.

Thanks, cowboy, that was just what I needed.

Yeah. He was just what the doctor ordered, apparently.

But…it hadn't felt like that with Charlie. First of all, because she'd made them wait instead of taking what she had clearly wanted. Second, because it had felt so…comfortable. He knew her. Who she was. How to make her laugh.

He liked women. He liked to bring them pleasure, and he damn sure liked to lose himself in his own. He liked their bodies and the sounds they made and the way they smelled and tasted. He liked their smiles and touches and looks. But sometimes…sometimes in the middle of all of that, he felt a little as if he was outside looking in. As if he was watching. But it hadn't felt like that with Charlie.

Ironic, considering that last night with Charlie he actually had been watching.

That smile took over his mouth again. The one he couldn't stop.

He was being an idiot, worrying about Charlie. She was just *Charlie.*

Walker switched off the TV, grabbed two beers and headed over.

"Hey there," he said when she opened the door. He raised his eyebrows at the sight of her in nothing but a black skirt and black bra.

"Hi, Walker. Is that for me?"

Keeping his eyes on her bra, he handed her a bottle and followed her in.

"I'm eating my dinner. I hope that's not rude." She plopped down onto her couch and picked up a box filled with salad.

Yeah. This was definitely comfortable. He grinned. "In your bra?"

"Well, you know, I don't want to unleash these bad boys. I probably wouldn't be able to reach past them to eat. Better to keep them contained for now."

"Clearly. But I was more wondering what had happened to your shirt, rather than why you hadn't gone full topless. Not that I'd mind. I encourage that whenever possible."

"I didn't want to get salad dressing on my shirt."

"Makes sense." He twisted off the cap of the beer and settled onto the couch next to her.

"I saw my brother tonight. It's been a while."

"What's he up to?"

She stabbed at her salad. "Being an asshole."

Walker choked on his beer.

"I'm serious. He's just… We were never that close because he's five years older. And a mama's boy. But now he's devolved into a thirty-four-year-old sexist, greedy ass. He's on his third divorce and probably already working toward a fourth wife."

"Yikes."

She waved her fork. "I'm sorry. Ignore me. I'm in a bad mood."

As far as he was concerned, she could be in as bad a mood as she liked, as long as she was wearing that sexy little bra. The satiny material dipped low over her breasts, letting him see the faint rise of her flesh above it. He'd put his mouth just there last night. And lower.

"What's going on with you?" she asked.

His gaze flew up to meet hers. "Sorry. I was... Uh."

She laughed. "It's fine. I don't get men ogling my breasts too often, so feel free to look. But I meant what's going on with your day?"

"Oh." Now he didn't know where to look. His eyes bounced up and down for a moment before he forced them to stop and meet her gaze. "I took some work at an old job the past couple of days. I think the guy might offer me winter work if I want it."

"That's good, right? I know winter is slow. But you don't sound happy."

No, he wasn't happy. He collapsed back against the soft cushions of the couch and took a swig of beer. "I don't know. It's not what I want."

"Ranching?"

"No, not that. I like the work. I like being outside, love being on a horse. But...I don't know. It's not lodge work. It'd be a long winter. I've spent most of the past thirteen years working with guests. A lot of hands look down on that kind of thing, but I like it. The variety. The people."

"You're good with people. You always have been."

"Thanks."

She poked him with her toe. "So why'd you leave the last job if you liked it?"

He sighed and ran a thumb around the neck of the beer bottle. "I was let go. It was the end of the season, and…well, you know the stuff I'm not good at."

"No. After last night, I know a lot of stuff you're *great* at, but I didn't notice any deficiencies."

"Heh." Either the beer had hit his blood quickly or he was blushing. Thank God for his beard. He rubbed a self-conscious hand over it. "That's encouraging."

"Oh, you should feel encouraged. I know I am. So tell me what you're not good at."

His smile faded. "Come on, Charlie. You know."

"I'm sorry, I don't know what you mean. Honestly."

"Anything that requires brains."

"Walker!" She gasped, sitting straight so quickly that she fumbled her box of salad and nearly dropped it before she set it down. "Are you kidding? I can't believe you just said that."

"It's true."

"It is *not* true." This time, instead of nudging him with her toe, she kicked his leg. "Don't ever say that."

Walker finished off his beer in one swallow. "What do you want me to say? That I have a learning disability?"

Another kick. "Yes! You *do* have a learning disability."

"All right. I'm dyslexic. That doesn't mean I'm not stupid, too."

She pushed up to her knees and shoved his shoulder. "Goddamn it, Walker! I can't believe you're saying this."

Laughing, he grabbed her hands so she'd stop beating him up. "It's okay, Charlie. Jeez. Cowboys don't need to be smart. Nobody expects us to read big books or write essays. I'm a damn good cowboy. It's just that at a guest ranch, there's sometimes paperwork. Hell, you have to file a two-page report anytime someone gets a splinter. I always put that kind of thing off. I missed things sometimes and it caught up to me."

"Walker." She said his name softly, so he let her hands go. They settled on his shoulders as she climbed onto his lap. Her skirt hiked to her hips when she straddled him. Oh, yes. He remembered this.

But this time, she didn't unbutton his jeans. She didn't reach for his cock, which was already getting hard for her. She only frowned at him, a vastly less enjoyable experience.

"Walker," she said again, her voice sweet and soft and wrapping around him as her hands twined into his hair. "Stupid men aren't good with people. Stupid men don't attract women like flies. Do you think I…" She leaned in and pressed her mouth to his, a whisper of a kiss. "Would sleep with a stupid man?"

He slid his hands up her thighs. "You haven't slept with me, Charlie."

"Mm." Her mouth opened for him as his thumbs

slipped over the impossibly soft skin of her thighs. She licked at his tongue, barely giving him a taste before she withdrew. "Are you trying to get a sympathy fuck, Walker?"

His laugh was half a groan, because now her pussy was pressed against him, but still so damn far away.

"Maybe if I resist, you'll tell me how much it hurts. How much you need me to touch it."

He groaned into her mouth, then swept his tongue deep inside her.

"Mm," she hummed into him before pulling back to trail her mouth along his jaw. "Do you need me to touch it?"

"God," he groaned. Was this what she liked? Teasing? Torturing? All foreplay and no sex? He would've hated that in high school, but now it was almost as delicious as it was painful. "Yes," he said, finally giving in. "Touch it."

"Oh. So bossy."

He growled at her.

"Okay, I'll touch it." Her lips closed over his earlobe and sucked gently. When she spoke again, he shivered. "But not until you admit you're not stupid."

Did she think he had a dog in this fight? He happily folded like a damn blanket. "I'm not stupid. In fact, I'm a goddamn genius. I play chess on the trail and read Shakespeare by starlight."

"That didn't sound sincere," she whispered.

"Oh, it was sincere. I promise you that."

"Walker." She leaned back just as he was trying to

slide his hands beneath her skirt to cup her ass. "I want to touch your cock as much as the next girl, but I can't do it unless I believe you."

"God, Charlie. What do you want from me? You were my tutor. You know exactly how dumb I am. No! Wait!" He tried to keep a hold of her thighs, but she slipped off his lap and eased her skirt down.

"You listen to me." Instead of reaching for his zipper, she pointed at his face. He thought he might weep. "You're a good man. You're smart and sweet and wonderful with people. So don't you take some job in the middle of nowhere if it won't make you happy. Don't do that!"

"I need a paycheck through winter. I'll find something better next spring."

He'd thought those were harmless words. Appeasing, even. In fact, he was already reaching to pull her back down to his lap, but Charlie's spine went straight and she put her hands on her hips to glare at him. "You can't work at a job that's going to beat you down. You look tired already after two days there."

"It was hard work, that's all. And it's temporary. No big deal."

"That's what people say to themselves. 'I'll just do it for a little while, just for the paycheck.' But then it'll be spring and you'll be busy. If you don't get work at the lodge, you'll have to make time to look for a position somewhere else, and you won't want to leave your current boss in the lurch."

He shrugged. "Summer, then."

"Walker!" She seemed shocked by the loudness of her own voice, and pressed her lips tight together before taking a deep breath. "Just…try to find something else, all right? Something that'll make you happy. Maybe branch out. What if you like people more than ranching? I could see if there's a position at the resort—"

"Charlie, that's enough. I'm a cowboy. I'll always be a cowboy. Winter work is just a temporary gig. It's nothing. Hell, I know plenty of men who drive down to find work in Texas for a few months. At least I'll still be in my own place."

She narrowed her eyes.

"I promise! I'm not going to throw my sorry life away for a few months of work. Trust me. I'll find something I like soon."

"Will you keep looking for a little while, at least?"

"I'm not sure why it means so much to you, but I'll ask again at the lodge if it'll get you back on my lap. Will it?"

"Maybe," she agreed with another hard look.

"No sex," he said, more than willing to embrace the heavy petting. "We'll only do what you want. I promise."

Her glare finally gave way to a grin. "I can trust you not to take advantage of me?"

"Absolutely."

Her giggle was unfortunately interrupted by a knock on the door.

"Walker," Charlie said as she reached for a scarlet-red blouse draped over the back of the couch. "You're adorable, you know that?"

He scrubbed a hand through his hair as he watched her slip away.

Starting to button up her shirt, Charlie looked through the peephole, then threw open the door. "Merry! Hi!"

Their neighbor's eyes went wide at the sight of Charlie's half-buttoned shirt. They went even wider when she spotted Walker on the couch. "Walker! Hi!"

He jumped to his feet as Charlie waved her in. "Evening, Merry." He reached up to tip a hat he wasn't wearing, then winced at the awkward gesture.

"I'm sorry," Merry said. "I didn't mean to interrupt."

When Charlie shrugged, Merry used the plastic container in her hand to point toward the open buttons of Charlie's shirt.

"Oh! Sorry. I was eating my salad."

Merry's eyes met his and then skittered away. "I'm sorry, I don't know what that means. But I'll leave you two alone so you can get back to…that."

"No, I was eating a salad!" Charlie pointed toward the box on the table.

Merry seemed to wilt. "Oh, thank God. I thought it meant… Never mind. Just… Here! I made you cupcakes! Welcome to the building."

Walker was still boggling over what strange activities Merry thought she might have interrupted, but Charlie just took the cupcakes and gave Merry a hug. "Thank you! Have one with me. Walker, you want a cupcake?" She turned toward him, then burst into laughter. "Look! You made Walker blush."

"I… Uh." Why was he flustered? They hadn't been— Well, he'd been hoping they might. But it wasn't as if Merry had knocked just as Charlie's hand had curved around his cock and slipped right into that sweet rhythm that— Okay, he was making it worse now. He cleared his throat and pasted on a smile. "I'll leave you ladies to your cupcakes."

"Come on, Walker." Charlie reappeared with a little plate that held three cupcakes. She handed one to him. "I know how you are. Don't pretend you wouldn't like to eat Merry's cake."

Merry choked and slapped a hand over her mouth to muffle her scream of laughter.

Walker felt his face get even hotter. "Charlie! Jesus."

She shrugged an insolent shoulder and handed a cake to Merry. "You talk a good game, cowboy. I thought you could take it. I guess not."

"I don't talk any game," he muttered.

"Oh, please. You're the biggest flirt I've ever met. Even in high school, you could get any girl to giggle with just a naughty suggestion."

Merry spoke from behind her hand. "You knew Walker in high school?"

"I sure did. Sit down. I've got stories."

Somehow his comfortable evening on Charlie's couch with her hand and her bra and her thighs and her mouth had turned into *this*. Two tall, beautiful women eating cake and laughing at him. What the ever-loving hell?

"You want another beer, Walker?"

"No. I'm going to excuse myself and get some sleep."

"Aw, come on," Charlie cooed. "It's only eight. Stay. Please?"

He was tempted for a moment. He liked Merry just fine, and Charlie was licking frosting from her fingers and watching him with pleading eyes. But then she licked her thumb, and he knew he couldn't take it. She loved to tease him, and she wouldn't let up. His cock was stirring again already, and as much of a flirt as he was, he wasn't going to sit here in front of Merry with an erection for the next hour, like some pervert.

"Nah, it was a long day in the saddle, and I've got a job hunt to continue tomorrow, remember? Thanks for the cupcake, Merry. Don't believe anything she says."

"Good night, Walker," they both sang as he left. He ate the whole cake in one bite as he closed the door on their laughter.

God. Charlie. He was never going to figure her out. But he damn sure wanted to try.

CHAPTER NINE

CHARLIE WOKE UP ready to run five miles. She hadn't felt this good in months.

Her lecture to Walker last night had inspired her. She'd been trying to keep him from making the same mistakes she'd made in taking the job at the resort, but maybe she could take her own advice. She didn't have to be miserable. She could go into work with a good attitude instead of feeling as if she were heading to an execution. It was a good job at a beautiful resort and she was no longer trapped in that studio apartment.

She was also damn proud of herself for not knocking on Walker's door last night after Merry had left. She'd wanted to. Badly. She'd wanted to push her way in, shove him onto the bed and fuck him until they both passed out from exhaustion. But she hadn't. This waiting game was fun. When they finally did it, she was going to go off like one of those glitter cannons at a pop concert, in a giant explosion of shiny fun.

Grinning in anticipation, she hopped out of bed to get dressed.

Unfortunately, her good intentions were met by rain. Not warm Nevada rain, but ice-cold, pouring Wyoming rain, so Charlie packed up a bag and headed for the resort to use a treadmill in the workout room. The pool and hot tub hadn't been filled yet, but the workout room was fully outfitted with high-end equipment and ready to be used.

She forced herself to smile as she drove up the long driveway that led to the parking garage. She even winked at the camera as she let herself in. This was fine. She could do this. She wasn't working in a meatpacking plant for minimum wage. She wasn't scrubbing dirty floors for twelve hours a day knowing all her hard work would mean nothing if immigration agents raided the place. She was, for the most part, sitting at a desk in the warmth and comfort of her own office, and compensated with a decent salary and good benefits. And, of course, watched over by the careful eye of her employer.

Her smile wavered. She put it back on and marched to the workout room.

The first three miles of her run went well. Unlike in most hotels, the Meridian workout room was on the main floor, with a beautiful view of the valley beyond. A misty view, but much nicer than a blank wall, and the sight of the wet day stretching out in front of her let Charlie lose herself for minutes at a time. And the music in her ears let her think. Her mind drifted to plans for building up her team of employees. She'd been so worried about her own experience at the resort that she hadn't spent enough time being a manager.

That would change this week. No matter what else was going on, she owed it to her employees to lead them.

When the music switched to a dark, sensual beat, Charlie's mind drifted away from work. She found herself watching her body in the mirror, thinking of peeling off her clothes for Walker and watching his face. She'd been skinny and tall her whole life, which had made her feel awkward in high school, but she enjoyed it now. She enjoyed the sight of her strong legs, the muscles flexing beneath the skin with every stride. They'd flex like that for Walker, too, if she worked hard enough.

And if her breasts were barely a small rise under her running top, at least they led down to a slim rib cage and flat belly. She wasn't curvy or soft or voluptuous, but that didn't mean she couldn't be proud when she stood naked before a man and let him look his fill. If a man didn't like it, he didn't have any business getting her naked anyway.

But Walker liked it. She smiled at her reflection and stepped up her pace. He was going to like it even more very soon.

"Charlotte?"

She yelped, and a quick stutter-step of shock nearly sent her flying off the treadmill. She caught one of the handholds and jumped her feet to the sides and managed to save herself from an ugly fall.

"Sorry," the man's voice said from behind her while she scrambled to turn off the machine.

"Oh, my God." She stole a quick look over her shoulder, saw Keith Taggert and collapsed against the controls to try to catch her panicked breath.

"I'm sorry, Charlotte. I thought you heard me come in."

She yanked her earbuds out. "I didn't hear you."

"Thank God you didn't fall off. That would've been a hell of a lawsuit." He laughed uncomfortably. His deep voice should have made it a booming laugh, but he always seemed to swallow it, as if he weren't allowed to have fun. He'd probably picked up that habit after his marriage to Dawn.

Charlie was suddenly aware of her running shorts and tight shirt. She hadn't gotten weird vibes from him, despite Dawn's obsession, but she'd never been half-naked and sweaty with him before.

Once she'd caught her breath, Charlie hopped off the treadmill and grabbed her water bottle. "What can I help you with?"

"Oh, right! There's a society benefit tonight I'd like you to attend if you could."

"A what?" Her brain immediately flashed to a nineteenth-century ball. Women danced by her eyeballs with feathers in their hair.

"A Night Under the Stars. It's an annual event."

"Oh, I'd have to be sure I can find something appropriate to wear. Is it—?"

"That's not a concern. This is Wyoming! It's held at a big ranch every year. In the barn. Just wear your best jeans. There will be plenty of fur coats there, of course, but no evening gowns, I promise."

He couldn't be asking her out on a date, could he? Not with all of Jackson society in attendance. But Dawn's paranoia had gotten under Charlie's skin.

"Tonight? I'd have to check my schedule. Maybe I could meet you there?"

"Sure. If you can let me know in the next hour, that would help. I bought six tickets. Two for me and Dawn, of course, and four for others in management. I'd like a strong presence from the resort, just to be sure people are aware that we're on the scene."

"Oh! Yes, of course I can go. Anything for the resort."

"Perfect. I'll drop off a ticket at your office."

She felt so relieved she almost didn't notice the way his eyes tracked down her body as he left. But she was half-dressed and damp. It was a normal guy reaction. It didn't mean anything.

She'd completely convinced herself of that after another quarter mile on the treadmill when the door to the room burst open again. Even with her earbuds in, Charlie jumped and vaulted off the machine.

It wasn't an attacker, though. Or not a dangerous one, at least. It was Dawn, eyes blazing and teeth bared. Her gaze speared every corner of the room before her grimace settled into a frown.

"What's wrong?" Charlie panted.

Dawn shook her head and looked around the room again. "I thought…"

Charlie wiped her forehead. "You almost gave me a heart attack."

"Sorry. I just thought someone else was in here."

"Who?"

"No one," Dawn answered dismissively. "It's nothing."

Charlie raised a doubtful eyebrow.

"Are you going to be ready at nine? You're supposed to give me another lesson on the surveillance equipment."

"Yes," she said flatly as Dawn turned her back on her and rushed out.

Charlie knew exactly who Dawn had been expecting to find in here. Her husband. She'd spied Charlie on one of the hallway cameras, and then she'd seen Keith going into the workout room a little while later, and she'd thought... What? That she'd catch them having sex on a weight bench?

The woman was delusional.

But Charlie suddenly felt more excited about tonight. A society party would be the perfect place to gather information, to urge people to repeat rumors over bubbling glasses of champagne. Parties made people talk. They wanted to be naughty. Charlie just had to give them the opportunity.

Afraid to take one more step on the treadmill, Charlie gathered her things and headed to her studio, now that she finally had a use for it.

The place felt empty when she let herself in. Dead. Dust motes danced on the sunbeams that snuck through the blinds. She was alone. She knew she was. But goose bumps trailed over her skin as if a cold finger had traced down her back.

A home was a place of safety. A refuge from the uncertainties and danger and heartbreak of the outside world. It was meant to give shelter in every way. But this place sheltered her from nothing. It didn't even provide the most basic level of privacy. She circled the room slowly, looking for evidence that anyone else had entered, but she hadn't left carefully enough. She couldn't remember if that lamp had been moved or if she'd shifted it when she'd packed up so quickly. Her bed was only half-made, but that was normal. Everything looked normal. But she still took her clothes into the bathroom to change there.

The hot shower was a relief after that tense run, and truth be told, the showerhead here was about ten times better than the one at the Stud Farm, but even the oscillating showerhead couldn't wash all her worries away. She was still a tight bundle of nerves half an hour later when she stepped out of her studio and started for the stairs, but when she looked down the hall, she spotted a familiar figure turning to head down another hallway.

What the hell? Had that been her *brother?* Why would he be here?

Charlie let the stairway door close and stared down the hallway where Brad had disappeared. Was it possible he'd come to apologize?

She felt immediately guilty for the way she'd left the night before. She'd lost her temper. She'd said some cruel things. She'd stolen a salad.

"Shit," she muttered. If he wanted to apologize, she'd say sorry, too. She put her shoulders back and set off to find him.

The short hallway he'd headed down was empty, so Charlie followed it past the service elevators to a longer corridor beyond. This one was dotted with beautiful tables that would soon hold fresh flowers. She knew this hallway. The Taggerts' offices were here. Maybe Brad had only asked to be pointed in the direction of management offices.

Curious, she walked down to the windows at the end, just to be sure there weren't any other hallways ahead. But she found nothing but closed doors and no Brad.

"Huh." She headed back to the start of the hallway, then walked toward the lobby. The place was like a ghost town, and there was no sign of her brother.

Maybe she'd imagined it. She'd review the tapes and see. She retraced her steps, but as she passed the management hallway and started past the service elevators, she heard voices. The first sign of life in ten minutes.

Charlie backed up and peeked around the corner, suspicious now. And rightly so. The men's voices grew louder, and then her brother stepped out of Keith Taggert's office. Keith followed him out, slapping a hand on his back.

"Well, I do appreciate the effort," Keith said. "Dinner next week?"

"Sounds good," Brad agreed.

They shook hands, and Charlie backed around the

corner as Brad headed toward her. Unsure why she felt the urge to hide, she hurried past the elevators and straight for the stairwell. After she ducked in, she caught the edge of the door with her shoe and held it open one inch to watch what her brother did. When he stepped out of the short service elevator hallway, he didn't head toward her apartment. He walked toward the parking garage entrance.

He hadn't been looking for her. He hadn't stopped to knock on her door.

Charlie raced down the stairs to the basement where her own office was, just in case, but Brad didn't appear. He'd come to see Keith.

Why? Sure, they knew each other, but what were the chances of Brad showing up here the day after she'd spoken to him about the Taggerts?

She stood in the hallway for a long moment, face crumpled into such a confused frown that she finally had to shake it off in fear of getting a headache. But still…

"What the hell?" she muttered as she ducked into her office and closed the door. Overwhelmed by the ridiculous stupidity of this whole situation, she leaned against the door and closed her eyes.

When had her life become a Scooby Doo mystery? Everything had been so damn normal up until nine months before. She'd been doing everything right. Making the right choices. But somehow it had all fallen down around her. She'd lost her job, her reputation, her security. She'd even lost her life savings on hiring a criminal defense attorney. At least that had paid off. The charges had been dropped. She wouldn't even have to testify in the trial. She'd been fooled so thoroughly that she didn't have anything to contribute to the defense *or* the prosecution.

Charlie made her shoulders relax. She took deep breaths to force her pulse to slow. The only reason her brother could've been here was to help her. To speak to his old friend about how she was being treated. To ask if there was anything going on with Dawn that would make her behave badly to Charlie.

Brad had come here to help. He'd felt bad about their argument, and he'd decided to make it up to her. It was the only logical explanation.

Charlie felt bad about the argument, too. He'd deserved her anger. He'd said awful things. But part of her anger hadn't been about Brad. She'd thrown it all it him, but part of it had been for herself.

Because she'd lied a little. She hadn't known her boss was married. He'd kept that a secret, separating his work and personal life with purposeful precision. Not so hard to do when you supervised nearly a hundred people at a giant resort. But she had known when she'd started flirting with her boss that it probably wouldn't hurt for him to like her. When it had gotten more serious, when she'd slept with him…it had felt like a triumph in more than one way. So she had lied to Brad. Sleeping with her boss had probably contributed to her promotion, and she'd thought there was no harm in that, because all that had mattered was she'd known she could do the job.

She'd been so damn wrong. If she'd been qualified to do that job, she would've realized something was going on. And if sleeping with him had really been uncomplicated, his betrayal wouldn't have destroyed her quite so thoroughly.

So despite what she'd said to Brad, she hadn't done everything right. She'd screwed up, and she'd compromised herself, which had been a sign that she could be taken advantage of. And so she'd been taken advantage of.

She'd call Brad tomorrow and feel him out. See if he had anything to say about the Taggerts.

Today, all she really wanted to do was get through the day and then head back to her new apartment, to her new friends. To one new friend in particular.

But now she had a charity function to attend. Damn. She'd hoped to finally give up her play at being a tease tonight, but she supposed it would have to wait one more day. But tomorrow… Tomorrow she'd show Walker just what he'd been waiting for.

"It'll be worth the wait," she said, trying to psych herself into feeling better. It wasn't exactly a glitter cannon at a pop concert—yet—but she did feel a little better. That was good enough for now.

CHAPTER TEN

WALKER'S HEART BEAT hard as he looked over the beautiful women surrounding him. He took in their bare arms and soft smiles. The shiny hair spreading over tanned shoulders. He'd missed this kind of contact. The knowledge that he had a role to play. That they needed him. He enjoyed that. He always had.

The gelding tossed its head, letting Walker know he was holding the reins too tensely. He relaxed and tipped his hat at the nearest lady. "Anyone want a ride?"

Yes. They did. He helped a thin redhead onto the very gentle gelding and mounted his own horse to lead her out of the barn and around the inner fencing of the ranch.

"You look very comfortable, miss. Are you a rider?"

"Oh, no." She giggled. He'd guess she was over forty, but her skin was flawless and she didn't have the tight-lipped restraint of a lot of rich women. Each of the riders had paid a hundred dollars to charity for the privilege to ride a tame horse around the yard for five minutes. None of them were riders, but everyone loved the romance of being on horseback.

"Do you work here?" she asked.

"Not regular, miss," he said, playing up the cowboy talk to give her her money's worth as he rode alongside her. "I fill in on occasion when they need another hand."

This place was the first dude ranch he'd ever worked at. He'd dropped in to let the manager know he was working up on the cattle ranch now, but that he'd really like to move down to the lodge. He'd volunteered that he was up for anything, and this charity event was about as anything as it got. Leading society ladies around on a pony. Hauling tables and stages behind the scenes. Posing for pictures when someone wanted to post a photo of a Genuine Cowboy to a Facebook feed.

Most of the hands hated this kind of work. He loved it. It was a party. He got to hang around with pretty ladies and listen to music and pilfer the occasional fancy finger food. And then he got paid. How could anyone hate that? Plus, if tonight's gig got his foot back in the door, he couldn't regret it.

"I'm from New Jersey, but we're thinking about buying a horse property here," she said.

"It's a beautiful place. I don't know anyone who doesn't love it here. Unless you're looking for wild nightlife, I guess. We throw a good party, but it's pretty quiet around Jackson after midnight."

"Oh, no!" She laughed. "I'm not a party girl. And I've always wanted to learn how to ride a horse. So thank you."

He tipped his hat. "All in a day's work."

"So…when people buy a horse, do they hire a cowboy like you to take care of it?" She blushed as she asked it.

Walker winked at her. "That calls for more of a stable hand, miss." Not that it was the first offer of its kind he'd gotten. "Or a trainer."

"Oh. Of course. That makes sense."

"Look at that." As they rounded the lodge, he pointed toward the Tetons. "You've caught the very last of the sunset."

"Oh, it's beautiful!" She gasped, her embarrassment forgotten. "Oh, my God."

"It never stops being beautiful. If you buy out here, you won't regret it. And we have more riding instructors than we know what to do with. You'll be a pro in no time."

"You really think so?"

"Absolutely. Look at you!"

She looked out over the fading panorama, totally relaxing into the horse. Walker did the same. They'd reached the quietest part of the inner yard, past the teaching corral where a gate headed into trails that snaked through the hills.

God, he hoped like hell he could get hired on again here in the spring. But for now, he'd enjoy this one night of going round and round, making people feel special.

"Thank you," the woman said a few minutes later, offering him a sincere hug before she made way for the next rider.

"Have a good evening, miss," he said in farewell, then tipped his hat to the next woman. Two hours later, his pockets were overflowing with tips, and Walker was damn near overjoyed he'd been offered this gig. Shit. Even if it didn't lead to a permanent job, it'd been damn fun and damn profitable.

Now that the charity auction and dinner were done, it was time for the dancing. Walker led the last horse away just as the band swung into a Rascal Flatts song. On his way back, the event manager of the ranch grabbed his arm.

"You're done with the horses?" she asked, looking over the clipboard in her hand. She'd worked here for twenty years, he'd never once seen her smile and the woman was probably capable of running the whole state single-handedly. "Can you dance?"

"Pardon?" he asked.

"Dance." She gestured toward the barn. "Two-step."

"Of course I can two-step." What the hell kind of cowboy couldn't two-step?

"Okay. Get in there and mix it up a little. These fancy men don't know what to do with themselves on the dance floor and their wives want to dance."

"Sure," he said, not sure at all. "So I'm still on the clock?"

"Yes!" she snapped as if his stupid question was holding up the festivities.

"And all I need to do is dance with ladies?"

"Jesus, Walker, just get in there already."

Sounded fair to him. Walker headed for the tack room first, to wash his hands and scrub a damp towel over his face and neck to catch any stray dust or straw.

He took off his shirt and shook it out for the same reason, then sniffed to be sure he still smelled decent. But leading horses around in a circle was hardly strenuous activity. He still smelled fine, thank God, so he shrugged his shirt back on, made sure he looked presentable and headed off to dance for money.

"I'll be damned," he murmured. He'd never thought this would be on his résumé. At least he wasn't dancing for tips, though. He assumed.

The barn was darker inside now, and more sparkly, but it didn't take him long to spot an older woman in a lacy dress tapping her foot next to the dance floor. "Ma'am," he said as he approached. "Care for a turn around the floor?"

Three dance partners later, he spotted a miracle. It was Charlie, of all things, standing only a few feet away in a stunning low-cut silver top, laughing at something with the man beside her. Walker nearly stumbled during the waltz, but caught himself just in time to make a joke to his partner about tripping over his own boots. She patted his butt in response. Fair enough.

When the song ended, he wound his way back to the spot where he'd seen Charlie. She was gone, but he caught the flash of her silver top moving through the crowd and followed as she made her way toward the bar.

Her shirt was a thin, metallic fabric that flowed around her as she walked, flashing through the crowd like the glimpse of trout beneath water. "Charlie!"

She swung toward him, the shirt clinging now, reminding him of the shape of her body beneath her clothes. "Walker?" Her face lit up and she jumped forward to give him a hug. "What are you doing here?"

"Working. What are you doing here?"

"The same. Networking for the resort." The flowing sleeve of her shirt started to slide down her shoulder.

"Here." Walker slipped it back up, watching his rough fingers against her smooth skin, entranced for a moment. "It's good to see you." He smoothed his thumb over her collarbone, fascinated by the contrast. She was so soft. So damn soft. It was as if they weren't even the same species.

Her hand came up to cover his and hold his fingers there.

"Do you want to dance?" he asked.

"Right now?"

"It's just a two-step."

She shook her head. "I'm working."

He didn't want to take no for an answer. "Me, too. Come on." He tugged her toward the dance floor as she laughed.

"Maybe one dance."

"Just follow me," he said, but before moving any farther, he stopped, pulled her against him and kissed her. It didn't occur to him that he had no right to. Not until she stiffened against him and he thought she might pull away. These were her people…coworkers and potential clients and people in higher social circles than he'd ever be. She couldn't be seen kissing the help. But before he had time to regret it, Charlie relaxed, and her hand curled around his wrist, and she kissed him back.

The relief that swelled inside him felt surprisingly close to his heart. He'd never be her man, but at least he could have this for a while. That was enough.

WALKER'S MOUTH BRUSHED hers again, and Charlie sighed against him. She wanted to melt into him. She wanted to slide his hand down to her breast and open her mouth for his tongue and make him wild. She couldn't even believe he was here, and now she was weak-kneed and wet for him, before even a minute had passed.

"Charlie," he whispered.

"Yeah?"

He tugged her forward and she followed, still dreaming of more, but then she realized he was leading her toward the dance floor again. "I've never seen you dance, Walker."

He only grinned and swung her into his arms. "It's not so hard."

One of his hands curled around hers, and the other curved around the nape of her neck. "Ready?"

Walker stepped her into the flow of dancers. Considering that she'd been dancing at the saloon the night before, she felt oddly stiff as she moved. It was Walker, after all. And she'd spent quite a few hours of her teenage life imagining that he might ask her to dance at homecoming or some other formal. This seemed momentous.

He must have felt her tension, because he whispered, "Relax, Charlie."

She tried to. She made herself stop thinking. She closed her eyes so she wouldn't see the horror on his face when he realized his mistake and made an excuse to dance her back to the sidelines. In high school, she'd been an athlete, never a dancer, never the pretty, graceful girl. She'd feared those school dances just as much as she'd hoped for that attention.

But this wasn't high school, she reminded herself. She was a girl who danced now. She was a girl who faced her fears. And now…

Now she was dancing.

Walker was turning her around the floor as if he had total control of her body. His fingers were a firm brand against the base of her neck and he held her so near his body that she had to follow his movements.

"Wow. You're a strong lead, Walker."

"Thank you, ma'am."

"Really. That's…" Her surprise melted into a wet, warm mess of thoughts about what he'd be like in bed. His movements were so sure. So strong. Not an ounce of hesitation in his step. He moved her where he wanted her to move and made her feel as if she was gliding gracefully under his hand. They turned round and round the floor. He never let her hesitate.

She wanted him between her legs. She wanted his hand holding her steady for his thrusts instead of his steps.

"God," she whispered.

"What?" Walker responded. She realized the music had ended and he'd guided her to a stop.

She shook her head as the band took up a slower pace, and Walker's hand slid down to the small of her back to ease her into a slow dance.

"This is nice," he said, his mouth close to her ear. "It feels like a date."

She smiled and realized she wasn't done teasing him, after all. "A date? That can't be right."

"Why?"

"I don't date cowboys anymore. Not since college."

"Why not?"

She chuckled and leaned up to brush her mouth along his jaw. "Because, Walker...I have it on good authority that cowboys don't go down."

She heard his breath suck in in surprise; then his chest shook on a rumble of laughter. "Who told you that?"

"Some rodeo cowboy I went out with once."

He shook his head and looked down at her. His hand slid lower on her back until his fingers were resting against the top of her ass. "Darlin'," he drawled, "you've been dating the wrong cowboys."

She started to laugh, but lust crashed through her at the thought of Walker's beard brushing her thigh, his tongue sliding along her most sensitive spots. But she was determined to be cool. "You like doing that, Walker?" she murmured, brushing her cheek against his beard, trying to imagine it was her thigh feeling that softness.

"You have no idea how much I like it."

God. She was wet. Her nipples were hard. She wanted to pull Walker outside into the night, shove him against the barn wall and make him touch her. Make him feel what he'd done to her.

This was ridiculous. This man was a damn menace to society. She couldn't believe he was allowed to walk around free, spreading his sex charm all over unsuspecting women.

He guided her toward the edge of the dance floor, pulling her through the crowd to a quieter spot near the wall. "You're such a tease, Charlie. I think you take pride in driving me crazy. I want you. You don't have to tease me anymore. I give in. I'm fine with any limits you want, just…"

Was that what he thought? That she wanted limits? Ha. Good. Better than him knowing the truth: that she'd do anything to have him right now. Anything.

"Let me come over tomorrow," he whispered. "Please."

"Tomorrow?" she croaked. No, she wanted him tonight. She *needed* him tonight. If he was working late, she'd leave her door unlocked. He could sneak in after midnight. She didn't care. She'd wait. She'd set her damn alarm. "Not tomorrow," she said, but her next words were cut off by the sound of Walker's name. Being said by a woman. Who definitely did not sound pleased.

Walker's head turned, leaving Charlie blinking in

the light his hat had been hiding. "Fuck," she heard him mutter.

Charlotte eased away from him and immediately spotted the woman she'd seen at the Crooked R with Walker. The blonde stood about ten feet away. Next to her, close to the woman as if they'd been speaking, was Keith Taggert.

Crap.

Charlie and Keith stared at each other in shock. The other woman's eyes blazed.

Walker was the first to break the spell. He turned back to Charlie, his mouth grim. "I'm sorry."

"It's no big deal," she said.

"I'd better get back to work. Will you be all right?"

"I'm fine."

He waited until she looked up at him, then nodded. "I'll talk to you later, then, if you're sure you'll be okay."

He shot the other woman a look that Charlie couldn't read, then hesitated a moment before moving back toward the heart of the party.

"He worked for us until a few weeks ago," Charlie heard the woman quietly explaining to Keith. That woman had been his lover…and his boss? Oh. That made his tale of unemployment a little more interesting.

Charlie caught Keith's gaze and made a little grimace of contrition. She had to remind herself that she hadn't actually been making out with Walker. She hadn't been doing all the things she'd been thinking.

It might not have been entirely professional to be cozied up to a cowboy, letting him whisper in her ear, but it hadn't looked quite as bad as it honestly was. Nobody knew what she'd been thinking about. Nobody knew what they'd been planning.

But Keith was frowning at her, not responding with sympathy or understanding. The woman touched his arm, and he jerked back and glanced around the party as if to check on who was watching this awful little scene.

Charlie decided she'd better return to her assigned schmoozing and started to walk away, but Keith took a step toward her. *Shit.*

"I'm sorry," she said as soon as he got close. "He's an old friend. I didn't mean to embarrass you or—"

"No, it's fine. I understand."

"You do?" She'd expected him to engage in an epic freak out as his wife would have.

"Of course. You're a young, single woman. You should be enjoying yourself."

"I should? I thought you'd be… I know there's a lot of talk around, and you gave me a chance. I don't want you to think I don't appreciate that."

"Charlotte, I wanted to hire you because I thought you'd gotten a bad deal. You're a local girl, and when I heard the story, I asked Dawn about you. She told me she'd known you for years, and I figured if you'd been friends with my wife, you were the kind of person who deserved a second chance."

Charlie knew she was standing there with her mouth

open, but she couldn't make her muscles work. What the hell? Dawn had said over and over that she was the one who'd gotten Charlie hired. That she'd talked her husband into it despite his reservations. She'd made clear that any misstep on Charlie's part would likely get her fired and Dawn would look like an idiot.

She shook her head. "I thought Dawn was the one who wanted to hire me."

"Oh, God no. I mean…" He flashed a sheepish smile. "Don't get me wrong. She likes you, she just had a few reservations about the accusations. But I get you."

"You do?"

"You're loyal. That's an admirable quality and something that's missing in ambitious people these days."

"Well…" She supposed maybe she was loyal. But mostly, she'd just been blind in her last job and now she was grateful for this one.

"Look, you popped up on my radar because of the police investigation and all that other nastiness. Sure. But your brother called and suggested I hire you, and I asked Dawn about you and she had such positive memories of your character. Now that you're here, I agree with both of them. You're amazing. Professional. Dedicated."

She nodded dumbly, too stunned to do anything else. Her brother had called to *suggest* her? Why had he played it down?

Her mind spun. This whole time, Dawn had been pretending it had all been her idea, but the truth was that she'd been dragged into it by Keith and *Brad?* Dawn had wanted Charlie to feel insecure, as if her position at the company was at Dawn's whim and could be terminated at any moment. It wasn't true.

Keith touched her elbow. "Listen, Charlotte. This is just my first resort of many. I've got plans for Utah and Colorado, and then Europe. And you're in on the ground floor. If you put in the hard work, your possibilities are limitless. You can help me plan and roll out each resort. You could end up in Europe if that's where you want to be. I'm loyal to those who are loyal to me. I want you on my team, all right? So don't look so nervous."

The flood of relief that overtook her was so strong she felt embarrassed. Tears sprang to her eyes, and she was relieved for the relatively dim lighting in the barn. Maybe this didn't have to only be a job she got through. Maybe she could have the future she'd always planned on, despite the awfulness in Tahoe.

She looked away, touching on several people in the crowd before she saw Walker's ex-boss watching with narrow eyes from a few feet away. Charlie ignored her.

"Thank you," she said to Keith. "I really appreciate knowing that you believe in me. It means so much."

"I do believe in you. You're good at what you do. You work hard. You're way ahead of schedule. If there's anything you're ever worried about, or anything you see that's worrying you, please come to me. Day or night."

Oh, that would go over well with Dawn. But Char-

lie nodded and blinked the moisture from her eyes.
"I will."

"Promise?"

She smiled. Keith had struck her as uptight and boring, but she suddenly wanted to give him a hug. She
wasn't dumb enough to act on it, but she did take his
hand and squeeze it. "I promise. Thank you."

When she walked away from Keith, she took a wide
berth around Walker's ex-employer, but she'd apparently tried to avoid the wrong woman. Only ten steps
into the crowd, she walked right into the claws of
Dawn. "What the hell was that?" Dawn hissed, digging
her fingers into Charlie's arm to force her to a stop.

"Excuse me?" Charlie tried to yank her arm free,
but Dawn refused to let go.

"You are such a little slut. My God. Don't you have
any shame?"

For a moment, Charlie considered one of the many
self-defense moves she could use to break Dawn's hold
on her. She wasn't an expert, but she'd had some basic
training. But tempted as she was to use physical force,
she didn't want to draw attention, so she relaxed her
arm until it was limp in Dawn's hand. Dawn's grip
slowly loosened.

"I just had an interesting conversation with your
husband." Charlie twisted her arm free and stepped
back a few inches.

"A conversation? Is that what you call it? Practically
fucking a big stud in front of him to get his attention?"

"Oh, my God. There's something seriously wrong with you."

Dawn's eyes went so wide that Charlie could see the whites all around her irises. She'd hit a nerve. "Don't you speak to me that way! Have you forgotten that I am your last resort? Ha. Literally! I brought you into this job. One word to my husband and you'll be out."

"That's funny. Because Keith just told me that he was the one who insisted on hiring me."

Her crazy eyes blinked. The smirk disappeared. She shook her head. "No. I hired you."

"Your husband wanted to hire me and he did it even though you objected, and that's why you've been acting this way."

"That's not true!"

"It is true. You would have gotten rid of me by now if you could. That's why I drive you crazy."

Dawn's mouth twisted into a growl. Her finger stabbed Charlie's breastbone. "I was fine with him hiring you until I found out the whole story! What man wouldn't want to bring in a slut who sleeps her way to the top?"

Charlie opened her mouth, about to tell this woman off once and for all, but this wasn't the place. If she got into a screaming match with the owner's wife and was later fired, that would only add another layer of tarnish to her already rough reputation. So she took a deep breath and spoke calmly. "Listen. I promise you that I have no designs on your husband. Not only that, but he's never been anything but a complete professional with me. I swear."

"I don't need you assuring me of my husband's fidelity!"

"Fine. He checks out my tits whenever he can and drools over my womanly wiles."

"You… You…"

Alarmed by the fluorescent shade of pink that took over Dawn's face, Charlie held up her hands. "God, I was just kidding. I don't have any breasts to check out, in case you haven't noticed. At least one thing hasn't changed since high school. Just calm down, Dawn. He's never said or done one inappropriate thing. He's not interested."

"Then why did he want to hire you? And why has he been so…" She waved a frantic hand.

Charlie didn't want to know what kind of "so" he'd been. That was above her pay grade.

"And when did you get so…" Another frantic hand wave. Her perfect little nose wrinkled.

"When did I get so what?"

"We had the same ideals when we were young. That's the only reason I agreed he could hire you. I thought maybe you'd retained some redeeming qualities, but I was wrong. You turned out just like all those other girls."

"I didn't turn out any way. I just grew up."

"Badly."

Charlie threw her hands in the air. "Well, I'm so sorry I've ruined everything for you! I know life married to a rich, successful man must be so damn difficult to bear, and now I'm here making it worse because I'm single and I hang out in bars."

"That is not my issue and you know it."

"Then what is it?"

"You're single, and you go to bars, and you sleep around, and you flaunt your ass around like a stray cat in heat *and* my husband knows you like married men. *That's* my issue."

Instead of fury, weariness washed over Charlie. She wanted to sit this girl down and explain to her that it was the twenty-first century and women could enjoy their lives just as much as men. They could be single and have sex and make money and still be nice, fulfilled, genuine people. But those crazy eyes were not open to seeing sexual equality for women. Not right now. Not in the face of Charlie Allington, husband hunter.

She couldn't let that stand. "I don't like married men, Dawn. I had no idea my boss was married. Nobody did. It was a big resort. He kept his private life a secret so he could rotate through all the new cocktail waitresses as they came on board. Obviously, I didn't know about that part, either. But more important than all of that…if you don't trust your husband, that has nothing to do with me. Please leave me out of it. I'm begging you."

"Don't talk to me about my husband."

"Fine. I'll talk about you instead. You can't spend every single day thinking about him and what he's doing and how to make him behave. You think he's doing that for you?"

"It's not the same," she muttered, her eyes searching the crowd behind Charlie.

"Why?"

Her wandering eyes finally found Charlie again. She looked her up and down with disdain. "Do you even remember the things we talked about in school? How we wanted to meet good men and get married and be successful, and not waste our lives screwing around with these stupid boys?"

"Sure, but—"

"Well, I did that, Charlotte. I met a good man. A successful, ambitious man who loved me, and who loved that I had worked hard and stayed focused and saved myself for something special. For *him*. I supported him. I left college to help him build his business. I had his children and I stayed home every single day until they were in school. I invested myself in this partnership. This is what I've chosen to do, so don't tell me I can't spend my days worrying about how he is and what he's doing. That is my job. To make this work. To make sure it doesn't fail. And I am just as important to our success as any deal he might make or any fortune he might invest."

Wow. Charlie blinked in shock. "Behind every great man…" she said. Dawn nodded, obviously missing the emphasis Charlie had put on the word "behind."

"So," Dawn continued, "don't waltz in here thinking I missed the boat because I didn't go off to the big city and drink myself into a stupor so I could lose my virginity to some sweaty stranger. Don't think I'm missing out just because I've never met a guy at a bar or partied in Vegas or…"

Charlie leaned a little closer to Dawn. "Fine. But don't think I'm evil because I have. If you think being single and slutty is such a shitty life, then why feel threatened by it?"

"I don't feel threatened," Dawn said, but she'd gotten distracted again. Her eyes homed in on something like a death ray.

Charlie followed her gaze and was surprised to see Dawn staring at Walker, who was in close conversation with his ex-lover. *Shit.* Something in Charlie's chest twisted at the sight. How stupid was that? Walker could talk to whoever he wanted. He wasn't Charlie's boyfriend. He never would be.

But she still heard the words "Who is that?" coming from her mouth.

"That's Nicole Fletcher," Dawn said, her voice flat. "She's an old classmate of Keith's. Kind of a slut, people say."

"Aren't we all?" Charlie muttered.

Dawn didn't answer. It was probably too obvious a question.

She watched Walker and Nicole speak for a few more seconds. He wasn't in flirtatious mode, that much was clear. Not that it was any of her business. Any woman who was stupid enough to fall in love with that man would live with a breaking heart every day of her life.

"Are you two sharing that cowboy or something?"

A solid mark. Maybe Dawn really did have her number. Maybe Charlie was just a worthless slut. Charlie sighed, feeling defeated by all of it. "Look, Dawn, you didn't want me here. I get that now. It kind of makes sense. Actually, it makes perfect sense, and I'm sorry if I've caused trouble. But I'm here now, so can't we just call a truce? Please?"

Dawn shrugged, already moving away from Charlie. She spared her a glance over her shoulder. "Keep your friends close and your enemies closer," she said as she walked away.

That didn't sound like much of a truce. Charlie grabbed a glass of champagne from a passing waiter. This was a war she didn't want. She could rise above it. She was smart and amazing and determined. She could do this. She could do anything.

Two hours later she trudged into the Stud Farm in utter defeat. She'd tried to enjoy the rest of the evening. She'd tried to schmooze about the resort. But all anyone had wanted to do was gossip about people she'd never heard of. Hell, even when she'd tried pointing the gossiping tongues toward Dawn, she'd failed. A couple of people had laughed and implied that Dawn was a prissy bitch, but otherwise the woman never seemed to have set a foot wrong in this town. She was the consummate socialite wife. The most Charlie had gotten was "Did you hear she's already gone half gray? If she didn't have that amazing hairdresser, she wouldn't look quite so perfect all the time, let me tell you."

"Gawd," Charlie groaned as she toed off her heels and stretched her poor, squished toes. All she wanted was a hot bath and then a soft bed. Thank God she hadn't invited Walker over. She wouldn't have been doing much mind blowing. Unless his number-one turn-on was limp snoring.

Dawn had defeated her. There was no mystery to solve. No reason behind anything. The woman was just bored and eaten up with jealousy. Over her husband or Charlie's adventures or something else that no one knew about. There was no evidence to acquire. Nothing she was missing. Dawn just needed therapy.

Charlie probably did, too. She'd assumed the worst about her brother because he was a gruff talker and… sometimes an asshole, truth be told. But he'd helped her out and hadn't even taken the credit. She'd have to find a way to repay him.

Damn it. She hated being wrong. Especially with Brad.

She tossed her shirt on the couch and unfastened her jeans as she headed straight for the bathroom to fill the tub with hot water. She was tying up her hair and sinking into the steaming water before the tub was even half-full. "Oh, God, yes," she moaned as she slid deeper. This tub wasn't nearly as nice as the jetted number she'd left behind at the resort, but the water felt so good on her tired legs that she nearly wept.

Maybe she was getting too old for wearing heels for five hours. Maybe she was getting too old for all of it.

Was it possible that Dawn was right? Had Charlie taken her life in the wrong direction?

She could've married some rich man and been living in the kind of luxury she now protected. Granted, she hadn't envisioned the society-wife life for herself. When she was young, she'd planned to go to college, have a good career and then meet a nice man and settle down in the country.

Then she'd gone to college in Colorado and fallen in with a fast crowd.

She burst into laughter at her own ridiculous thought as she switched off the faucet and sank farther into the tub.

A fast crowd. Right. What she'd fallen in with was the tiny group of women isolated within the Systems Security program at school. Charlie had learned that she could be successful and smart and still have fun. She didn't have to choose between being perfect or being her mother. There was a middle ground, and she'd found it. She and her girlfriends had gotten the same grades as the boys, and they'd had fun while they did it.

The bath cheered her up, and she was almost ready to fall peacefully into bed when she heard a noise from the other side of the wall.

Walker was home. She closed her eyes and listened to the creak of floorboards as he moved about. A door opened very close by. She jumped when the sound of his shower suddenly rumbled through the wall.

She couldn't help smiling then, picturing him as he stepped into the tub and the sound of the water changed. God, he was a gorgeous man. All muscle and dark hair and smiles. Maybe she did have the energy, after all. Maybe she could go knock on his door as soon as the shower stopped. Better yet, just walk in. He never seemed to lock his apartment. She could walk in and drop her towel and tell him she was ready for him.

But then she heard it. A low grunt that rumbled through the apartment wall. Then a soft gasp that she only heard because she was holding her breath.

Was he having *sex?* Was he with that woman?

But no. She'd only heard one set of footsteps and definitely no heels. He was alone. He was getting himself off. He was thinking about Charlie.

Despite her earlier jealousy, she was almost sure of that. The way he'd held her tonight. The things he'd whispered. She tipped her head and let it rest on the cool tile of the wall so every sound would have to go right through her.

He grunted again and murmured something. Something low and urgent. It could have been her name. It could've been anyone's name, but she didn't care anymore. Didn't care whose name he said or who he thought of. Because she could picture him then, wet and hard, his fist wrapped around that gorgeous, thick cock. Stroking it.

Charlie slipped a hand between her legs. She was

already wet, slippery despite the water. She bit her lip to keep from crying out at the pleasure, but that didn't stop the feeling. It didn't stop her thighs from clenching or her hips from jumping. Her other hand toyed with her hard nipple, pinching and teasing it as she stroked herself.

She wished she could watch him. God, she'd love to see him as he jerked off, one hand braced against the shower wall as water sluiced down his back.

"Walker," she whispered as he grunted again. God, she wanted him inside her. Wanted to barge in and stop him from getting himself off so she could have it all. His cock, his come, his gasps of pleasure. She wanted him making that sound because he was pushing into her body, because she was squeezing around him. She wanted him whispering her name as he tried to hold back.

She squeezed her nipple harder, her teeth sinking into her lip as she tried to hold back a cry. He thought she was trying to slow him down, but she wanted everything with him. Every taste, every sound, every feeling.

Charlie rubbed herself faster, pushing her hips up as she clenched her teeth. She imagined him watching as she touched herself, urging her on, pumping his cock as he—

She heard another faint sound from his side of the wall, then a curse and a strangled moan. He was coming. Right there. Oh, God. "Yes," she whispered as her own orgasm built inside her. "Yes."

And then she came. Biting her lip, her eyes clenched shut as she tried not to scream. She came as she pictured him, naked and wet just a few feet away, come still dripping off his fist.

Yes. One more day. She could wait. But just barely.

CHAPTER ELEVEN

WALKER STOOD IN the parking lot of the roadside restaurant, watching his breath cloud his vision every time he exhaled. A cold front had moved in overnight, which was good news for him. It meant he'd have steady hard work soon, as ranchers hired extra hands to drive cattle down from high grazing land. But there was no work today. No excuse not to meet his brother for breakfast.

Not that he didn't want to see his brother. Micah only came through town a few times a year, making the circuit of hospitals in the Mountain West, reviewing critical-care systems or so he'd explained several times to Walker.

Walker had no idea what he did. All he knew was that Micah was good at it. He was great at everything. The best little brother a guy could hope for.

So, no, Walker didn't want to avoid his brother, but a visit with Micah meant that Walker would have to see their dad, too. A quick drive over to the care facility, and then an excruciating eternity of staring awkwardly at the floor. There was nothing dangerous about it. Nothing scary. But his pulse pounded as if he were standing at the edge of an airplane door, waiting to jump out.

His heart thundered so loudly that he couldn't hear himself think, so he stood still for a moment, looking up at the big Hot Food sign that blinked weakly in the cold sun. Micah always wanted to meet at this same dive. Walker thought of him every time he passed it.

"You look like a damn mountain man," Micah said as soon as Walker stepped through the door.

"Micah. It's good to see you, too." His brother stood and hugged him, a gesture Walker was thankful for every single time. They certainly hadn't learned that kind of affection from their dad. "You look great. How's Timothy?"

"Still putting up with me. How's your flavor of the month?"

Walker smiled. "Pretty tasty."

"Ha. You never change. Good thing Dad never gave a damn about grandchildren. Neither of us seems likely to give him any."

"Yeah. Not that he'd notice at this point."

Neither of them bothered with looking at the menu, they just ordered the regular and settled into the coffee with a vengeance.

Walker tapped his mug. "I'm glad you're here, but I wish we could just hang out. There's no reason to go see him, you know. He doesn't know we're there."

"Yes, he does. He's still in there, Walker."

"Ha. You think? I don't know who that old man is. He's not Dad."

"He's still happy to see us."

"Yeah." Walker looked out the window at the passing traffic. "That's exactly what I mean."

They fell into silence. There wasn't much to say on the subject. Their hard, mean bastard of a father had been reduced by old age to a confused man who was a damn sight happier than he'd ever been when he was healthy. Their parents had married late. Dad had been fifty by the time Walker was born. Unfortunately, age hadn't softened him early enough for Walker's sake. He'd still been made of granite and rage all through Walker's eighteen years at home.

"How's work?" Micah asked as the waitress set down half a dozen plates on the table.

"Oh, you know. I'm picking up jobs here and there. It's fine."

"You're not at the ranch anymore?"

"No. I'll find something permanent in the spring."

"I still think you should've kept Dad's land. The house wasn't much, but you could've run a hundred head of cattle out of there."

Walker changed the subject. They'd had this discussion a dozen times. "Anything new for you?"

Micah shrugged. "They made me a VP last month."

"Jesus, man. No wonder you can afford that amazing place on the water in Seattle. Congratulations. You deserve it."

"Thanks. Are you going to come out sometime? Or do I need to drive a herd of cattle into the yard to tempt you?"

He'd never managed the time off before, but... "You know what? Maybe I'll drive out this winter, if you're willing to put me up."

"Really?" His brother's face lit up, and Walker decided then and there that he'd make the time.

"Yeah. Don't bother with the cattle. You've only got a patio anyway. They'd make a mess of it."

"I'm glad, Walker. Really."

"If you're sure."

"Please. We'd love to have you. You know that. But you'll have to promise to behave. Half of my friends have a crush on a photo of you I have in the living room."

Walker grinned. "Yeah? That might be nice. All the attention without any of the temptation."

"You sure? Some of them are damn hot men."

Walker burst into laughter and raised his cup in a mock toast. "I guess we'll find out. But after all the years I've spent in bunkhouses, I can't imagine I could ever find any male part appealing."

Micah waggled his eyebrows. "Oh, bunkhouses. Nice. Remind me again why I didn't become a cowboy?"

Walker shook his head. "I'd have beaten your ass before I'd have let you waste your brains on driving stock. Seriously, Micah, I'm proud of you. And so was Dad, when he was still clear."

Micah's smile faded. "Dad was proud of you, too."

"Bullshit. He hated having me for a son. Called me an idiot every day of my life."

"Walker…"

He waved his brother off. "Don't defend him. He was a miserable bastard."

Micah finally gave up on whatever speech he'd been about to make. His shoulders dropped. "He didn't understand."

"Yeah. No shit." There hadn't been any such thing as dyslexia to their father. There hadn't been learning disabilities. There'd only been thick-skulled stupidity and laziness. There'd only been a stubborn, shiftless kid who needed a slap upside his head every day and an occasional good beating.

Their mom had sometimes shaken her head and clucked her tongue about her husband's words, but that had been it. Walker had at least been able to shield Micah. That was why Micah was more sympathetic. More forgiving. Because he'd seen a calmer side to their dad. Walker had drawn the fury, and he'd been damn glad to be the one.

But by the time he and Micah were teenagers, things had calmed down slightly, if only because Walker had been big enough to fight back. And by then, they'd both been mostly out of the house. Micah had taken classes at the community college in addition to high school. And Walker had spent every waking moment out with friends or working. He'd worked hard. He'd saved up to move out. And he'd saved up even more to send his little brother to college. It was the best thing he'd ever done.

Micah was an amazing man doing amazing things.

Walker was so proud of him. Walker might be destined to be nothing but a muddy ranch hand for the rest of his life, but he'd helped raise his little brother. Taught him how to ride and fight. He'd taken him fishing and hunting and camping. And he'd helped pay for the education that Micah had deserved and their father had scoffed at.

Micah set his coffee on the table. "We should get going. I think he has physical therapy at ten."

He wanted to tell Micah to go without him, but he'd tried that before and it had ended with an argument that had left Walker feeling like an asshole. "All right," he said, "but I'll meet you over there." He needed the time alone to brace himself for the visit. And the time alone after to stuff all his emotions back down where they belonged.

"Sure. I've got to hit the road after anyway."

"You just got here. Stay for dinner, at least. Better yet, stay the night. I've got a couch that's almost long enough for you."

"Tempting," Micah said, as he stood and waited for Walker to follow him out.

"Come on. It's been four months since you've been through."

"I'm sorry, Walk. I'm already running late. I have to get to Helena for a lunch meeting tomorrow."

"No relief from travel with the promotion?"

"Oh, there's some talk of hiring another team member, but so far I'm basically doing two jobs. So no."

"Figures. I'll see you over there."

Walker closed himself up in his truck and took a deep breath as his brother pulled away. It'd only be a thirty-minute visit. Best to get it over with.

The senior care center was at the outskirts of town, next to the hospital. A small place, but modern and clean. They'd talked of moving their father to Washington to be closer to Micah. After all, it wasn't as if Walker ever dropped in to visit. But here in Jackson, they knew some of the nurses and attendants, so they didn't have to worry that their dad would be neglected or mistreated. So here he stayed.

When Walker pulled up to the center, Micah was already going through the doors. He knew better than to wait for Walker, but this time, Walker forced himself to get out of the truck and walk right inside. No hesitation, no pacing around, no psyching himself up. He simply walked through the lobby and straight to his dad's room.

Of course, his dad wasn't there. He never was. It was only the stranger in his dad's skin. A thin old man who seemed to be collapsing in on himself. A ghost who smiled as if that came naturally to him.

"Oh, hello," the old man said to Walker. He looked back to Micah with that same smile. "Two visitors on the same day?"

"Dad, it's Walker," Micah said patiently. Their father just gave him another pleasant smile and shifted his slippered feet. His bare ankles were thin and pale and hairless.

Micah sat down for a conversation. He even reached

for his dad's hand. But Walker didn't sit down. He paced to the window and looked out at the view of pine trees and a parking lot.

He couldn't reconcile this frail body with the past. His dad had always been a giant. A mean son of a bitch with a temper to match his strength. When Walker was small, his dad had been a vengeful, flawed god. Unfathomably powerful. Now he was a harmless stranger dying slowly of congestive heart failure and Alzheimer's.

Walker snuck a look over his shoulder and felt rage boil up inside him. He didn't even have the right to be angry at this man. His father's final, parting cruelty had been removing himself from the path of that rage. Walker had lots of things to say to his dad, but if he said them, he'd be raging at a helpless innocent. He'd be screaming at a man who had no idea why or what he'd done. He was free of it.

Every time Walker saw him, it only made the anger worse. The fury grew inside him and pushed at his body from the inside out. He should've punched the bastard back when he'd had the chance. He should've hurt him. Made him sorry.

He stared out at the trees until they went blurry. Then he stared some more.

After an excruciating half hour, a nurse finally broke up the reunion. "I'm sorry, gentlemen, but it's time for Mr. Pearce's therapy."

Walker turned and walked out without a word.

When he got to the lobby, he breathed in deeply. It didn't smell like bleach and urine out here.

"Hey." Micah's hand rested on his shoulder. "You don't even look at him anymore."

"He's not Dad. And if he was, I wouldn't set foot in this fucking place no matter how many times you asked."

"Walker," Micah said, but he didn't add anything else. They'd had this discussion many times. Micah had forgiven their dad. Walker didn't even want to.

"I miss you, Micah. You should try to switch up your schedule now that you're the big man on campus. Come through more often."

Micah pulled him in for a long hug, ending it with a painful slap on the back. "Come see us this winter, all right? I mean it. You do the long-distance driving for once."

"I will."

As he watched his brother step through the doors, Walker heard his father's voice echoing down the hall. Some helpless, petulant tone he'd never heard out of that man's mouth when he'd been himself.

He clenched his jaw and walked out without looking back. Micah could do this on his own next time. Walker was fucking done with it.

CHARLIE HIKED THE laundry basket higher on her hip and raced up the cellar stairs. She wasn't crazy about the stone-walled utility room in the basement of the Stud Farm, but a little Stevie Wonder made it all better. Singing along to one of his best '70s songs, Charlie danced across the entryway and cheerfully hopped up the stairs toward the second floor. It was her day off and she wasn't going to let a creepy cellar ruin her good mood.

It was a glorious day. Cold and windy while she was alone and cozy in her little apartment. Nothing could ruin it.

Except a stranger waiting at the top of the stairs to murder her.

She shrieked and nearly tripped to her death before she registered that it was Walker. He raised his eyebrows and said something she couldn't hear over the music. This iPod would be the death of her.

Knees shaking, Charlie took the last few stairs, set down the basket and pulled her earbuds out. "What?" she croaked.

"I said 'good song.'"

"God. You didn't hear me singing, did you?"

"Oh, I sure did."

She cringed. She had the worst singing voice in the world. Too bad she loved music so much. "I'm sorry about that."

"No, it was entertaining."

"Shut up, Walker."

He grinned unabashedly. "What are you doing here?"

"It's my day off."

"Mine, too," he said with a raised eyebrow.

"Wanna help me fold laundry?"

He looked down at her basket. She'd piled all her unmentionables on top. "Just try and stop me."

The way his voice dropped reminded her with sudden and violent force of how she'd gotten off the night before. Her blush had nothing to do with the lacy panties he was eyeing and everything to do with the ones she wanted him to tear off.

"Let's do this." She picked up the basket and led him toward her lair.

Turned out she didn't have to do much leading. As soon as she set the basket on the coffee table, Walker spun her around and kissed her. A long, deep kiss that had her dizzy within seconds. "I've been wanting to do that since last night. You have no idea how crazy you made me."

Oh, she had some idea. Smiling, she rose on her toes to kiss him again. She slid one hand over his beard, marveling at how soft it was. She wanted to feel it everywhere.

His kiss was more urgent today, his hands a little rougher when they slid over her hips and down to her ass. Had she really driven him that crazy? Apparently she had, because he was hard as a rock against her belly.

"Charlie," he said against her jaw. "I'm sorry. I want to touch you again. Tell me to stop anytime. I swear I will. But I want to touch you. Please."

God. Poor man. He still thought she wanted to take it slow. He was in for a surprise. "You can touch me, Walker."

"Thank God," he groaned. "I want to. So much."

She pushed him toward the bedroom, and he went willingly, tugging her along as he kissed her and walked backward through the door.

She wished she was wearing something sexier than yoga pants and a T-shirt, but he seemed to like the feel of her ass through the pants, and at least she was braless and her shirt was easy access. He had it off and over her head before she'd even fallen back onto her bed.

"God, I love your tits," he said as he followed her down to the mattress.

"You're easy to please," she murmured, then lost herself in a gasp as his mouth closed over her nipple. Yes, he was definitely rougher this time. He sucked her harder. His teeth scraped over her and she shuddered against him.

"I'm sorry," he murmured against her skin. Then he drew her in again.

The contrast between nice Walker and sexual Walker made everything inside her tighten. They'd been friends so long, and she'd wanted him so long, and how many times had she fantasized that he'd say *I'm sorry* as he took advantage of her? God, yes. He was sorry but he couldn't stop himself from touching her. He was so sorry, but he *had* to.

By the time he moved to her other breast, Charlie was squirming for more. She needed his hands on her pussy. She needed his mouth, too. Oh, God, she needed that and he'd *promised* her.

And now his mouth was moving down, his beard

sliding over her belly as his hands went to the waist of her pants.

"Is this okay?" he murmured. He slowly peeled the fabric down, exposing her hip bones first, then the top of her panties. "This is okay, right, Charlie?"

She didn't say yes or no. She wanted him like this, uncertain and desperate as he stripped her. She wore only her panties now, and he looked at her for a moment, his blue eyes shining and hot, cheekbones flushed above the edge of his beard. His hair was sweetly mussed from her clasping fingers. He was gorgeous. Even with all his clothes on, he was the kind of centerfold a girl could get off to.

Walker laid one of his hands over the front of her underwear. He just held it there, watching as his thumb traced the edge of the silky fabric. She watched, too. His hand was so wide, his blunt-nailed fingers thick, and the skin so scarred and dark against her most delicate flesh. He could hurt her if he wanted to, but he never would. Not unless she asked him very nicely.

As they both watched, his fingers stole beneath the edge of her panties and slipped down. She moved her thighs apart and eased up onto her elbows to watch. His fingertips traced over her plump lips, just the edge, then back up. Teasing her. Testing her. She held her breath as he did it again. Then his fingers slid along wetness and brushed her clit.

"Oh," she gasped. Walker watched her face. She was breathing hard and fast already.

"I want to taste you," he said, before he leaned forward and pressed one nearly chaste kiss to her mound. Then another. When he opened his mouth over her, she felt the shocking heat and wetness of him through that thin fabric.

She gasped his name and he licked her. His tongue slipped over her clit as she watched him, tormenting her through her pink panties. "Oh, God. Walker." He did it again, and now that the fabric was wet, it felt even better. But not good enough. Not nearly good enough. Then his fingers slipped over her slick lips and this time, he pushed deeper. Just a little. Charlie's hips bucked toward him in shocked pleasure.

Now his mouth closed over her and he sucked until she was whimpering. "You want to leave your panties on, Charlie? It's okay if you do."

Fuck, he was teasing her. Working her clit with his lips and tongue, torturing her pussy with his fingers. "No," she gasped.

"Are you sure? I don't want to go too fast for you. We can leave them on if you feel shy."

"Please. Just…take them off."

He sucked at her one more time as his fingers slid slowly up and down.

"Please," she begged again. "Please, I want to."

Walker nodded and then he finally dragged her underwear slowly down. She was mortified to see her thighs were already trembling. His hands smoothed over them as if he'd noticed, too. But then his eyes were locked on what he'd uncovered. Her bare pussy, open and wet for him.

She saw the flash of his teeth in his beard, heard the low rumble of his growl. He stood and took off his shirt, his boots, his jeans, but his gaze stayed glued to her the whole time.

Her eyes, on the other hand, were roaming restlessly over him, catching on pleasing sight after pleasing sight. She'd need days to get her fill of just looking. Then weeks to memorize him with her hands. A few more to taste every inch of him. The innocuous parts like the inside of his wrist, the top of his hip. And the dangerous parts like his mouth, his fingers and that gorgeous cock he'd just released from his briefs.

Oh, God. Yes, weeks just for that.

He retrieved a condom from his jeans, and for a moment, she thought he was going to skip all the foreplay and just fuck her. Frankly, she was fine with that. She needed to feel him inside her. All her nerves went tight in perfect anticipation of him pushing into her.

But no… He set the condom beside her and met her gaze. "I'll stop whenever you want. That's just in case. Okay?" She nodded, and when he knelt between her legs, she scooted farther back on the bed, eager to give him room to work.

He put his mouth to her inner thigh first. Then a little higher. Then he sucked at the hollow at the very top of her leg. His beard brushed the sensitive skin between her thighs. "Just in case…" he whispered, dragging his mouth along her sex. "You like this…" His tongue flicked over her clit.

She tensed, her breathing filling the silence of the room.

"…as much as I know I will."

Another faint little lick of his tongue. Charlie whimpered.

"Look at you, Charlie. So bare and vulnerable."

Yes. That was what she liked about it. She was so sensitive like this. So—

He opened his mouth against her and sucked at her clit. The pleasure was so shocking that she cried out. Loudly. His eyes flickered up. And then he smiled, mouth still pressed to her flesh, his eyes crinkling with delight. He sucked at her again and pressed his tongue to her, and Charlie couldn't stop the animal groan that tore from her throat.

Charlie let her head fall back when he started working her with his tongue. His thumb slid over her slick flesh, up and down, up and down. Then he pressed a little deeper, but just a little. His thick thumb traced her opening, teasing her with the possibility.

"Oh, God," she panted. "Please."

"Shhh," he murmured. "Take your time, Charlie. I could stay here all night."

Then his tongue was on her again and she was crying out and whimpering. When he kept teasing her and offering no satisfaction, she gave up her coy act completely and blurted out, "I need you inside me. Walker, please. Fuck me. I need you. All of you. Now."

He only chuckled and kept up his teasing, the laughter brushing his beard against her screaming nerves.

Finally she felt her release building. That strange, sweet wave of awareness prickling under the skin of her neck and then her chest and belly and thighs. The tension riding beneath her skin until it all built up into that one spot under his mouth, and then—

She screamed, her hips bucking against the arm Walker had wrapped around her thigh. He sucked at her again, bringing on an even stronger climax, a hoarser scream, as the pleasure pulsed through her, over and over, seemingly endless. When he sucked again, she twisted her hands into his hair. "Oh, fuck, stop. Please. I can't…"

Walker lifted his head and offered her the most ridiculous, full-of-himself grin she'd ever seen. "Told you you've been dating the wrong cowboys."

She groaned.

"Want to go again?" he asked, dipping his head toward her.

Charlie let out a squeak and tugged at his hair. "No! I need a minute. It's…sensitive. Just give me a minute."

He pushed up to his knees and reached for the condom. "Too sensitive?" he asked as he stroked his hard cock.

"Oh," she said, already transfixed by the sight of him. "No. Not too sensitive."

"Good."

He rolled the condom on, watching her face as he did. "Say yes, Charlie?"

He was so sweet. Hadn't she already begged him to fuck her? "Yes," she said clearly, reaching for him as he stretched over her. She wound her fingers into his hair and looked him straight in the eye. "Yes, Walker."

"Thank God."

Holding her gaze, he gripped himself and she felt the delicious slide of him against her slick flesh. He notched himself just there, just where she needed, then pushed slowly in.

Oh, God. She was so glad he'd only teased her before, because his cock sliding in felt like everything she'd ever wanted. As if she'd been missing it for years. She winced as he stretched her, and Walker eased back, but she didn't want it easy. She slid her nails down his spine.

"Fuck me," she urged, and Walker's hips jumped forward.

He cursed under his breath and tried to pull back again, but she lifted her hips and took him deeper. He surged into her with a hiss of pain or pleasure that got mixed up with her own shocked gasp. He felt bigger than she'd even expected, and she was thankful for the moment he took to press his forehead to hers and breathe.

"Walker," she whispered, just for the joy of saying his name while she was so filled with him. She raised her hand to his jaw, to stroke his beard and urge his mouth to hers.

Tasting herself on his lips, she kissed him deeply, and Walker rewarded her by slowly, so slowly, moving inside her.

Her eyes fluttered closed. She needed the darkness.

She needed to just feel him. His tongue against hers, his hands cradling her head and his cock moving inside her. Sliding, stretching, filling. In that moment, there was nothing else in the whole world except his body and hers.

"Walker," she said again, as he kissed her chin, her cheek, her jaw.

"You feel so good, Charlie. Damn."

Raising her knees, she curved her legs around his hips to take him deeper even though her heart beat harder at the thought, warning her he was deep enough. But he couldn't be too much for her. She wanted him so badly. And when he groaned and thrust harder, Charlie threw her head back and cried out with tortured pleasure.

"I'm sorry," he murmured against her throat. "I'm sorry." When he tried to gentle his thrusts, Charlie dug her nails into his ass to urge him on.

She didn't want it gentle, even though Walker seemed determined to hold back. What was the point of having a big, rough, beautifully hung cowboy in your bed if he wasn't going to give it his all?

Her nails seemed to spur him on. He braced himself on his hands and fucked her harder. When she dragged her nails up his back, his hips slapped into hers.

"Oh, God, yes," she groaned. "Like that."

"Fuck. Charlie. I don't want to hurt you."

"No," she whispered into his ear. "Please. Hurt me."

Walker twisted his fist into her hair. "Damn you," he growled. "Damn you." And then he gave her exactly what she wanted.

He was shaking.

His hands trembled when he wasn't holding her, so Walker gripped her harder. Her nails bit into him, the pain brightening the pleasure of sinking himself over and over into her body.

Sex normally calmed him, but this wasn't calm. This was *need.*

But it was Charlie, and his frantic brain kept telling him to slow down, to be careful with her. But Charlie was the one clutching him tighter, whispering yes, yes, the harder he took her. Begging him to hurt her, to fuck her.

He clenched his teeth at the awful pleasure her words released inside him. He liked women. He'd always been careful with them, conscious of their pleasure, but now he just wanted to get as deep as possible. To get more of her tightness stroking him, sliding, squeezing his cock.

More. Harder and deeper and wetter. *More.*

The need clawed at him from the inside as Charlie clawed his back, and he couldn't take it anymore. He hooked an arm beneath her knee and hiked her leg higher, opening her to him completely.

She choked out his name, but she was still pulling him toward her, so he took her just the way he wanted. Fast and hard, loving the way their flesh grew slick with sweat, the way her hips jerked up to meet his. And, God, the way her neck arched and her mouth twisted with awful pleasure. He wanted to fill her with his body. Make her his. Just for that moment, maybe, but all his, filled with him in every possible way. He grunted with every thrust, waiting for her to protest, but she only pulled him tighter.

Her hips urged him on. Her cries drove him wild.

"Charlie," he growled, the knowledge that it was her making it feel more deliciously wicked. "Ah, God, Charlie…I'm going to come."

"Yes," she moaned. "Come for me."

Her words commanded his body, and his orgasm turned him rigid as he buried himself inside her with one last thrust. He grunted once, twice, as the pleasure tore through him, as it ate him alive for a dozen heart-beats. And then…it felt as if everything stopped for a moment. His heart. His breath. Everything.

He came back to himself in slow measures. First his pulse and pumping blood. Then the sound of his ragged breathing. Then the feel of Charlie's arms and legs, slippery and tight around him. He stayed like that for a long minute, then another, not wanting it to be over.

When he finally pulled out of her, he winced at the grip of her around his sensitive cock. Charlie's leg slipped slowly down his hip. Her fingers slid up his back. Her hands were shaking, too.

"That was…" she started, then drew in a shudder-ing breath.

For one horrible second, Walker felt a sharp stab of fear. Then Charlie smiled. "That was exactly what I needed."

He choked. Dropped his forehead to hers. Then he

laughed. "Damn. You ever tried a turn on the rodeo circuit? I don't think I could've thrown you if I'd tried."

"Were you trying?"

"Ha. No." He kissed her nose before he collapsed next to her on the bed and slipped off the condom. "Jesus, I needed that more than you could know."

"Yeah? Then I'm happy I could help." She turned on her side and laid her hand over his chest.

Walker pulled her closer until her whole body was warm against his. "I'm not feeling one iota of stress right now, I can tell you that. You're a miracle worker."

She petted his chest. "Is it the job hunt?"

He hesitated for a long moment, trying to decide if he should tell her. But he was too damn relaxed to lie. "Yes. And I saw my dad today."

"Oh. You don't get along?"

"We get along fine now that he can't remember how much he hates my guts."

"Walker!" Charlie sat up and slapped his shoulder.

"I'm serious," he said, though his seriousness was awfully challenged by the sight of her bare breasts.

"No one has ever hated you," she said, shaking her head and giving him another slap. "Ever."

"You are so wrong about that. But it doesn't matter anymore. Alzheimer's."

"I'm sorry."

He tugged her back down. "Just lie with me. It feels nice. Anyway, I got to see my brother, and that's always good."

"I don't think I knew him."

"He was a couple of grades behind."

"Is he a big strong cowboy like you?"

"No. He's a big, strong, medical-systems expert who lives with his husband in Seattle."

She sat up again. "Are you kidding me?" Her eyes went wide.

Walker braced himself for a judgment he hadn't expected from her. Other cowboys, sure. That kind of shit he could handle. But not from her. He felt a little of his happy warmth fading away.

Charlie shook her head. "I can't believe this. Walker Pearce's little brother is married and settled down?"

"He…" Relieved laughter shook through him. "Yeah. Hard to believe, huh?"

"Impossible." She smoothed a hand over his beard. When her fingers crossed his mouth, he kissed them. "You're close to him?"

He shrugged. "He's my little brother. I'd do anything for him."

"That's so sweet."

"He's a good guy. Reminds me of you, actually. He's really smart and always in charge. He knows where he's going in life and won't let anyone stop him. In other words, he's nothing like me."

Charlie's brow crinkled. Her lips parted, but she didn't say a word. What could she say? *Oh, Walker, you know you're smart and ambitious, too.* Yeah. Right.

He slipped a hand behind her neck to tug her down for a kiss. "Did I mention how much I needed that?"

"Well, I'm glad I was here, then."

"I didn't mean it like that."

She laughed against his mouth and trailed her hand through his chest hair. "It's okay, Walker. I know you're not my boyfriend. But, God, I hope you'll drop by and use me for a little stress relief again soon. Because… that was good. Really good."

His conscience twinged a little at Charlie Allington calling herself his sexual stress relief, but male pride won out and he smiled at her review of the performance. "When did you get so wild, Charlie?"

"Oh, you know. It took a few years. Practice makes perfect."

"It damn sure does," he murmured, kissing her again.

Giggling, she slid off him and curled under the covers.

"Can I have some of the blanket?" he asked.

"I suppose. But then I won't be able to look at you." Her hand slipped up his hip and belly and traced one nipple as he watched.

"But I'm cold."

"Oh? How cold?" Before he could answer, she leaned close to trace his other nipple with her tongue.

Walker shivered as goose bumps chased across his chest. "Not that cold."

"Mm. Good. I like touching you."

Another goofy smile spread over his face.

"You're so furry. And big."

"Yeah?"

"Oh…" Her hand trailed down, following the line

of hair from his chest to his groin. Then she slowly, carefully wrapped her hand around his cock. "Yes. Definitely."

He couldn't believe it when he felt his cock swelling in her hold. That was a fast recovery even for him. "Shit, Charlie. Look what you've done now. You trying to kill me?"

"Aw. I'm sorry. Want me to stop?" When she let him go, he grabbed her hand and wrapped her fingers back around him.

"Not yet. I'm still worried about that job hunt, after all. I've still got all this stress…"

They both watched as his cock stretched under her fingers.

She squeezed him. "Is there a way I can make it better?" she cooed.

Walker groaned at her teasing words and the tight grip of her hand. "Let me think about it. In the meantime…" He kept his hand curved around hers and worked it up and down. Slowly. "Just like that, Charlie."

He was going to go to hell for this, surely. For working sweet Charlie Allington's fist over his cock. For fucking her. And for wanting to fuck her again. But damn if he wasn't going to enjoy the downhill trip.

CHAPTER TWELVE

CHARLIE HEARD THE shower turn on in Walker's apartment and smiled at the thought of the last time she'd heard it. Had that only been last night? It felt like weeks ago. She was a changed woman, after all. Or at least a very sore, happy woman.

Her smile turned into full-on laughter at the memory of Walker's boyishly pleased grin when he'd made her scream like a climaxing banshee. God, he was so damn adorable.

She reached for her hair dryer and round brush. Normally she let her natural waves fly, but if she was going to go on a postcoital date with Walker, she wanted her hair shiny and flowing around her shoulders. She wanted him *entranced*. He'd already come twice, so she couldn't rely on his lust to make her seem beautiful. She'd have to put in the hard prep work.

Her two orgasms had calmed her restless mind considerably, and as the dryer droned in her ear, melancholy thoughts dogged her. Walker hadn't just given her his body. He'd exposed more vulnerabilities.

He'd said he'd been stressed, and she believed him. He'd seemed...different today. More sexually aggressive. Less flirtatious. More intense. The time with his father had shaken him, and he really had needed that release.

He'd shaken her, too, in several ways.

First, that had definitely been the best first-time sex she'd ever had. Holy *cow,* had it been the best. Yes, Walker was well endowed. In fact, he was probably the biggest she'd ever had, but that wasn't why it had been so good. Or not the only reason anyway. It had just been so *hot.* And fun. And comfortable. And intense.

She couldn't quite figure out how those things all fit together, but maybe it was just Walker's special gift. Maybe he made all the girls feel that way.

Charlie winced. She didn't want to be jealous over him. She *couldn't* be jealous over him if she wanted to hold on to her sanity. She'd known that after the first hour she'd ever spent tutoring him.

God, he'd made her feel special and so cute back then, the way he'd smiled at her with those crinkly eyes and teased her about being so smart. She'd known him, of course. Everyone had known Walker in high school. But they hadn't run in the same circles and hadn't taken the same classes. He'd been the big man on campus. Not in the star football player sense, but in the sense that a hundred people said hi to him each time he walked down the hall. And Walker had a friendly response for every single greeting, no matter who the person was.

Walker smiled at everyone, but for a few minutes on that first day in the library, a tiny hope had flamed to life in Charlie's aching chest. That his eyes crinkled just a bit more for her. That his teasing touches meant he'd only been waiting for the chance to meet her.

Thank God the homecoming queen had come over and propped her hip on the table right in front of Charlie that day. Thank God Charlie had watched Walker lean forward and whisper something naughty enough to make the girl blush. Charlie's fantasy was stomped out and dead before it could grow. A mercy killing. Quick and kind. Because if she hadn't seen the light that day, she would've fallen head over heels in love with him. He'd told her constantly how amazing she was. How much he admired her. Even now her chest felt tight and warm at the memory.

She couldn't fall in love with him. She wouldn't. And she wouldn't be jealous, either.

But she really, truly wished she'd never seen his ex-lover. Nicole was blonde and curvy and sophisticated, and Charlie didn't want that woman's beauty mixed up with her memories of Walker from today. She didn't want to imagine him doing those things with another woman. Saying the things he'd said. The way he'd said them.

Unfortunately, her only choice was to refuse to imagine them. Because he'd done them to other women. He'd been doing those things since high school. He'd likely done them to that homecoming queen, as well. All Charlie could do was be glad for the knowledge he'd racked up. Because he'd racked up plenty.

But it wasn't just the sex that had shaken her. He'd

insulted himself again, in ways that truly disturbed her. Walker wasn't stupid. Emotionally, he was a masterpiece. Like the way he'd made everyone around him feel good in high school. The jocks and cowboys and nerds and goths. Even the teachers he'd frustrated with his lack of effort. They'd loved him and they'd gotten frustrated because they'd *wanted* him to succeed.

Stupid people weren't good with others. They weren't perceptive and quick to assess any situation. And they damn sure weren't good at charming women. He'd struggled with his dyslexia his whole life, and he'd compensated for that by applying his intelligence in other ways. But somehow he couldn't see that.

He also couldn't see how screwed up Charlie was. He thought she was bright and in charge and capable of taking on the world. She'd deceived him with her promising start all those years ago. Hell, she'd deceived herself, too.

She wasn't going to take on the world. She'd peaked before thirty, just as her mother had. Maybe by forty Charlie would follow in her mom's footsteps and be thrice-divorced and working as a convenience-store clerk. And by fifty, desperate to marry another man, any man, because all the money she'd ever made had been spent helping leeches fix their cars or pay off child support. And then a slow, slow descent toward a wretched retirement.

Yeah, that might be her bright future. But Walker still looked at her and saw promise. She couldn't tell him the truth right now. Maybe later, if she ever managed to get her life back on track. Maybe when she was flying off to Aspen to open another resort. Then she'd tell him about that little bump in the road that was her current life.

But right now…God, right now she just couldn't. He was the last person who still thought she was amazing.

What she could correct was this ridiculous idea he had that he was a dumb cowboy going nowhere. If he wanted to work with people, that's what he should do. And if he still had trouble with getting his thoughts down on paper, that problem needed to be addressed. Hot cowboys could be so stubborn sometimes.

Half an hour later when Walker knocked on her door, she was dressed and ready to go. His eyes swept down to take in her tight white tank top and skinny jeans and heeled boots. "Gorgeous," he said as she grabbed her coat.

"Not bad yourself." He looked delicious in a tight blue T-shirt and worn jeans.

"You sure you're going to be able to swing a bat in those heels?"

"Watch me," she answered with a wink.

His gaze fell to her ass. "Oh, you don't have to worry about that."

She took in all the small touches of being on a date with Walker. The way he ushered her in front of him down the stairs and held open the front door and offered his arm for her hand as they walked down the sidewalk.

"Hey!" a shrill voice called, ruining the moment

of chivalry. "I guess there's a fox living in this damn henhouse."

"Evening, Miss Rayleen," Walker said as he turned them toward her.

"Are you eating my little chickens, Walker?" the old woman called from the porch of the saloon. When Walker frowned, she broke into a howl of laughter that made Charlie giggle.

He shot her a look of censure.

"I'm sorry! What am I supposed to say? I think you've still got feathers in your beard."

"Good Lord," he muttered as Rayleen made her way down the stairs and hurried over.

"I'll be damned," Rayleen muttered, her eyes sweeping down to Charlie's hand on his arm. "You two really are doing it, aren't you?"

"We're going out," clarified Walker.

"Oh, I see." She took the unlit cigarette from her mouth and tucked it behind her ear. "It's all sunshine and innocence, huh? Walker's going a-courtin'?"

"Something like that. You know I'm a nice boy, Miss Rayleen."

"Nice, indeed. Is he as *nice* as I've heard?" she asked Charlie.

Charlie grinned. "I don't kiss and tell."

"No? Do you screw and tell? Because I'd like to hear all the details about this big boy."

Charlie was glad for the support of Walker's arm at that moment, because she would've fallen over laughing if she hadn't been holding on. Especially when Walker choked out Rayleen's name on a horrified gasp.

Charlie shook her head. "Walker is—"

"Don't tell her about it!" he interrupted.

"I wasn't going to!"

Rayleen hooted. "I knew it! You two are doing the deed. You've got good taste, Charlie. A girl after my own heart. Pick the biggest stallion in the barn and break him in."

"I..." She didn't know what to say to that. "Okay."

Rayleen smiled and slipped the cigarette back into the corner of her mouth. "Well..." The cigarette bobbed. "I guess I've got my gossip for the day. You kids have fun. And keep it wrapped up, stud."

Walker just stared, openmouthed, as Rayleen walked back to the saloon.

"Try to get a cock shot, Charlie!" the old woman called over her shoulder.

"Okay!"

Walker's head whipped around to offer Charlie the same horrified look.

"I'm sorry!" she cried. "I didn't know what to say!"

"You don't say *okay!*"

"Hey, you're the one who confirmed we were sleeping together. Sheesh. What about my reputation, Walker?"

"Oh, shit." His shocked expression snapped immediately to concern. "I'm so sorry. I don't really think she'll—"

An Important Message from the Editors

Dear Reader,

Because you've chosen to read one of our fine novels, we'd like to say **"thank you!"** And, as a **special** way to thank you, we're offering to send you **two more** of the books you love so well plus **2 exciting Mystery Gifts** – absolutely FREE!

Please enjoy them with our compliments...

Pam Powers

Romance Reading...

TWO BOOKS FREE!

Each of your FREE books will fuel your imagination with intensely moving stories about life, love and relationships.

We'd like to send you **two free books** to introduce you to the Harlequin Reader Service. Your two books have a combined cover price of $15.98 in the U.S. and $17.98 in Canada, but they are yours free! We'll even send you **two exciting surprise gifts**. There's no catch. You're under no obligation to buy anything. We charge nothing – ZERO – for your first shipment. *You can't lose!*

Visit us at
www.ReaderService.com

YOURS FREE!
We'll send you 2 fabulous surprise gifts (worth about $10) just for trying "Romance"!

The Editor's "Thank You" Free Gifts include:
- *2 Romance books!*
- *2 exciting mystery gifts!*

Yes! I have placed my Editor's **"Free Gifts"** **seal** in the space provided at right. Please send me 2 free books and 2 fabulous mystery gifts. I understand I am under no obligation to purchase any books, as explained on the back of this card.

PLACE
FREE GIFTS
SEAL HERE

194/394 MDL F47H

FIRST NAME	LAST NAME

ADDRESS

APT.#	CITY

STATE/PROV.	ZIP/POSTAL CODE

Thank You!

DETACH AND MAIL CARD TODAY

ROM-10/13-EC3-13

"Walker. I'm just kidding. I don't care about my reputation, and if anyone else does, they can kiss my ass."

He watched her for a moment, as if checking to be sure she meant it. Then a slow smile spread over his face. "They might be tempted. It's a pretty nice ass."

"Yeah? Well, if you play your cards right, you can have first dibs."

He slapped her butt and then helped her into his truck. "Come on, then. Let's get this date started."

"Didn't you have another big shiny black truck in high school?"

He climbed in and started the engine. "It's my vice, I'm embarrassed to say. I've never saved up to buy a house, but damn if I don't always find the money for truck payments."

"It's very pretty," she said, stroking a hand over the glove compartment. There wasn't a speck of dust on any of the vinyl that she could see.

"I like pretty things." He winked at her and tipped his hat.

"Aw. I bet you say that to all the girls."

"Only the pretty ones."

Charlie had to laugh at that, because it clearly wasn't true. He flirted like crazy with even old Rayleen. God. The man was incorrigible. And very sweet.

She was going to have to nail her heart down with railroad spikes to get free of this without any attachment. He reached over to take her hand, and one of the spikes fell over with a dull clunk. Damn it.

A few minutes later, he pulled into a parking space

and walked around to open her door. "Mini golf or batting cages?"

"Batting cages," she scoffed. "Are you trying to get out of it now? Afraid I'll embarrass you?"

"Ha. I'm afraid you'll embarrass me when you fall on your ass after you swing and miss."

She gave him a hard shove, but he didn't even budge, he just offered her an arrogant smile and tugged her toward the coin machine.

"God, this reminds me of high school," Charlie said.

"Oh, yeah? Maybe later you'll let me feel you up in my truck."

"Maybe. But just a little."

She kept walking, but he caught her wrist and pulled her back.

"Hey," he said softly, then leaned in to kiss her. Very slowly. Very sweetly.

Charlie's pulse fluttered. "What was that for?" she asked when he raised his head.

He cleared his throat. "I just thought I'd get it over with early. Get the nervousness out of the way. It's our first date."

Charlie burst into laughter. "Oh, Walker. I can't believe you said that with a straight face."

"Fine, then. I wanted to kiss you. All right?"

"Yes, all right. But you don't have to seduce me, you know. I'm already putting out."

"But could you put out more?"

This time Charlie tugged him down for a kiss. "Yes," she said against his mouth. "But I should be clear…I need this to be exclusive, Walker. Just while we're doing this. That's all."

He pulled back with a frown. "Of course."

"It's just that…I saw you talking to your ex last night. Nicole?"

His arm stiffened under her hand. "Right. That was nothing. It was just…you know."

"It looked serious last night. And it's okay if it was. You just can't have us at the same time, all right?"

"Sure," he said, sounding a little distant. "Of course."

Shit, she shouldn't have brought it up. His arm was stiff against her as they walked toward the cages. "Hey, I'm not trying to get possessive. I swear."

"Yeah. I get that." But he was still uncharacteristically quiet as he stopped at the coin machine and fed bills into it.

He probably had to deal with this shit all the time. Being spectacular in bed and sweet outside it. That kind of behavior could make a girl think she was special.

"Hey." She nudged his arm. "Did you ever hang out here? It brings back memories. I'd come here with my friends from track and hope some older guy would notice me and ask me out. Someone with facial hair, even." She reached up to pet his beard. "Now look. All my fantasies coming true. I only had to wait a dozen years."

He relaxed and nudged her back. "Silly girl. If you'd just told me you wanted to get a little dirty, I'd have helped. As a favor to a friend. You know, you tutor me, I tutor you."

"Oh, yeah? God. Teenage boys are such an untapped source of generosity."

"It's true."

"Especially in the 'I'll let you put your mouth around my penis' area of community service."

Walker nearly collapsed with laughter, putting one hand on the wall to support himself as he stumbled to a stop. "Oh, Jesus, Charlie," he choked out past his laughter. "I totally would've let you do that."

"Yeah, I know. You were probably citizen of the year, even without me."

He shook his head, still trying to choke back the laughter that echoed against the cement wall. "In my dreams. But I'm still willing to give it a go if you feel like it'd be a valuable experience."

"As a matter of fact, I do, so I'm glad you're open to it."

That stopped his laughter. He leaned against the wall, his eyes on her as a smile played over his mouth. "God, you turn me on."

She tried not to preen. After all, she'd never met a man who didn't love a blow job. It was nothing to feel proud about. But, damn, this man was hot, and if he wanted her on her knees for him, she was going to treasure every bit of the experience.

"Come on, before we get caught making out and everyone at school finds out."

He tipped his head. "That looks like an empty birthday party room over there."

For a moment, she was tempted. Just one moment. But that moment would've turned into a dirty, sweaty, frantic encounter if she hadn't gotten off so thoroughly just an hour before. Thank God for orgasm-induced dignity.

"Walker," she said in a tone that pretended exasperation.

"Hey, you know how we older guys are."

She grabbed his hand and tugged him toward the cages. "Time to get your butt kicked."

She missed the first swing, of course. Walker was too kind to laugh, but Charlie still felt her competitive beast kick in. She set her jaw and took an even harder swing at the next ball. The satisfying crack sang through the bat and set her bones vibrating.

"Woman, that was a home run!" he shouted.

"There's more where that came from."

When he responded, "That's what he said," Charlie choked on a laugh and missed the next ball.

"Oh, can't take the heat!" Walker called from behind the chain-link caging.

She decided right then and there that she couldn't lose. Charlie hit the next eight pitches in a row and only missed the last two. By the time she stepped out of the cage, her arms ached, but she was grinning from ear to ear.

Walker smiled right back at her. "Do you have any idea how hot you look doing that?"

"I hope that will be some comfort to you when you lose," she countered.

"No, but it's going to add to the pleasure of winning."

He missed his first swing, too. Charlie wasn't as gracious and laughed out loud. He missed his second pitch because he was too busy pointing at her and telling her to behave. After that, he only missed twice more. They were tied. This was even more fun than she'd expected.

Charlie ignored her aching shoulders and took the bat from his hands as he held the gate open for her. "Again?" he asked.

"Oh, yes. Again."

His hot gaze let her know he wasn't thinking about the batting cage. Good. Neither was she. She was thinking that later he'd be her prize or she'd be his. And they'd both win no matter what.

Her adrenaline was pumping as she took a stance and raised the bat. The machine ground loudly away ahead of her. The first ball flew. She narrowed her eyes and slammed it back the way it had come.

"Goddamn, you're sexy, Charlie."

She spread her legs a little farther and wiggled her hips. Walker groaned. She hit the next pitch. And the next. Her heart beat hard with lust and awareness and competition. She wanted to beat him at this game and she wanted to be pushed to her knees and taken hard from behind. Wanted triumph and submission all at the same time. An altogether delicious contradiction.

She only missed three pitches.

Walker missed four.

She bit her lip as he came out of the cage, and tried her best not to laugh as he exchanged the helmet for his cowboy hat. Walker threw her a serious glance. She pressed her lips tight together. It didn't help. Before she knew it she was grinning so hard her cheeks hurt.

Walker reached for her and tugged her close. "You got something to say, Charlie?"

She shrugged and pretended to be unaffected by the press of his hot body against hers. "You're pretty quick on your feet for a big man. But not quick enough."

"Yeah." He spread his hands over her shoulders. His thumbs traced along her collarbone. "But that's not what you're looking for, is it? Speed?"

Her nipples tightened at that faint slide of his skin against hers. "No."

"Especially not for your victory round."

"Oh, I get a victory round?" she asked.

"Don't you want to celebrate your dominance?"

Her instinct was to say no. Definitely not. She'd gotten her victory and now she wanted to be used. But then she thought of him lying beneath her. Thought of riding him. Using his cock just the way she wanted for as long as she wanted. With what they'd already done today, he could last a very long time....

Yes. She definitely wanted to lord it over him. Charlie pressed her hands to his wide chest, sneaking her fingers beneath the edges of his coat. His body heat was trapped here. "You're a gracious loser."

"You have no idea how gracious."

"Oh. Maybe we should skip mini golf so we can get dinner out of the way."

He smiled and ducked his head closer. His beard brushed her cheek and she fought off the urge to snuggle into him with a needy groan. God, he smelled so good. "Come on. Let's get dinner out of the way."

"All right. But I need to powder my nose first. Don't move."

A few minutes later, after powdering the sweat off her face and fixing what the batting helmet had done to her hair, she hurried back to where she'd left Walker. She wasn't surprised to find that he'd wandered off. He'd done it every time she'd left him alone at the school library, too, always looking for someone to talk to or interact with. She strolled past the batting cages and over to the snack bar, but there was no sign of a big, sexy cowboy. The place wasn't that crowded on such a cool, late-season night, and just as she'd decided he was in the men's room, a wild burst of high-pitched laughter caught her attention. It sounded like the excited squeals of a pack of small animals. Charlie scanned the area until she spotted the source.

On a wide expanse of grass that families used for picnics in the summer, a dozen kids were gathered in a densely packed group. In the middle of them, rising like Godzilla from the sea, was a roaring Walker.

The kids screamed again as he grabbed one child and hefted her over his shoulder.

"Me! Me!" Several of the others called, tugging at any part of his clothing they could reach. She noticed how frail some of the arms were, and that several of the laughing kids were in wheelchairs.

He leaned down to place the girl safely on the ground, then reached toward a little boy sitting in what looked like a very rugged, high-tech wheelchair. Charlie watched him glance toward a man who stood at the edge of the group, and when the man nodded, Walker scooped up the boy.

Another boy grabbed Walker's hat and ran off with it, so he chased after the boy, roaring, while the child cradled in his arms shook with hysterical laughter.

Charlie walked over to the man at the edge of the lawn. "Hi. I'm Charlie. Do you know Walker?"

"Charlie," the man said. "I'm John. A pleasure." His hand rose as if he'd tip a hat he wasn't wearing. He seemed to be close to forty, and he had the tan skin and lined eyes that told her he'd spent some time in the saddle. "Walker's worked with my brother on and off over the years. He came over to say hello."

"Are you with the kids?"

"Yep. It's their last full day at the ranch, so we're having a little party."

"The ranch?" she asked.

"The Ability Ranch."

"The what?"

He smiled. "We've got a ranch north of town that does equine therapy and lots of work with disabled and traumatized kids and adults. The kids come out and stay for a few weeks at a time."

"Oh!" Charlie shook her head. "I've never heard of it. I've only been back in town for a few weeks."

"It's a pretty amazing place. And we always need volunteers." He raised an eyebrow at Charlie.

"Oh, no," she said, then realized how panicked she sounded. "I mean, I don't know anything about kids. Or horses. You should talk to Walker."

"I have. He's not interested."

"What?" she gasped, looking back to Walker as he chased the kids with another child slung over his shoulder.

"I know. He should think about it. Hell, he should think about working there. He's really amazing with the kids. Lots of people feel nervous around children with obvious disabilities."

Charlie nodded, but she kept her eyes on Walker. Her heart fluttered at the sight of him among all those tiny bodies. He didn't seem intimidated by them. Strangely, he fit right in. "What kind of jobs do you have there?"

"Well, hell. All kinds. But we're almost always short an instructor or two."

Her mind spun. Her pulse picked up. He could be good at this. He already was.

Walker was lowering a boy carefully back into his chair; then he scooped up another kid before he'd even straightened. As he stood, the next shrieking kid balanced on his shoulder, Walker's eyes swept up to meet Charlie's gaze. He smiled right at her before swinging the boy around in a big circle.

"Damn you, Walker," she whispered, feeling her heart start to melt all over her guts. It was going to make a terrible mess in there. Everything was already starting to ache. "Shit." This was going to be bad.

"CAN YOU REALLY eat all that?" Walker asked in admiration as Charlie rubbed her hands together over the giant barbecue platter that had just been placed in front of her.

"Let's find out," she answered, starting on a piece of brisket.

"You're an amazing woman," he said, meaning it. He didn't know any other woman who'd order a gigantic platter of ribs and barbecue on a first date. Or any date, but Charlie hadn't even hesitated when she'd ordered.

She finished the first chunk of brisket, then reached for her margarita. Walker set into his own ribs.

"God, this is great," she groaned. "You can't get barbecue like this in Tahoe."

"No? I bet life is a little wilder there than in Jackson, though."

She froze for a moment, her eyes meeting his, but then she smiled. "Not all that wild. It was pretty quiet."

"You don't seem like the quiet type, Charlie. Not anymore. I bet you found trouble when you wanted it."

She coughed and reached for her margarita. "Not really. So you've eaten here before?"

He almost pressed her, wanting to tease her about this new fun Charlie he liked so much, but he let it go.

"Yeah, I've been damn happy since this place opened last year. For a few weeks, the other hands and I would sneak away every Monday night for the all-you-can-eat special."

"Oh, man. I bet they cringed when they saw a herd of cowboys coming in."

"A herd?" he asked.

"I don't know. What's the correct term? A gaggle? A pack? A cuddle? A *spur* of cowboys?"

"Probably a posse."

Charlie laughed as she dug into her ribs. "Do you miss your friends there?"

"Sure. Like I said, I got used to being around people all the time. There are some good guys out there."

"Yeah… You know I've been thinking about something tonight."

"Oh? Does it have anything to do with the kind of stuff teenage boys like? Because I've been thinking about that, and I've got to tell you that grown men are okay with it, too."

She laughed and pressed a sauce-covered hand over her mouth.

"I could tolerate it, at least. I mean, I'd like to try." He liked making her laugh, especially when her face was smudged with barbecue sauce and her eyes were so bright, and he could still feel the way her body had tightened around him when he'd fucked her.

She shook her head, eyes still twinkling. "No, I wasn't talking about that. Though I'll take your comments under advisement."

"Please do."

She grabbed a napkin and wiped the worst of the sauce off her face. "What I was thinking was… Tonight. Those kids you were playing with…"

"John's kids?"

"Yes." Charlie put her elbows on the table and leaned forward. "You're amazing with people, Walker. You were amazing with those kids."

"Only if you consider giving a few kids a piggyback ride something spectacular."

"It's not just that. You're just so *easy.* With everyone. And those kids…they loved you and they'd only known you for five seconds."

Walker cleared his throat and grabbed his beer to drown out the strange mix of pride and embarrassment flooding through him. "Thanks," he said once he'd gotten some beer down his dry throat. "I like kids."

"I talked to John a little bit, and I was thinking that you should consider applying there."

Walker shook his head. "I don't know what you mean. They don't own cattle, do they?"

"No. I meant that you could work with the kids. Teaching them about horses and how to ride. You'd be around people every day, doing exactly what you like to do."

For a moment, he was still blessedly confused, and then the humiliation of what Charlie was saying slammed into him, full force. "You want me to be a *teacher?* Charlie, I can't do that."

"Sure you can!"

"No. I can't." He tore half the meat off a rib and ducked his head to stare at his plate while he chewed.

"You wouldn't be a teacher, per se," she pressed.

The back of his neck burned.

"When you were at the guest ranch, you taught people how to ride, didn't you? You gave lessons?"

Walker swallowed and reached for a drink. After scrubbing the napkin over his mouth, he felt calm enough to speak. "No. I wasn't a riding instructor."

"Well, what did you do? You taught them something."

"I put on a little performance every day, showing them how to throw a lasso, how to rope a calf. And then I'd lead them on trail rides. Teach them how to groom a horse. Sometimes we'd brand cattle."

"See? You've already taught people!"

Jesus, she looked so happy. As if she really believed he was capable of this. She didn't understand. She never had understood. At least his dad had named it for what it was.

"Charlie. It was a show. We helped people play at being cowhands for an hour or two a day. And then we'd go out and do the real work before coming back to serve them dinner around the campfire. I'm not a teacher. I'm not qualified and I never will be."

"But you're good with horses," she pressed. She kept eating her dinner as if nothing important was happening. "And you're good with people. It'd be perfect for you."

Walker's heart beat hard. He didn't want to have to

explain out loud that he was dumb, that no one would ever want him working with their children, that no one would ever even think about hiring him for such a thing.

Sure. Hire a dumb cowboy who could barely read to be a teacher. Perfect. He couldn't even teach *himself* anything.

"I'm good with horses, yes," he said flatly. "And cows. And other hoofed animals. I am not capable of being a professional teacher or working with people's kids."

"But—"

"I'm a cowboy," he snapped.

"Yes, but that's not all you have to be." She reached for his hand. "You could be so much more than that."

Before her fingers could slip through his, he drew his hand back, feeling as if he were coming out of his skin. He wanted to get up and pace away. Go outside and let the wind cool him down until he wasn't pissed and embarrassed anymore. "If me being a cowboy isn't good enough for you, then say it flat out, Charlie."

"What?"

"Every time we see each other, you tell me I could be something more. Maybe I could. I seriously doubt it, but maybe I could. But that's not the point. I am not something more. If you don't like it—"

"Of course I like it!"

"It's getting hard to tell, honestly. I'm a cowboy. That's what I do. It doesn't pay well and it's not glamorous, and I go out and get rough and dirty and tired and hurt, but I'm damn good at it. I don't read. I don't analyze. I don't improve the world or build new technology or contribute ideas. I'm sorry if that's too little for you to accept."

She stared at him, openmouthed, before she slowly shook her head. "I didn't mean that, Walker. I'm trying to help. I know you're a cowboy, but you're more than that, too. You're—"

"No. I'm not. That's all I am, and all I'll ever be. You know that better than anyone."

"You know, you could try some more classes...."

His heart raced into panic. He set his jaw and tried to hide the fact that he wanted to jump up and flee. "Yeah. Tutoring didn't work so great for me, remember?"

"I was just another kid, Walker. And now that you're an adult, you're probably more focused. It wouldn't just be about trying to get a passing grade in a class you didn't want to take in the first place. It would be a way to get better at your work."

"That seems a little drastic for a ranch hand."

"But..." He knew what she meant to say, but she must've taken his earlier words to heart, because she let her words die in her throat.

"I really don't want to talk about my damn *learning disability* on a date. I've heard enough about it to last ten lifetimes. But thank you." He said it as flatly as he could. This conversation was over as far as he was concerned, but he had the feeling that Charlie would keep pressing if he gave her an inch.

Still, he felt bad almost immediately. She watched him, her eyes dark with hurt after his hard words, her forehead drawn tight in disbelief.

"All right?" he said, forcing a smile. "No hard feelings."

"Sure, but…I didn't mean anything bad, Walker. I swear."

He nodded, and they both focused on their dinners. When the waiter offered dessert, they declined. Walker tried to tease Charlie about not finishing her food, but she only smiled and picked at the potato salad with her fork.

"Do you want a to-go box? I know how fond you are of them."

"No, I'm good."

This date was all backward. It had started with Charlie in her pajamas. Then they'd had sex. And more sex. Then this date. If they'd done it in the right order, the evening would've gotten no further than this awkward moment of waiting for the check to arrive. They both breathed a sigh of relief when he finally paid and they could leave.

He tried to let go of his mood as they drove back to the Stud Farm, but now he couldn't stop thinking of all the other things she'd said since they'd started messing around. That he wasn't her boyfriend. That it was only stress relief. That he wasn't the marrying type and she wasn't possessive. All of it was a continuation of things he'd heard from women his whole life.

Not that he'd never had more than that. He wasn't a leper. But it was starting to become a common theme.

Thanks for the ride, cowboy.

Yeah. He got it. And hell, he was up for a good time, but what if he wanted more than that?

What he needed to do was stop dating women who were so far above his station. He couldn't help being attracted to them. The quick wit. The intelligence. The confidence and bright humor. It drew him in. As if he were a magnet attracted to the opposite charge. He wanted to be near them, but it was too much. He felt dull in comparison. He was just a big package of physical labor. He'd been fine with that his whole life. He'd embraced it. But the role he'd shrugged on so easily for so many years was starting to chafe.

"Listen," he said as he pulled up to the apartment. "I apologize, but I'll have to drop you off. I need to talk to someone about a job."

"Right now? It's eight."

"Yeah, I know."

Charlie's crossed arms tightened. "Walker, I'm really sorry. I honestly didn't mean to offend you. Can we go upstairs and talk? Or not talk, even?" Her smile faded when he didn't answer.

No, he didn't want to *not talk* with yet another woman. Not even with Charlie. Not tonight. "I really need to get going."

Her face fell. "Okay. But…I had a really good time today."

"Me, too," he said with sincerity. He couldn't deny that part of it, not even to himself.

He felt like complete shit as he got out and opened Charlie's door. He walked her to the circle of porch light and up the stairs to open the door for her. She gave him a kiss on the cheek and left him there without a word.

Yeah, it was late, and he was a fool not to walk her in, take her to her door and hope to be invited inside. He was an idiot not to kiss her until she forgot she'd already come twice and she needed him so much she grew desperate.

But he had to put a stop to this foolishness that he was going to become something *better*. He'd bought into it himself now, and that was too much. He was hesitating over taking this job working cattle, as if it wasn't good enough anymore.

In a few days, he'd be on roundups for a good two weeks of work, bringing cattle down from the high country into the valleys for winter. He needed solid winter work lined up right now before someone else snatched it up.

Walker got back in his truck and called up Kingham. "Mr. Kingham, are you still looking for a hand to help out this winter?"

"Couldn't find anything better?" Kingham groused.

Walker shrugged, not caring that the man couldn't see him. He hated having to ask this old bastard. Walker could tell after only two days of work that the guy had no respect for the cowboys or the animals.

"Fine. I pay in cash for the roundup and then I'll

put you on permanent payroll. There are only enough bunks for the lodge hands. You'll have to find your own bed."

"Got it."

He only felt resignation as he hung up. Maybe that one cowboy had been right. Maybe lodge work had made Walker soft. He rubbed a hand over his face and let his head fall back against the headrest.

It was just work. Nothing to feel stressed about. The same damn work he'd been doing since he was fourteen. It was brutal and basic and there was no shame in that.

So why did he feel ashamed?

Something had changed recently. Nothing to do with Charlie or even Nicole. He was telling himself that it was because he couldn't find the right position, the right place to work, but things had felt off for months, long before he'd gotten fired.

Things had felt off since he and Micah had finally sold off their dad's land.

He looked up as a light came on in Charlie's apartment. He should go on up and apologize. Ask if she'd let him back in. But he didn't want to spend time with someone who found him wanting tonight. Hell, he didn't want to spend time with anyone, and that was unusual.

Right now all he wanted was his damn dog.

That was what he'd argued with Nicole about at the charity party. He'd asked how Roosevelt was, and she'd used that as an excuse to tell him he was a self-ish asshole.

Jesus. He couldn't win.

He'd begged Rayleen to let him keep the dog in the apartment, but even if she'd said yes, he couldn't have pulled it off. There were just too many days he wouldn't be around to let the dog out. If he had a yard, Roosevelt would be fine, but in an apartment? No. Plus, technically the dog probably didn't belong to him. He'd raised it from a pup, but Roosevelt was a ranch dog.

"Shit," he cursed, trying to decide if he should just go on to the saloon and get drunk.

But there'd be friends at the saloon. People who'd want to talk. And he didn't want friendly faces. He'd rather drink among strangers. Flirt with girls who didn't know anything about him. Maybe get into a fight over a hot piece of ass who didn't even know his name. At a place like that, he had only his assets and none of his faults, and no one wanted him to be anything more.

The curtain in Charlie's window twitched. He clutched the steering wheel for a moment, torn between staying and going.

In the end, Walker started the truck and drove on.

CHAPTER THIRTEEN

SHE WOKE UP to sun, thank God. The temperature didn't matter to her, as long as it wasn't raining. She had to get out for a run, and if she'd been forced into that workout room again, she would have lost her mind.

Last night had gone fantastically wrong, and Charlie was still reeling. She had to get out in the fresh air. She had to breathe.

If pressed, she would never have guessed that Walker could've been that sensitive about anything. She'd also never have guessed that any amount of irritation could keep him from free sex. His very favorite hobby was flirting. And he damn sure seemed to enjoy sex. But she'd pissed him off so much he'd walked away from it.

Or at least from her. She didn't know where he'd gone last night, after all. Maybe to see some woman who didn't care that he had trouble with reading. Or maybe to see Nicole.

Charlie pulled on her running clothes and dug a hoodie and gloves from a packing box in her closet.

It was okay. If he'd gone to see Nicole, then this little fling was over. That was all. No hard feelings.

But if he hadn't, then Charlie needed to apologize and explain. She didn't think he was dumb. She didn't think there was a damn thing wrong with him except stubbornness. He had dyslexia, but he'd be able to read and write much more easily if he applied himself. Not well enough to read a book in a day, maybe, but well enough that it wouldn't interfere with what he wanted in life.

"That's none of your business," she muttered as she pulled on her shoes. "You're not his girlfriend."

Then again, she was his friend. Surely that counted for something.

Pissed at herself and at Walker, she grabbed her headphones and headed out the door.

Walker's door opened at the exact same time. They stared at each other in shock. Charlie's shock quickly exploded into dismay. "Oh, my God! Walker, what happened to your face?"

He gave her a rather tight-lipped smile, probably because the left half of his bottom lip was swollen. She rushed across the landing to look closer. "Oh, no." She reached carefully toward his black eye but didn't touch it. "Are you okay? Were you in an accident?"

"Not exactly."

In addition to the purple-and-black bruise around his eye and the fat lip, there was an angry red cut across one of his cheekbones. "Were you in a fight?"

"Yeah."

"Walker! Where the hell did you go last night?"

He shut his apartment door and sighed. Then, instead of answering, he shrugged on his shearling coat and adjusted his hat.

"Oh. I see. None of my business?"

"Shit, Charlie. I don't know. I just… I was pissed at you. I'm sorry."

She nodded, waiting for him to go on and dreading it.

"I just wanted to get out of here and not think for a couple of hours."

"But you don't want me asking where you went. I see." Her heart fell. Damn. She'd known this wasn't for forever. She'd known it wasn't love or commitment, but she'd hoped it was *something*. "That's fine," she made herself say. "I get it. I know this isn't a serious relationship, but I told you I couldn't be one of many. So no hard feelings."

He caught her arm as she started to turn away. "It wasn't like that."

"Well, whatever it was like, I hope you enjoyed it."

"I didn't have sex with anyone."

"Okay. So what did you do?"

"I…went out to the ranch."

"The Ability Ranch?" For a moment, her poor confused heart jumped into a happy dance. "Walker, that's so great! I'm sorry I—"

"No. I meant the Fletcher Ranch."

Her heart froze in midjig. Then it dropped like a stone. "Ah. Right. Of course."

"It wasn't about her, Charlie. I wanted to see my dog. That's all. I—"

"But it became about her," she interrupted, gesturing toward his black eye. "I don't think anyone would cause that much trouble over your dog."

"Yeah. I thought her husband was still out of town, but—"

"Whose husband?" she asked, but she realized the answer before she'd even finished asking.

"Nicole's."

"She's married." Her voice had dropped to a darker tone even in her own ears.

Walker's eyes widened. "She, uh… Yeah. I thought you knew about that."

"No. Why would I have known that?"

He shook his head, his face turning pink beneath the bruises. "I just… There've been some rumors going around since I was fired."

"You mean because you were fired for sleeping with the boss's wife?"

"No!"

"Right." She tried not to be judgmental. She tried not to feel irritated and hurt. But it didn't work. She punched him in the shoulder. Hard. "*What the hell,* Walker?"

He didn't even react to her fist. "I know. But it's not what you think."

"You weren't sleeping with the man's wife? Right there under his nose?"

"I wasn't. I didn't."

"Walker…" Her shoulders slumped. "You can't lie

to me about that. Anybody could see by the way she looks at you."

"We never actually..." He shook his head. "I swear. It just...got out of control. And I don't know if that's why I was fired. No one should've known."

"Your boss's wife? Are you insane?"

He took off his hat, then put it back on, shifting from foot to foot like a little kid caught in a lie. "It's not something I thought about. It just happened."

"Once?"

His flushed skin told her everything she needed to know. "Their marriage is bad. He cheats on her. I guess I told myself it wasn't my responsibility."

She tipped her chin up, her gaze on his bruises. "I guess someone thinks you deserve a little blame."

"Yeah."

"So you got into a fistfight with your lover's husband?"

"No. When I pulled up last night, my dog found me right away. He ran right up to the truck like I'd only been gone a few hours. We were playing around...." He paused to smile. "That dog loves to fetch a stick more than any other dog on earth, I swear. A couple of buddies came over to talk. It was cool. I was only going to stay for a few minutes, but this asshole stable manager who's never liked me ran up to the lodge to tattle. Came back and said the owner told him to escort me off the property."

"So you calmly exited the scene?" she asked drily.

"Well. I meant to. But that bastard put his hands on me, and I wasn't in the mood for that kind of shit."

She frowned resentfully at him. "Are you okay?"

"Sure."

"Really? No broken ribs or anything?"

Now he looked offended. "No way. I broke his nose and he went down like a tree."

"Yeah, well, it looks like he got in a couple of good licks before he dropped, Sugar Ray."

He made a noise of irritation. They stood silently on the landing for a long, awkward moment.

Charlie took a deep breath. Then she asked the question she wasn't sure she wanted an answer to. "Did you go out there to see her, Walker?"

"No. I swear."

"Then how did you know her husband was supposed to be out of town?"

Confusion flashed over his face, and for a moment she thought, *That's it. He got caught in a lie and he can't recover and now I'm going to have to give him up.* The grief was immediate.

"She brought it up at that charity event. Then we argued. That was the end of it."

She wanted to believe him, but that was the stuff gullible women were made of. How many times had she asked her ex these kinds of questions—where were you yesterday? Why didn't you call me back?—just hoping he'd give an answer she could believe? And he always had. It was the desire for belief that was the problem, the warning, the flag.

"Charlie, I didn't even see her at the ranch last night, much less do anything I shouldn't have. As a matter of fact, I was alone with her a week ago and I stopped it. I told her it was over."

She nodded, but she stared down at her hands. "But a married woman, Walker?"

"I know. I'm sorry. I'm ashamed of it. Ashamed that people think there's more to it. That's a damn good learning tool. If you don't want people to know, it's something you shouldn't be doing in the first place."

Yeah, she had her own experience with that. "I'm glad you're not hurt too badly."

"I'll survive."

She touched one careful finger to his mouth. "Are you working today?"

"Yeah."

She nodded, and then he was shifting again, rubbing a hand over his beard. "I'm sorry, Charlie. About last night and…just everything I guess. I have to hit the road, but can I buy you a drink later?"

"Yeah. That might be all right."

He left then, and she stood there for a long moment, listening as his truck started and he pulled away to some brutal, low-paying job that he'd throw his all into. He was more than that, even if he couldn't see it. Walker was heading fast down the same path of hard living so many reckless cowboys took. There was nothing she could do to stop that and no point in trying. She had her own mistakes to make up for.

She pulled on her hat, turned on her music and headed out for a run, praying that the cold would numb her. And it did. For a little while.

CHAPTER FOURTEEN

IT WAS A good day at work. Finally. Despite the way it had started, Charlie was eight hours in and she was still in a good mood.

Part of it was that she'd gotten out of her office and done a little physical work, coming up with camera locations and angles for the last of the banquet room areas.

She'd felt so energized by scrambling around on ladders for two hours that she'd gathered up her senior security people and walked the perimeter of the entire resort. First the lodge itself, then the outbuildings, then the lines of the actual property. A lot more thought went into security than people knew. Or at least, a lot more thought went into it when Charlie was in charge. People were vulnerable on vacations. They let their guards down, made foolish choices they'd never make at home. Charlie watched out for them, even if they had no idea she was there.

As they'd toured the resort, she'd pushed her employees to discuss weaknesses in the planned security and areas that needed improvement. It had started to feel a little bit more like a team, as if she actually had friends and support in this place. Despite her aching finances, she'd ordered pizza for everyone and commandeered one of the meeting rooms to discuss her plans for the opening weeks.

Her mood also hadn't been hurt by the relief she'd felt after talking to Walker this morning. He hadn't gone out and met up with some other woman. And he'd apologized for getting angry the night before. They were still friends. Things would be okay.

And now that she no longer felt sick over the way they'd left it, she could enjoy the fact that she was sore and weak and a little raw from the way Walker had used her the day before. Charlie smiled as she strode down the hallway toward her office.

God. That had been…extraordinary. Just the thought of it made her feel giddy. Walker was like catnip for pussy.

"You look happy."

Charlie's heart sank at the sound of Dawn's voice, but Dawn just shot her a wry look and brushed past her. Maybe after their discussion at the party, Dawn had decided to lay off. Maybe they really had called a truce.

If so, Charlie was relieved. So relieved that when she opened her email and found the background report on Dawn waiting in her in-box, she actually felt a twinge of guilt. But just a twinge. By the time she opened the file, Charlie's heart was quickening with anticipation.

What would she find in here? A secret drug problem? An addiction to shoplifting? Maybe a series of involuntary commitments to mental health hospitals? Really, the possibilities were endless.

Or…actually, they were pretty limited, because a quick scan of the pages left her slumped in her chair and pouting at the screen. Dawn Taggert was as pure as the driven snow. Certainly purer than Charlie, just as she'd been asserting, and purer than most of the public. No citations for underage drinking, no speeding tickets. Not even a failure to provide proof of insurance at a traffic stop.

"Annoying," she muttered as she read the report more closely.

Still, there were a few nuggets of information. Her first child had either been conceived before her wedding or been born a few weeks early. "Scandal!" Charlie crowed, desperate for anything.

More important, though Dawn's credit was good, there had been ups and downs. Keith's fortunes hadn't been a steady climb, apparently. He'd filed for bankruptcy seven years before, and there'd been a few defaulted car payments a year ago, and then a lawsuit filed by some sort of real estate holding company. Charlie would have to look into that.

She wrote down the dates of the financial problems, then closed the document and hid it in a folder with an innocuous name. Just in case.

The evidence seemed to indicate that Dawn wasn't quite as crazy as she seemed. It was a temporary affliction, brought on by…what? Maybe she was just going through the occasional bout of depression and anxiety, like everyone else Charlie knew. Certainly, Dawn wouldn't be the type willing to go to a therapist and expose her vulnerabilities. She probably thought of that as something "other people" did. Like picking up big cowboys for a friendly sex romp. Or two.

Oh, well. Her loss.

Just as Charlie was about to pack up and go, an email from Keith chimed into her box. He needed her expense reports and budget sign-off tonight.

She glanced at the clock. Almost six. "Crap," she groaned. She'd taken a full day when she needed to do budget work at her last job, and he wanted this done in a few minutes?

What the hell was the hurry? If this hadn't been her first month on the job, she'd just matter-of-factly tell him she couldn't get it back to him until tomorrow. But it was her first month, and she had to make a good impression.

Damn it. *I'll be sure to get that to you this evening,* she wrote back with a grimace at the clock.

All she had to do was sign off on it and say yes to the expenses. Keith had told her it was all pretty much automated. She'd known a few managers who did that, but it wasn't her style.

A little anxious, she opened up the spreadsheet. The numbers appeared in rows and columns of black and red that meant absolutely nothing without context. Thousands of dollars in hourly and salaried wages. Benefits. Contractor costs. Equipment. Even the cost of office space within the resort itself.

She clicked on the Wages tab, and it opened to reveal a list of half-blacked-out Social Security numbers with the hourly pay for each employee. None of them made very much, unfortunately. She closed that and opened the Equipment tab.

"Holy shit." Was that how much the extra cameras had cost to order and install? No wonder she'd had to exchange half a dozen emails with Keith and the construction manager about it. She closed that tab, too.

She didn't bother clicking on the Salaried Employees tab. She was planning to hire an assistant manager before ski season, but for now, Charlie was the only one on salary in her department, and she was more than familiar with the pitifully low total at the end of the column.

But the whole thing, altogether? It added up to her being in charge of a ridiculous amount of money. Considering how small her security department was, she was shocked, but this was the opening phase. There were start-up costs, and some of those equipment expenses had been accrued before she'd even been hired.

Shit. She didn't even have anything to compare this to. Scowling, she fired off another email asking Keith if he had the numbers from the month before, then clicked through the spreadsheet again several times before her computer chimed.

All expenses for previous months have been included in the development and construction budget.

Charlie groaned and rubbed both her hands over her face. Maybe it didn't matter if she was rushed. What the hell could she tell from one month's worth of expenses anyway?

She didn't like it, she didn't want to be rushed, but the truth was that it had nothing to do with Keith Taggert. She was still shell-shocked from Tahoe, and she'd promised herself that she'd set that aside. She wanted to do her job well, be thorough and *not* assume that everyone in the world was trying to screw her over.

Keith was rushing her, but the resort was opening soon. Everything was rushed. She needed to be a big girl about it.

The bottom line was that the budget seemed to be in the black, and the expense report numbers lined up fairly closely with the budget numbers.

Two hours later, she'd looked at the expenses up, down and sideways. At least now she could tell herself she was ready for next month.

Someone passed quickly by her office, and when she glanced up in surprise, Keith Taggert's head popped into view as he backtracked. "Oh, hi, Charlotte. You're still here."

"I am. Just finishing up the expenses."

"Everything look good?"

"Everything looks great!" she said, adding extra enthusiasm to cover her irritation.

"Good." He stood there for a moment while they smiled at each other.

"Can I help you with anything?"

"Nope. I was just making the rounds before I leave."

"Great. Okay." She fiddled with the mouse. "I'll just get this to accounting, then."

He waved goodbye and left while Charlie typed up a quick approval of the budget and sent it off. She then printed out the documents, signed them and stuck them in a manila envelope to drop off on her way out.

At least she had the numbers in her head for the next managers' meeting. And at least she could go home.

She'd meant to call her brother and ask if he could meet for dinner, but it was after eight now. Tomorrow maybe. Tonight…God, tonight she wanted to run right home and jump Walker's bones. She wanted to text him and tell him to strip down and shower up and she'd be right there. But Merry had texted at seven-thirty and proposed pizza and margaritas with a few of the girls, and that was a good thing. After last night's tension, it was good to make Walker wait. He could spend his evening wondering if she'd really take him up on that drink.

Charlie packed up and started making a mental list of margarita makings she'd need to pick up. And then she'd have to find her big pitcher. It was probably still in a box somewhere like half of her other things. And how in the world was she going to find her citrus juicer?

Charlie had already locked her door and was turning away when her brain ejected a stray thought, nicely packaged and wrapped with a shiny ribbon.

She froze and frowned down the hallway toward

the elevators. Then she swiveled her head and looked toward the surveillance room.

Where had Keith been heading when he'd passed her office?

She stood straight and frowned down the hallway. He'd definitely been walking toward the surveillance office, and there wasn't anything of interest past it. But after he'd spotted Charlie, not only had he stopped, but he'd turned around and walked back in the other direction.

She walked to the surveillance room and looked in. Most of the monitors were dark and no one was on duty. There was no need to watch the monitors. If someone from the construction crew dared to steal anything, it would be right there on the hard drive in the morning.

She walked the rest of the hallway, just to be sure she wasn't forgetting anything, but there was nothing here that should've interested the owner of the resort. He'd said he was just making the rounds, but she didn't remember seeing him down here after hours before.

Charlie stopped to look at the monitors one last time.

Was he spying on his wife? Were they playing some sick game of trying to ruin or control each other?

More important…couldn't Charlie just get a normal damn job for once?

"God. I need a drink," she groaned. Luckily, she knew just where to get one.

CHAPTER FIFTEEN

"Who wants a margarita?" Charlie shouted over the music blasting from her stereo.

Four hands went up, just as she'd expected. She passed out glasses to all the women and filled them to the top with homemade deliciousness. "Here's to girls' night, ladies!"

The apartment swelled with the cheers of the women as they all reached to clink glasses.

Charlie didn't have to worry about the noise. Merry was her downstairs neighbor and she'd organized it. And if Walker was home, then...well, he could just deal with it. He was used to the screams of all sorts of women, after all.

"Jenny," Charlie called, "what time do you have to be at work?"

"Not until ten! I've got an hour!" the bartender answered.

Rayleen snorted. "Hell, not even then if I say so."

Charlie clinked glasses with her. She wasn't sure why Rayleen scared everyone so much. She seemed sweet as pie to Charlie. A little feisty, sure, but funny as hell. "Thanks again for letting me rent here. I hope I can find some way to repay the favor."

"Well, you could start by bringing fewer chickens around this place and a lot more cocks. Where's all the man meat at this party?"

Charlie choked on an ice cube.

Rayleen's grand-niece Grace patted Charlie on the back. She was a striking woman with wildly cut, bright red hair and watchful eyes that missed nothing. "Sorry. My aunt has that effect on people."

"I know," Charlie said once she could speak again. "She's awesome."

"See?" Rayleen interrupted. "I'm awesome. You can stop calling me a mean bitch behind my back."

"Sure. As soon as you stop calling me trash."

Charlie's shoulders tensed in anticipation of the imminent argument. This was obviously some long-simmering tension. But just as she was holding up a hand to stop it, the two women burst into laughter.

"Charlie," Grace chuckled, "if you ever hear that people soften with age, I want you to think of my aunt and laugh and laugh."

Rayleen elbowed her. "I don't know what you're laughing about. You're a hell of a lot harder than I was at your age. You're gonna be one cruel witch by the time you get to be this old."

"Nah. I'm offsetting my grumpiness by getting laid. Speaking of… Did you call Easy back yet?"

When Charlie saw Rayleen's face go pink, she leaned forward in nosy curiosity. "Who's Easy?"

"Some beat-up old cowboy," Rayleen snapped.

Her niece shook her head. "He is not some old cowboy. Rayleen has a crush on him, and he called to ask her out, but she's afraid to call him back."

"That's bullpucky! I'm not afraid."

"Then why haven't you called him? You're half in love with the man."

"That's ridiculous!" she protested, but her cheeks were scarlet now. "You can't tell if you even like a man before you've taken him for half a dozen test drives. Sheesh. *Love!* What a joke."

"Right. So apparently Easy is finally ready for that test drive. And after a year of you teasing him, you're turning out to be all talk."

"I'll call him when I'm good and ready!" she snapped, waving an irritated hand as she rose to head for the kitchen.

Grace rolled her eyes at Charlie. "She's scared."

"I think it's sweet."

"She's been teasing poor Easy mercilessly about how he's too old to take her on, and he finally called her up and asked her to go to the movies. That was almost a week ago. She hasn't called back."

"How do you know all this?"

Grace winked as she pulled out her cell phone. "My boyfriend and I live in a little ranch house next to Easy. I'm going to text Easy and rat Rayleen out. He was planning to come to the saloon tonight and force an answer out of her."

"But she's so nervous."

"Good." Grinning, Grace typed away on her phone. "It's because he means something to her. Not very many people mean anything to her. Not very many people put up with her. So I'll be damned—" she typed a few more letters and hit Send with a triumphant gesture "—if I'll let her fear keep her alone any longer."

"Won't she be mad?"

"She's always mad. At least this mad could turn into something much, much happier."

Poor Rayleen. Charlie felt anxious about the whole thing and it had nothing to do with her love life. Grace's phone dinged.

"What did he say?" Charlie asked when Grace grinned.

"He's at the saloon, so he'll be here in just a few seconds. She won't have time to escape."

Charlie drank the rest of her margarita to calm her nerves. She wasn't cut out for springing dates on the elderly, it seemed.

Poor Rayleen was just over there minding her own business and in a few minutes… Or actually, she wasn't minding her own business, she was scowling into Charlie's fridge as she pushed things around on the shelves. "Ever think of buying some real food?" she yelled. "Maybe if you cooked once in a while, you could lure some men in here instead of all these women!"

"I have other ways to lure!" Charlie yelled back.

She thought Rayleen muttered something about skinny jeans and whore shoes, but she couldn't be sure over the music.

"See?" Grace said. "She needs a better way to spend

her time than nosing through your fridge and shout-
ing insults."

"She's fine. I think she's cute."

"Cute," Grace snorted, but there was no missing the
indulgent smile on her face.

A hard knock on the door cut through the music.

Jenny hooted. "Did someone order a stripper?" She
danced over to the door and flung it open. A white-
haired man stood there with his cowboy hat clasped to
his chest and a bouquet of flowers in the other hand.
"Easy!" she said.

"Evening, Jenny. I'm looking for Rayleen."

All eyes turned toward the kitchen. Rayleen was
frozen in the open door of the fridge, a bottle of olives
clutched in her hand, her jaw dropped in shock.

The old cowboy stepped inside with a tip of his head
toward the whole room. "Ladies," he said politely, but
his eyes went straight to Rayleen. "Miss Rayleen, I believe we have a movie to see tonight."

Her grip tightened on the olives, and for a moment,
Charlie expected the jar to fly straight at Easy's head.

"It starts in thirty minutes," he added. "And it's the
last showing of the night."

All the pink had left Rayleen's face. Just as Charlie
started to worry she was going to pass out, the color
returned to her cheeks with a vengeance. "Damn it,
Easy. I never said I'd go to the movies with you."

"No, but you will."

She didn't move or respond. Charlie considered her

poor perishables for a brief second, then decided this whole situation was much more delicious than yogurt.

Easy nodded as if something had been decided. He put his hat on his head and walked across the room to the kitchen. "Woman, you've been daring me to try something for over a year. If you didn't want to draw my attention, you shouldn't have waved your red cape every damn time I saw you. We're going to the movies. Here are your flowers. Say good-night to your friends. I might not have you back before morning."

Charlie actually gasped, but everyone else just snickered. And then Jenny started to clap.

"You tell her, Easy!" Grace called out over the friendly applause.

Rayleen looked at the room as if an elephant had just dropped from the sky. Her expression made clear that no one had ever spoken to her like that.

It took a few heartbeats, but she finally recovered and snatched the flowers from Easy's hand. Her chin inched up. "Fine," she snapped, taking the arm he offered.

For all his big talk, Easy slumped a little in relief.

"But," Rayleen added, "let's not pretend a man your age can even hold a conversation all night long, much less take on a woman like me in bed."

Easy rolled his eyes and walked her to the door. "We'll see who cries uncle first."

"If you think I'll be talking about my uncle, you've been dating some nasty freaks, you old coot."

And with that, they were out the door, their bickering echoing off the entryway ceiling.

"Holy shit," Charlie breathed.

Jenny stood in the open door and waved. "Bye, kids! Have fun!"

Merry shook her head. "That. Was. *Awesome.*"

"And way overdue," Grace muttered. She and Merry grinned at each other and then clinked glasses.

"What's the story?" Charlie asked in awe.

Grace shrugged and refilled her margarita from the pitcher. "The story is exactly what you saw. They've been acting like that for years, playing gin rummy together, snapping at each other like irritated dogs. I think Rayleen is embarrassed that she actually likes him, and Easy isn't sure he wants to take on a crazy woman. But they can't stay away from each other."

"Aw!" Charlie actually felt tears prick her eyes. "That's so cute."

"Ha. It's also annoying if you have to be around it for any length of time. You just want to yell, 'Take your clothes off and work out this damn tension already!'"

Merry snorted. "Didn't you actually yell that a few months ago?"

"Maybe," Grace said with an insolent smile. "She's my aunt. I figured I owed it to the rest of you to step in."

"Hey!" Jenny called from the doorway. "Eve is here! And there's Walker!"

"Oh, God," Charlie said. "Invite him in. He'll be the perfect addition to girls' night."

Eve, who was introduced as Grace's boss, came in carrying a bottle of wine and a cake. Charlie liked her immediately.

Walker got as far as the doorway, then stopped, looking over at them with a wary eye. "What's going on here, ladies?"

"If you're going to start with that line," Merry drawled into her drink, "you'd better be wearing your tear-away police uniform, stud." Then she looked at him over her shoulder and gasped. "Oh, my God, Walker, what happened to your face?"

He shook his head. "Just a little barnyard fight. It happens." His eyes caught Charlie's for a moment and he looked away.

"I hope the other guy looks worse than you do," Jenny said, patting his cheek.

"He does."

"Good. Then come in. You look like a man who needs a margarita." She dragged him in, but he still looked doubtful.

"This looks like girls' night."

"It is," Merry said. "You can be the entertainment. Are you going to dance for us, Walker?"

He waggled his eyebrows. "Come on, girls. You know you're not ready for this jelly."

They collapsed in snorting laughter while Walker did a pretty good imitation of resisting Jenny's pull, but eventually he collapsed onto the couch next to Charlie. "Seriously, ladies. I need a shower. I probably smell like I've been pushing cattle onto a truck all day."

Charlie nudged him with her hip. "Yeah, if there's one thing we women hate, it's a big dirty cowboy in our midst. Just awful."

"Horrible," Jenny agreed. "No one wants to see that."

"I was more worried about the scent."

Charlie leaned closer and breathed him in. There was a hint of hide about him, but mostly it was crisp air and...sweaty Walker. "You'll do," she said softly. "Have a margarita and stay awhile. At least we'll keep you out of trouble."

Trouble with married women was what she meant, and he seemed to understand because he cleared his throat and accepted a glass without another word. If he'd been planning a quick escape, he changed his mind when the pizza arrived. Soon enough they were all stuffed and tipsy and laughing about sex stories over their cake. There really wasn't any other reason to have a girls' night, in Charlie's opinion. She didn't know if anyone had kids, but she damn sure didn't want to talk about them.

She'd missed this. She'd had girlfriends in Vegas, but she hadn't seemed to assemble many in Tahoe. Her idea of a good time by then had been curling up on the couch with a bottle of wine to watch a scary movie by herself. Her boyfriend had been a workaholic, or so she'd thought. What he'd actually been was married and spending time with his family.

But Vegas... Yeah, that had been good for a few years. Of course, Vegas had set a very high bar for girls' nights, but you couldn't go watch male strippers *every* weekend. Even that had gotten old. Or Charlie had gotten bored. But this…this was nice. And immediately comfortable, despite the fact that she hadn't known any of these women more than a week.

A few minutes later, Merry was telling a hilarious story about a dirty talker that had half of them in tears.

"But come on!" Charlie protested. "Dirty talk is fun!"

"Oh, I know. But this wasn't the right kind of dirty talk."

Walker leaned forward, elbows on his knees. "What's the right kind?"

"You know." Merry blushed and waved him away, but she couldn't resist. "It's supposed to be interactive. And hopefully have *something* to do with the person you're with. Not just some weird running monologue you trot out every time."

Charlie screeched, "Like what?"

"Well… It was like a pep talk. 'Oh, yeah, you like that, don't you, you dirty whore? Oh, God, yes, you love it. You always love it. You love it just like this.' He never paused for a response or anything. It was just the same thing every time."

"Oh, no!"

"He never even opened his eyes. It was like he had to turn me into a bad girl in his mind."

Charlie wiped tears from her eyes. "Really? Did he spank you, too?"

"Oh, God, no!"

"What?" Charlie protested with a giggle. "There's nothing wrong with a good spanking every now and then."

Walker leaned even farther forward. "There's not?"

Charlie turned to grin at him. "Wouldn't you like to know?"

"Yes. I really, truly would."

"Aw!" Jenny interrupted. "Don't tease Walker!"

"If he can't handle girls' night, then he should leave." Charlie aimed a sly smile in his direction.

"I'm not going anywhere," he countered, crossing his arms and leaning back into the couch.

"Maybe he can learn something," Grace said as she cut herself another piece of cake. "So many men seem to be under the impression that we want to be treasured in bed."

Merry stuck her lip out. "There's nothing wrong with being treasured."

Charlie nodded. "True. But when you meet a very special man, and you have very special feelings for him...sometimes it's okay if he wants to use you like a little whore." They all erupted in screams of laughter. Grace shoved Merry so hard that Merry nearly fell out of her chair.

Charlie's eyes were too full of tears to see Walker clearly for a moment, but when she finally looked at him, he was staring intently at her. Her amusement suddenly flamed into hot awareness. Thank God her cheeks were red from the margaritas, or everyone would think she was blushing.

"Fine," Merry said. "That might be true. *Sometimes.* But Shane's the only one who knows for sure."

"And me," Grace said. "You did tell me about that one time he made you get on your knees and—"

"Stop!" Merry shrieked. "You're the worst best friend ever!"

"Oh, right. Like the rest of us have never done that."

Merry giggled and covered her mouth. "I know *you* have. But I've never been a dirty girl before."

Grace poked her with a toe. "It's fun, isn't it?"

None of them needed any answer except Merry's ridiculously wide grin.

Yeah. It was fun being a dirty girl. Charlie snugged her hip a little closer to Walker's.

He was blushing now, too, but he maintained his stubborn posture on the couch, determined not to be ousted from the party.

"Are you a dirty girl, Walker?" she cooed.

He shook his head. "I don't even know how to answer that."

They moved on to teasing Grace about how she was shacking up with her boyfriend out on an actual ranch, and the dirty talk died down into laughter about which of the women was going to get married first. But Charlie was still more than aware of Walker at her side. Eventually he dropped his hand and slipped it between them so he could rub his thumb along her thigh.

Fun girlfriends or not, Charlie suddenly wished them all gone. She wanted to be with Walker. In the biblical sense.

But just as Grace was declaring she would only be a ranch partner and never a ranch wife, Walker pushed to his feet. "Now that all the pizza's gone, I'd better make my escape. I've got an early day tomorrow. And I still smell like cow."

They all called out in dismay and tried to talk him into staying, but he waved them off with thanks for the pizza and drinks.

"Charlie," Jenny said slyly as he made his way to the door. "Do you have something going on with Walker?"

"I wish," she said as he opened the door and tossed her a wink.

"You two seem awfully cozy."

Charlie laughed. "Come on. You know how it is with Walker."

He closed the door on their laughter, while Charlie fought the urge to call him back. *Please stay. Stay all night.*

She wanted him like that. In her bed. Big and strong and so close she could touch him anytime she wanted. So warm that she knew he was there even in her sleep. She wanted to wake up to the feel of him behind her, already sliding into her wet body before she'd even opened her eyes.

God. She wanted that.

"That's weird," Grace said. "Charlie is staring at her front door like she wants to eat it up. I wonder what that's about."

She blushed while they all laughed, but there was really nothing to be ashamed of. Who wouldn't want to eat Walker up? He was one big, lickable treat. She'd consider it a privilege.

WALKER WAS GETTING more sensitive with age. Or maybe he had some sort of chemical imbalance. Every time Charlie implied that he was only built for temporary fun, he bristled. Ridiculous, considering how often he'd said it himself. Oh, he'd had the occasional girl-friend here and there, but it had never lasted more than a couple of months. And that had never been a problem.

So why did Charlie's words keep hurting his feel-ings?

"My feelings." He sneered as he got out of the shower and towel-dried his hair. He felt stupid even thinking it.

He'd forgotten about his bruises, and winced when the towel caught his cheek. After wiping the steam from the mirror, he stared down at his own tired face.

God. He was getting too old for this shit. He'd been itching for a fight last night, but he'd tried to mitigate that by going to visit Roosevelt instead of heading out to a bar. He'd tried to be smart. Sure, a good bar fight was a hell of a lot of fun, but it was more geared to-ward younger men who never thought about expensive dental work or the danger of being arrested for drunk and disorderly.

So he'd driven out to the ranch, and everything had been good for a few minutes. Roosevelt had jumped in wild circles of excitement, and Walker's mood had improved within seconds. Then a couple of friends had invited him to sit by the campfire for a beer. It'd been perfect. His dog at his side, a beer in hand, thousands of stars above.

Until that bastard stable manager had happened by.

Walker pressed a hand to his ribs and pushed. They were hardly sore at all tonight. The guy had gotten in a few good punches, but they'd only pissed Walker off. Like everything else these days.

But he couldn't stay mad at Charlie. She hadn't done anything wrong. She couldn't understand, and he didn't want her to.

He heard a faint shriek of laughter from the hallway and shook his head. Those women were crazy. And cute. And very, very bad.

He pulled on sweatpants and a T-shirt and was heading to the kitchen to wash the breakfast dishes when someone knocked on his door. Expecting more teasing, he opened it to find Charlie standing there alone.

"You left quickly," she said.

"Oh, yeah?" he drawled. "Did you want me to stay?"

He'd said it automatically, and wasn't expecting her quick "Yes." The jolt of happiness caught him by surprise.

"We were going to talk, remember?" she said.

"Ah. Right. I'm sorry. I guess I'm not much in the mood for talking."

"Me, either."

Her steady gaze sent a prickling of awareness over his skin, and he suddenly remembered how torturous it had been to sit next to her and not touch her. "Do you want to come in?"

She smiled and swept into his apartment, the tumbling waves of her hair trailing the already familiar scent of her shampoo. His pulse went wild.

"I'm sorry about last night," she said as she took a seat on his couch. "I really didn't mean to upset you."

"I'm the one who's sorry. The job search and everything else has me stressed. But that's all over. I accepted that winter job. It's done. So I'm right as rain again."

Her lips parted as if she meant to say something, but then her eyebrows drew together and she shook her head. "Okay. Sure. But will you at least think about what I said?"

"Charlie," he moaned, sprawling onto the couch beside her. "No."

"Why not?" She stretched out over him, her head against his shoulder and her hand on his chest.

"Because."

"But, Walker…" Her fingers spread. "You're so good with people."

"Charlie."

She kissed his neck. "And you like working with them."

He shook his head.

"And you're so damn big and amazing."

"Okay, I'll take that."

Her mouth whispered against him. Her fingers found his nipple and circled it. "Walker—"

"Stop, Charlie. Just stop. How about we talk about you instead?"

Her fingers froze. "What about me?"

"I don't know. I guess we could start with how naughty you are."

"Oh." He could feel her smile against his neck. "That."

"Are you a dirty girl, Charlie?" he asked, repeating her earlier question.

She giggled as he spread his hand over her back. "I don't know. Would you like it if I was?"

He smiled and let himself slide farther down the cushions until his head came to rest on the arm of the couch and Charlie was sprawled across him. "I'm not sure. I wonder if there's a way we could find out."

"Mm. Maybe." Her teeth bit into him, making him hiss. "I already found a clue." Her hand slid down his belly and curved around the shape of his cock through his sweatpants. He was already half-hard, and about to get much harder. "You like that, Walker?"

"I do. Yes. Definitely."

"Mm. But it's not really naughty, is it? That's just touching."

"Yeah. Just…" She squeezed his cock and it sure as hell felt naughty. "I suppose."

She let go of him and his fingers tightened on her back. "Wait—"

But now her hand slid his shirt up in very slow inches. He sucked in his belly as her hand dragged over his skin. She slid her body down, until her head met up with the skin she'd exposed, and she put her mouth on his stomach, just above his navel. "Does that feel naughty?"

"Yes," he said without hesitation this time.

"Really?" Her wet tongue touched him, then retreated. "But...that's just a little kiss."

"Yes, but..."

"And here, on your poor side." She kissed one of the bruises. "And here." Her tongue traced his navel, and he sucked in a breath. He looked down to see her watching him, her tongue darting past her smile to taste his skin again. When his muscles jumped, she laughed.

Walker's eyes narrowed. His heart beat harder. "You're right," he said. "That's not really very naughty. I thought you had something to show me, Charlie. I guess I was wrong."

Her smile faded and her eyes went a little wide. She didn't look so playful anymore. Now she looked... *serious*. "You want a dirty girl, Walker?"

He didn't answer. He just met her challenging gaze and watched as her fingers hooked into the waistband of his sweatpants. She tugged. And tugged again. His cock sprang free, and they both watched as Charlie wrapped her fist around the base. He wanted to groan. He didn't.

She gave a little hum of approval as she slid lower down his body. He kept an eye on her mouth, counting the inches as it drew closer to the head of his cock.

"Look at you," she breathed. "So hard for me."

Yeah, he was. Hell yeah. She held him so firmly he could feel the beat of his pulse beneath her fingers.

"You want me to kiss it, Walker? Is that what dirty girls do?"

Oh, shit, she was so damn sexy, looking up at him past her lashes, her mouth only an inch away. She licked her lips. His heart skipped and stammered.

"Yes," he managed to say.

And then she kissed him.

Just her lips at first. Just one gentle kiss, and then two, and three. Her lips parted, and he watched as her tongue swirled around the head of his cock.

"Yes," he said again. Her mouth opened, and heat engulfed him. "Yes, like that."

"Mmm." This time when she hummed, he felt it. A little vibration of approval that made him shudder. He forgot that he was supposed to be playing this game, and all he could do was watch as she took him deeper. As wet heat took him in and broke him down. And then she sucked.

"Charlie," he groaned.

She hummed again and took more of him. It was pure heaven. The best thing he'd ever felt. Charlie's mouth around him and her gray eyes flashing up and her tongue pressing. God.

And then she did something he'd never expected, and for a moment, he didn't know how to react.

Charlie took his hand and pressed it to the back of her head.

"Oh, shit," he breathed. Her fingers splayed over

his so that he was cupping her skull. His brain stopped working.

When she took him deeper, his hand followed her movement. The next time she did it, he urged her on with a light touch that grew firmer when she moaned her pleasure around him. "God, yes," he murmured. "Take more, Charlie. Like that."

She took more. Then more still when he pressed her down.

His heart beat so hard it felt as if his cock was swelling in her mouth, growing thicker and heavier as she sucked him. His chest felt strange and tight as he watched her, her head working slowly up and down. He felt like growling, like snarling like an animal. He was rough and out of control as he tried not to force her to take more.

"You like that, Charlie?" he growled. "You like doing that?"

She hummed around him again, her eyes flashing up to meet his gaze. Fuck, it was too much. Too good. The eager way she took him. The sight of his wet shaft sliding from her lips. The insane, unimaginable pleasure every single time her mouth pulled at him.

He wanted to come. He needed to. Just like this, her mouth around him and her approving sounds of pleasure. Oh, God. Yes. He needed that.

But he remembered the dirty things she'd said earlier, and the way she'd teased and taunted him, and instead of urging her to take him faster, he fisted his hand in her hair and drew her off him.

She watched him, panting, her lips wet and red from what she'd done. His heart thundered at the sight. He wanted to remember this forever. Sweet little Charlie, her eyes hot with lust, her mouth bruised from servicing him, her hair wrapped around his fist. Fuck, this was so wrong.

He almost eased her back down. His body was screaming at him to do it. To slide his cock between her lips and growl at her to get him off. But he ignored the compulsion and tugged his pants back up. "The bedroom," he said gruffly. When her eyes blazed, he knew he'd made the right choice.

He followed her to the bedroom and said, "Take off your clothes." It wasn't quite natural for him, telling a woman what to do. But natural or not, his pulse thrilled at the way she did what he asked.

Walker had his shirt and pants off within seconds, and he watched intently as she stripped for him. First her shirt, then her shoes and jeans. Then…everything. Until she was standing before him, long and lean and naked.

"So…" He cupped his hand over her jaw, then let his fingertips slide down her arching neck, her delicate collarbone, until he plucked at her nipple. She gasped. "Do you like being a dirty girl, Charlie?"

She smirked at him. "No." God, she was such a tease. He realized now that she'd been teasing him the whole week, pretending not to want all of this as much as he did.

"No? That's odd considering what you said earlier tonight."

"Maybe I lied."

"Your mouth felt pretty naughty a few seconds ago."

She shrugged, one shoulder rising even as her nipple got harder beneath his touch. "Beginner's luck, I suppose," she said. He pinched her harder. Her cheekbones were flushed pink now. Her hands tightening to fists at her sides as her breath came faster.

"Turn around."

She turned and he put one hand on the nape of her neck and slowly bent her down until she'd placed her hands flat on the bed. Walker moved to the dresser to grab a condom.

Charlie was a fantasy, bent over, her ass pale and smooth and exposed to him. And she'd really said that, hadn't she? That sometimes a girl wanted to be spanked. Sometimes she didn't want to be treasured? And fuck… The light from the lamp made it clear she was wet for him. Her plump flesh glistened.

Walker's head pounded with rushing blood.

He couldn't do this.

But he moved behind her and smoothed his hand over her ass. She looked small under his rough fingers. And so perfect and soft. He squeezed her. Hard. And then he slapped her.

"Ah!" she cried out, her fingers digging into his bedspread. But she didn't move. She didn't say no. He made contact again, smacking her so hard his hand stung. But even as the mark of his hand flared to life on her pale skin, she pushed back toward him.

"Charlie," he whispered. "Tell me you like it."

She shook her head. He wanted to stop. It scared him. But his hands were shaking and not from fear. He slapped her again, then over and over, watching her skin turn red. She whimpered, her breath shaking from her throat.

"Tell me you like it," he groaned, but then he slipped his hand between her legs, and he didn't have to ask again. She was hot and slick and she cried out when his fingers slid over her. "Oh, fuck, Charlie."

He reached for the condom and slid it on, then notched himself against her. He didn't ease in this time. He wasn't gentle. He just braced his hands on her hips and sank his cock deep.

Charlie screamed, throwing her head back as he pushed mercilessly in. The heat of her body squeezed and pulled at his cock as he started to fuck her. Her arms buckled and she went to her elbows. "Yes," he hissed as her hips tipped up for him. "God, yes. Touch yourself, Charlie. Do it."

He watched her slip a hand beneath her body and then she cried out and pushed back to meet his thrusts. He couldn't quite catch his breath then. The air rushed out of him as if he were working too hard. As if her body had overwhelmed him.

"Tell me you like it," he growled one last time, his fingers digging into her hips.

"Yes," she answered. "Yes. Yes. Please."

"More," he ordered.

"I need it," she sobbed. "Don't stop. Please. I need you."

Adrenaline poured into his veins, ratcheting his pleasure to impossible heights. She met each of his thrusts with a little sob, working herself against him, trying to get off. Not quite believing it, even as he did it, Walker raised his hand to his mouth. He slid his thumb along his tongue, wetting it; then he slid it carefully between her ass cheeks and pressed in. Slowly.

"Walker," she moaned. "Oh, God. Oh, God." But she didn't pull away. She pushed back. Taking him inside her. "No," she moaned. "No." But she arched her back, taking his thumb deeper with a low moan.

He thrust hard into her pussy, over and over, leaving his thumb buried deep inside her, making her feel him everywhere. Her moans became whimpers, and then eager cries, and finally she came for him, screaming, her body tightening around his cock, pulsing around his thumb. Her hoarse sobs filled the room, but a moment later, Walker's ears were filled with his own rushing pulse as he fucked her harder. Harder. Until he buried himself deep with a desperate grunt of pleasure.

Her body was still pulsing as he came, squeezing the come from him as he bowed into her.

He slipped his thumb free. She cried out one last time. He held himself still, trying to draw the pleasure out for one more long, perfect moment. She shook beneath him. She shook from what he'd done to her.

Oh, man. That had been too much. For him. And

clearly too much for her. He felt guilty as he slowly slid free of her body.

Charlie collapsed onto the bed in a pile of limp limbs.

Walker retreated to the bathroom to toss the condom and clean up and try to figure out if there were right words to say after sex like that. He couldn't think of anything, but he couldn't just leave her there alone. She must be shaking harder than he was, so Walker snuck back into the bedroom.

Easing down to lie on his side, he faced Charlie. "Hey," he said, reaching out to slide the hair off her face. Her eyes were revealed first, a little dark and stunned. Then her cute nose. Then her mouth…which stretched into a grin.

"Hey yourself," she drawled.

He blinked.

"Damn, Walker. That was hot. Like…really crazy hot."

He blinked again.

Charlie frowned. "Oh. Too weird for you?"

He curled his hand behind her neck and leaned toward her pretty mouth. When he kissed her, she sighed into him. "Why do you have to be so fucking perfect, Charlie Allington?" he whispered.

She sucked in a breath and shook her head. "Shut up."

"It's true. That was…really crazy hot."

Her grin returned, and then she laughed. He pulled her tight against him and tucked her head under his chin. She snuggled against him like a kitten, and Walker's heart twisted. This wasn't good. He liked this girl. He respected her. He was a little in awe of her and always had been. Mix that up with insanely delicious sex, and Walker was in big trouble.

Damn.

"Maybe we should argue more often," she said.

He shook his head and stayed quiet. He didn't want to talk about it, but as the silence settled over them, he knew he owed her more than that. "I didn't mean to argue with you," he said quietly. "I don't want to. It's just... Shit. My dad was always hard on me. He never believed in me. So I don't want to talk about all the stuff I'm not doing, Charlie. I work. I'm great at what I do. I need that to be enough, at least for myself, even if no one else agrees."

Her fingers tickled his chest when she stroked him. "I'm sorry. I know how it can be when dads are shitty."

"My dad didn't understand. He hated what was wrong with me, so I don't like to talk about it. I don't want to think about it. I'm done now. I'm not in school, I don't have to deal with the struggle, and I'm not going back."

"But I *do* understand," she pressed. But when he shook his head, she let it go. "All right."

"Thanks."

"I'm only agreeing to let it go so I can talk you into more sex."

"You really think that's all it would take?" he asked, then laughed when she punched him. He found himself smiling against her hair, breathing in the scent of her. Yeah, this was bad. "Can you stay tonight?"

She melted into him a tiny bit more. "Yeah. I'd like that. If I can sleep. It's been a while since I spent the night in someone else's bed."

He hadn't realized he'd been tense about her answer until he heard it. When she agreed, he felt...surprised. Grateful. He would have been less shocked if she'd said, *Nah, you know this isn't like that, Walker. You're not the kind of guy a girl cuddles with afterward.*

And maybe he wasn't. Maybe he was what he'd always been. The good-time guy. The booty call. The man you cheated with, but never depended on. The man who was exactly what you needed, exactly when you needed it, but never more than that.

He'd been all those things to other women, but for her...for her he could be something totally different, if only she'd ask for it. "You didn't have a boyfriend in Tahoe?"

Her eyes flashed up to his for a moment. "It ended a while ago. How about you? Did you have someone special before Nicole?"

He noticed that she didn't say "before *me*."

Charlie laughed when he didn't respond. "Yeah. I figured."

Walker wanted to tell her she was wrong, but how could he? He'd had a few girlfriends in his life, but only a few. With the hours he worked, and the weeks he was gone, it wasn't easy. And whatever way he interacted with other women seemed to qualify as flirting, even when he tried very hard not to flirt. His relationships had always been volatile and quickly over. So yeah…how could he assure her she was wrong when she wasn't?

"It's okay," she said, patting his shoulder. "I'm not very good at relationships. I'm better off being friends with a guy like you. I'm not even sure I really believe in love."

"You don't believe in love?" he asked. Did she think he didn't? That he didn't want it?

"Don't worry. I'm not initiating a very special relationship talk." Laughing, she leaned up to kiss him and then rolled onto her back. "You heard all the stories about my mom, I'm sure. They were all true. And lots more you didn't hear about. My dad was just gone. Moved on. I haven't seen a lot of good come out of love or whatever people think love is."

He wrapped his fingers around hers and stroked his thumb over her knuckles. "No?"

"What about your parents? Were they good together?"

"Oh, hell, I don't know. They stayed together. They didn't fight that often, which is a miracle considering my dad's temper. Or maybe it was because of his temper. But I don't know about the love part."

"Yeah," she sighed. "Me, neither."

He squeezed her hand. "I think you'd be pretty easy to love, Charlie."

"Ha." She laughed as if he'd been joking. "Look who's talking. Every woman loves you, Walker."

He made himself chuckle. "Don't believe everything you hear."

"All right." She brought his hand up to her mouth and kissed it, and Walker's heart did a strange turn in his chest. "I'll only believe half. And you can tell me I'm special. And I'll even believe it while we're here in this room. Deal?"

"Deal," he answered. And he wished like hell he was only playing along.

CHAPTER SIXTEEN

HE WAS WARM under her hand. Even warmer than she'd imagined. His chest rose and fell in a steady rhythm that made her heart hurt for reasons she couldn't fathom.

Charlie cuddled closer in the dark, and his arm tightened briefly around her, as if he knew she was there. But that was just his body's memory, borne of the hundreds of times he'd held other women like this. She wouldn't let it sneak inside her, the comfort of him. Of his heat and skin and smell and the way his mouth brushed over her hair when he held her.

She pressed her lips to his shoulder. He was asleep. He'd never know.

It was only 4:00 a.m. She should be sleeping, too, but she'd woken fifteen minutes before and her brain refused to stop working.

She wanted so badly for him to look into the Ability Ranch. Her heart beat hard every time she thought about him with those kids. He probably thought anyone could do that, but Charlie knew the truth. She turned into a nervous mess around kids. They were just odd strangers who invaded your space and were unpredictable and came with different rules depending on age and size and brattiness. Sometimes they cried. Sometimes they yelled. Sometimes they stared at you as if they knew something you didn't.

God. They freaked her out. Walker had no idea what kind of gift he had.

But if Walker's dad had treated him badly because of the dyslexia, she understood why he wouldn't want to deal with it. Why throwing himself back into the challenge of it would be too much.

She should let it go, but Walker was so damn amazing. And his problems seemed so much easier to solve than hers. Charlie's problems were legion and lingering and hard to even wrap her head around.

Like that thing with Keith Taggert tonight. What the hell had that been?

She eased off Walker's arm and lay on her back to stare up at the ceiling. Someone's porch light shone through the backyard trees and made shadows dance against the white room. It was a perfect, peaceful night in a wonderful man's arms, and she was thinking about the Taggerts.

Something about the situation—*everything* about the situation—niggled at her brain.

The conversation with Dawn at the party had slipped a couple of puzzle pieces into place, but those pieces had dislodged others. Dawn's behavior made much more sense now that Charlie knew Keith had been the one lobbying for her employment. But why would he really have wanted her?

She came at a discount. That was one good reason. Charlie had taken a steep cut in pay from her last job. In fact, she'd be embarrassed to tell anyone about the package she'd accepted. But considering the resort's budget, those numbers couldn't be the sole motivator.

So maybe his loyalty speech was the key. He'd scraped her off the bottom of the barrel, and now he thought she'd be a valuable, tireless advocate for his business. That could be it. It was a pretty solid theory. She was inclined to feel damn generous toward him.

And maybe, just maybe, it was because of her brother. Sure, he hadn't been the kind of big brother Walker clearly was. He hadn't protected her in childhood. He hadn't looked out for her. But maybe losing their father had changed something for him.

She brushed her hand against Walker's fingers and thought of the way he'd spoken of his brother. She couldn't quite understand that kind of sibling love, but maybe she could have a part of that. Her brother would never be her hero, but he could be something like a friend if she tried.

She'd call him today. For sure. She wouldn't forget this time.

Charlie closed her eyes and told herself she could go back to sleep. She'd thought through all of her problems. There was nothing to be done right now. But her brain kept turning.

Crap. She opened her eyes. There wasn't going to be any more sleep for her tonight. And she couldn't wake Walker this early. He didn't sit behind a desk all day. He had real work to do.

Before doing anything drastic, she looked at him. She could just make out his profile in the darkness. The black swirls of his messy hair stood out against the white pillow. He needed a haircut, but she was glad he hadn't gotten it yet. She liked the way it made him look wild and vulnerable at the same time, like a careless little boy.

She wanted to touch him. Wanted to wind her fingers into his hair and snuggle close and breathe in his scent. She wanted to wake him with her hands and her mouth until he covered her and filled her with his body. They could fall back to sleep together, limbs tangled and heartbeats keeping pace. In the morning, he'd tease her and kiss her and then she'd use his shampoo and smell him all day, as if she were still wrapped up in him.

But that would be one of those memories that would hurt when he'd moved on to someone else. She'd see some cute girl sneaking out of his apartment in the morning. Someone prettier and smaller and younger, and Charlie would hate that girl and hate him and hate herself and all her memories.

No. She couldn't do that. Her last lover had made her feel like a fool. She never wanted that again.

Charlie slipped out of bed and pulled on her clothes and made her escape. She meant to shower and go for a run, but as she dried her hair, she realized she had an opportunity. If she got into work before everyone else, she could check out those security tapes in private. If Keith had been trying to spy on someone, she wanted to know who it was. His wife? An employee? Someone else?

Yeah. This was an opportunity she couldn't miss. She stuffed her running gear into a bag and dressed for work instead. If it was nothing, she'd still have time to run before she needed to be in her office. Heck, she could even take a nap. This having-two-apartments gig was starting to work out. She should take advantage of it before they gave her room away.

A moment of guilt stabbed her when she quietly closed her apartment door and tiptoed down the stairs. She should've left at least a note for Walker, but even that assumed too much. It assumed he'd care that she was gone and why she'd left. No. Better to just pretend last night had meant nothing more to her than it did to him.

But good Lord, that man was hot. She was starting to worry that she'd be willing to sacrifice a lot for the chance to have him whenever she wanted. Her pride, certainly. Because even when the day came that she saw another woman sneaking down these stairs, Charlie wouldn't stop wanting him. God, maybe she actually would share him with someone else if it meant feeling his hands on her the way she had last night. Rough and needy and demanding.

Wow. Just…

Charlie shook her head as she stepped into the icy night air.

That had been so good and filthy and hot. Not just what he'd said and done, but the fact that it was *Walker,* who'd always been so sweet to her.

All the most sensitive nerves in her body woke to immediate arousal when she thought of tasting him. Sucking him. Pushing him so far that he'd growled filthy things at her.

Chuckling, she got into her car and started for work.

Oh, she was going to do that again. As many times as she could before it was over. She'd loved him in her mouth, loved the power of it getting all twisted up with the submissiveness of the act.

Yes.

She replayed every moment of the night on her drive to the resort. Every touch and sigh and taste. In fact, she was so turned on by the time she pulled up to the garage that she almost turned the car around and went back. She could pick up breakfast, then wake him with something even sweeter than donuts. They could have a perfect morning together before they had to part.

But no. She wasn't going to be one of those clingy women. How many girls had wanted everything from him? And how many of those had he walked away from? No. Charlie didn't get walked out on if she could help it. She did the walking. Unless, of course, the relationship ended up with an arrest. Once there were handcuffs involved, the semantics of it took on a smaller significance.

Regardless, she wasn't going to sit on his lap and feed him breakfast. She wouldn't fall that far. So just as the first hint of pink broke above the hills behind her, Charlie pulled into the resort garage and left that amazing night behind.

After dropping her bag in her studio, she headed straight downstairs to the surveillance room. Every office was still dark. If the resort were up and running, she would've at least passed by a housekeeping supervisor or two, but the place was eerily empty at this hour. Thank God.

She shut the door behind her and fired up the monitors. The feeds automatically drew her eye, but the rest of the hotel was dead quiet, too. Time to do what she'd come here for.

Starting with yesterday at 8:00 p.m., she worked back through the digital video. It was tedious and took forever, even when she pulled four feeds at once.

Once she'd made it through twelve hours of half the feeds, she started feeling stupid. There was nothing here. Keith owned the resort. He'd been making the rounds. There was nothing odd about that.

Charlie stood and stretched with a groan of frustration; then she forced herself to sit back down. There was no point doing this half-assed.

Thirty minutes later, she'd convinced herself she was on a wild-goose chase. She saw Keith in the videos, but he was only walking from office to office, or occasionally stopping to chat with an employee in a hallway. She made notes of each time she saw him, but the notes were about to make a quick acquaintance with the trash.

Charlie slumped in her chair and watched yesterday's video of an interior decorator instructing a crew on exactly where a giant statue of an eagle should be placed. Charlie would have to head down to the lobby to check it out. It was a damn impressive bird.

A glance at the clock told her the sun would be fully up by now. If she wanted to go for a run, she'd have to head out in the next five minutes or there wouldn't be time to shower before her shift.

"Shit." She ran her hands through her hair and took a deep breath. All right. She was done with all this. Her instincts were off, yet again. She should quit this job and open a cozy shop somewhere in the countryside. She could sell… Oh, hell, what did she know anything about? Dirty greeting cards, maybe?

The monitor glared accusingly at her. She glared back. "Damn."

Charlie pulled up the activity logs for the computer, then waited for them to load. And suddenly—just like that—all thoughts of a run vanished from her mind.

Keith had logged in at 9:00 p.m.

Keith had waited for Charlie to leave and then he'd come back to the surveillance room and he'd logged in to this computer and he'd screwed around with her files.

She wasn't losing anything. Her instincts were just fine. She just had to learn to trust them again.

"Motherfu…" Charlie sat forward and fired up the video feeds again. She called up every instance of Keith's appearance and then worked forward from there. Hours went by without anything suspicious. Then she saw it. A skip in the numbers. She backed up and looked again.

There. She backed up further. Ten minutes before the skip, Keith went into his office. Then there was a twenty-second-long skip. Fifteen minutes later, another brief skip in the time stamp.

Someone had come to see him. Someone's arrival and departure had been deleted from the feed. She marked the times, then started working through each camera.

Yes. The next camera down the hallway had the same two cuts, different by only a few seconds.

"That little shit," she growled. He'd been thorough. Really thorough.

She followed the logical path of video for someone proceeding from the garage to Keith's office. There were a few missteps, but she eventually tracked down every digital cut.

Staring at the list she'd made, she racked her brain for some detail he could have missed, but even the parking garage footage had been altered.

Then she remembered the elevators. Those camera numbers were in a different order and the feed went to different software. "Bingo," she breathed as she pulled up that program and opened the files.

It took her two minutes to identify the right camera, and then she had it. A light-haired woman walked onto the elevator, head down. She pushed a button, smoothed down her skirt and then looked up as the floor numbers ticked by.

"Holy shit," Charlie wheezed. The person who'd come to see Keith was Nicole Fletcher. More important, the person whose presence Keith didn't want anyone to know about was Nicole Fletcher. "Seriously?" Charlie barked. She couldn't get away from this bitch.

A memory from the charity party flashed over her. When she'd still been huddled with Walker, she'd glanced over to see Keith talking to Nicole. Nicole had touched his arm and he'd pulled away. Charlie had been so wrapped up in her own embarrassment that she'd overlooked that. She'd thought Keith's self-consciousness had been something to do with his employee making out in public.

But no…there had been that touch.

Keith was having an affair. Dawn had been smart to be worried; she'd just been worried about the wrong trashy woman in her life. It wasn't Charlie; it was Nicole.

Charlie shut the program down and backed up all the files to the server.

Keith wasn't as smart as he thought he was. She'd never have reviewed the video if he hadn't been so concerned about deleting it. And really, what the hell did she care who came to his office to visit?

"You're here early."

Charlie jumped in shock and spun to see Dawn standing in the door, already dressed perfectly in a trim little yellow skirt and sweater. "Uh. Hi."

"Good morning," Dawn responded.

Charlie waited for the next words, the little swipe at Charlie's character, but it never came.

She looked at the monitor over Charlie's shoulder. "What are you doing?"

Charlie snuck a panicked glance back to be sure she'd closed everything. "Just catching up. You know. Making notes on cameras." She scraped together all her paper and smacked it into a crooked pile. "Checking all the time stamps."

"The time stamps?"

Crap. Her heart raced. "Yes. I need to be sure they all line up."

"Hm. Anything odd?"

"No. Nope. Nothing at all." Oh, man. Now she was covering up a husband's affair. But really, this had nothing to do with her job. She didn't owe Dawn anything. In fact, she owed Keith a lot more.

Damn this place.

"Be sure you let me know if you ever see anything unusual," Dawn said softly.

"Sure."

"Because you still need to train me on how to handle suspicious events."

"Yes. Absolutely. Later, though. Today I'm checking security features in the rooms."

Dawn stared her down for a moment, but she eventually sighed and walked away without a word. Charlie let out the breath she'd been holding.

Keith hadn't been worried that Charlie would see a

woman coming to his office. He'd been worried that Dawn would see. Charlie was beginning to lose her faith in marriage.

She laughed at the thought. Then laughed harder. She'd never had any faith in marriage, and she'd yet to see anything that would change her mind. Her own parents had been disasters, whether they were together or with other people. Working in Vegas had given her a crash course in all the ways men and women could betray each other. People married for reasons she could rarely understand, and then they stayed married for even more mysterious motives.

As for love… God. She hoped it never happened to her. There was no motive to that at all. It was just a natural disaster that slammed over you and took you down. All she could do was dig a bunker and hoard supplies and hope she never needed to deal with that emotional apocalypse.

How many times had she seen her mom ruined by it? How many cycles of euphoria and joy, followed by denial, then frantic despair? Then her mom would jump right back in, eager to manufacture some new happiness.

Charlie had only come close once. With a man who'd lied about everything.

No, love wasn't for her. Love was the opposite of security, and security was Charlie's specialty.

She logged out of the system and grabbed her notes to retreat to her office. As soon as the door was closed, she popped her laptop back open and went straight to the search engine.

Her hands hovered over the keyboard. It felt creepy to search out information on Walker's old lover. Super creepy. He wasn't Charlie's boyfriend, and if he was, any insecurities she had would be a reason to talk to him about it, not snoop. But this wasn't about Walker and the curvy, beautiful blonde he'd recently fooled around with.

"Hmph," she grouched to herself. No, this wasn't about that at all.

She typed Nicole's name into the search field and watched the results pour in, dozens of references to Fletcher Guest Ranch. Pictures. Reviews of the ranch. A video interview with Nicole. Charlie took one look at Nicole's perfect makeup in the still shot and skipped over the video. She wasn't jealous. Exactly.

Ignoring the video, she clicked on an "About Us" headline, and there was a picture of Nicole with her husband, both of them smiling as if the ranch were a dream home for a dream couple who were still dreamy in love after all these years. Charlie clicked back.

Everything seemed to be publicity about the ranch, so she tried out the husband's name. Nothing came up. Then she tried Nicole Fletcher and Keith Taggert together. There were no hits for that, but there was an alternative suggestion.

She clicked on it and frowned as she leaned closer to read the legal language. Her frown deepened. And then her eyes flew wide at the sight of her brother's name. What the hell did her brother have to do with Keith Taggert and Nicole's husband?

It seemed to be a land development deal, and it contained a lot of real estate language she wasn't familiar with, but she eventually puzzled it out. Keith had bought the land for the resort from Brad for millions of dollars. And her brother had purchased it from none other than Nicole Fletcher's husband only six months before selling it to Keith. Her brother had made quite a bit of money in a very short amount of time.

So maybe Nicole had only been here to discuss business, but that didn't explain why Keith had deleted the evidence.

It was time for Charlie to make that call to her brother.

CHAPTER SEVENTEEN

"GODDAMN IT!" Walker slapped the cow on her hind-quarters and she double-stepped into the truck. He tugged off his glove and looked down at the finger the heifer had just ground into the gate latch. It was turning purple already, but he could bend it, so he tugged the glove back on and turned back to the truck with a growl.

Before he could get back into the rhythm of the work, his phone rang for the second time in an hour, and he cursed again. He waved to one of the other hands, who nodded and moved closer to the truck. Walker backed away to get the call.

"Yeah?"

"Mr. Pearce, it's Gina from the care center again."

"Right."

"I really think you should come by. Your dad is still struggling to catch his breath, and he's having trouble staying calm."

"My being there won't help him calm down."

"It might. It's hard to say when they're in this state. He might recognize you, or he might mistake you for someone else who's familiar. If it doesn't work, we can try a higher dose of sedative, but we hate to start altering his medications with the heart congestion."

His father had been going into congestive heart failure for months. They'd said it would probably take a few more weeks to get bad, but now his dad had become agitated and out of breath.

Walker tipped his head back and stared at the cloudless blue sky. "I'm over an hour away. Give him the sedative."

"I see. Okay. I'll call later and give you an update."

"Just call me if it gets worse."

"Oh. All right. That's fine."

Walker was done with this whole damn day. First, he'd woken to an inexplicably empty bed. Charlie had left without a kiss or a word or a text. Then he'd gotten the call that his dad was having problems. And then that they'd worsened.

"Just what I fucking need," Walker growled.

He resumed his place by the trailer and got back to work, but his finger throbbed as his blood pressure rose. It was only five-thirty. He'd be at this for another hour, at least, and then there was the drive back to Jackson, and...

Trying to shake off the distraction, he guided another heifer into the trailer, patting her gently to make up for shoving that other poor girl earlier. She hadn't meant to crush his finger. She'd only been panicked.

He tried to calm his temper. A bad mood could spook the animals. But he was pissed at Charlie. And now there was his dad....

"Shit."

When the last cow was on the trailer, he closed it up and motioned to his boss. "I'm sorry. I got a call from my dad's nurse. He's not in good shape. I have to head back."

"We're almost done here. You may as well go on."

He nodded as if he were relieved. The truth was that he didn't want to go to the care center at all, but the nurse's censuring tone had shamed him. He had to go check on the old man, even though it wouldn't make a damn bit of difference to him or his dad. It might make Micah feel better, though, and Walker didn't want to have to face his brother after behaving like an asshole.

Turning his stereo up loud to drown out his thoughts, Walker took off down the dirt road, enjoying the slide of his tires when he took a curve too fast. This was all he needed in his life. Hard work, a fast truck, a warm woman in his bed when he wanted it. Instead of being pissy about Charlie sneaking out, he should be thankful. A beautiful, sexy woman who didn't want anything more than sex? Heck, that was every man's dream, wasn't it? "Hell yeah," he muttered to himself. When the words rang hollow in his ears, he turned the music up higher.

An hour later, when he pulled up at the care center, his eardrums were buzzing, but his mind had cleared. He was conscious of his dusty jeans and boots when he walked in. The floor here was shiny and white and he worried he was leaving bootprints behind him.

He stopped thinking about his boots when he

reached his father's door and registered that the bed was empty and neatly made. Alarm flooded his body.

"Mr. Pearce?"

He turned to see a nurse hurrying toward him and braced himself for the words.

"Your father's doing better, but we moved him to the hospital for overnight observation."

"Oh." He slumped a little, and she smiled.

"I'm sorry, I would've called and warned you, but I didn't think you were coming."

"It's fine. He's next door?" The small regional hospital was only a few steps away.

"Yes. Let me get you his room number."

He managed to make it to the hospital without balking, but each step was heavier than the last. By the time he made it to his dad's room, he felt as if he were toting two hundred pounds on his shoulders. But he felt a surge of relief when he stepped into the room. His dad was sleeping. And he looked all right.

Walker took off his hat and sat in a chair next to the bed. He didn't bother with relaxing. He'd stay for a few minutes and then leave. He'd speak to the doctor, get the latest information; then he'd leave and call Micah with the news. Obligation fulfilled. He bowed his head and counted down the seconds.

A deep breath drew his attention, and Walker looked up to find his dad awake and watching. His face was swollen from the advancing heart failure, and with his cheeks filled out, he looked more like his younger self. Not so gaunt and sickly, despite the tubes feeding oxygen to his nose.

Walker stared at him for a long time, at those blue eyes that looked exactly like his. When his dad's mouth curved into a smile, Walker wondered if his dad had ever looked like that in his youth. If he'd ever been happy.

"Hey, you came back to see me."

"Hi, Dad."

His eyes flickered with confusion, but he kept smiling. "Where's your friend?"

"He's my brother. Micah. He's at work right now."

"Ah." His father nodded. "You look like fine men. Hard workers." He gestured toward Walker's clothes, but then his eyelids drooped.

Walker swallowed hard, trying to think what to say. His father's words meant nothing. They were a stranger's words and not meant for him.

He didn't want them, but they might mean something to Micah. "He just got a promotion," Walker said, his throat thick. "Micah. He's doing real well. He bought a house overlooking the ocean way out in Washington state."

His dad's eyes opened. "Yeah? That must be something to see. I've never seen any more water than the Great Salt Lake. It's salty, but it ain't the ocean."

"I haven't, either. I'm thinking of going out to give it a look, though. Maybe he and I could see what kind of fish we can catch out there."

"You should do that, son. That's what brothers are for. Do you have any other family?"

Walker met his eyes. He searched for his dad in there for a long time before he shook his head. "No. Just Micah."

"Yeah. I…" He paused, his brow dropping until his bushy white eyebrows nearly covered his eyes. "I don't know," he finally said, looking away. "I'm tired."

He looked more like himself now, frowning, irritated. Walker nodded and slipped his hat back on as he stood. "Well, I'll leave you to get some rest, then."

"Thanks. Listen, on your way out, will you ask someone to call my wife? She's out in Wilson."

Wilson. His parents had rented a place there the first year they were married. For a moment, for one awful moment, Walker considered saying the truth. That Mom was dead and had been for a long time. That she'd died tired and timid because of her asshole husband. Walker wanted to see the confusion on his dad's face. Wanted to hurt him. And that terrible truth made Walker's stomach flip over in his gut. "Sure. I'll tell them. I've got to go. I'm glad you're feeling better."

He didn't need to go anywhere, of course, but he needed to get the hell out of there. The man had tortured him when Walker was smaller and weaker, and Walker didn't want to turn into his dad now. Hurting the weaker person just because he could.

God, how he wished his dad was still hale and hearty. That Walker could talk to him as an equal, tell him exactly what he thought of him and his fucked-up parenting. Hell, he wished they could face each other as men and work it out with their damn fists, but if there'd been a moment where they'd been exactly equal in strength and stamina and brain power, Walker had missed it.

He checked in with the doctor and called his brother just as he'd promised himself he would.

"It was only temporary," he explained when Micah panicked. "He got agitated, and his blood pressure and respiration shot through the roof. But he's fine now. Or back to the way he was anyway."

"Are you sure? Do I need to be there? I should be there."

"He's fine. He'll be back in his room tomorrow."

"You saw him?"

"Yes, I saw him. And I spoke to the doctor."

Micah sighed. "Okay. If you're sure. But I'll try to swing through sooner rather than later."

"Good. And plan to spend the night."

"If I can. Thanks for taking care of him, Walk."

Walker hung up without responding.

For the millionth time in his life, Walker was damn glad his brother was around. Without him, Walker wouldn't have had a reason to try for better. He wouldn't have had anything to get him through childhood except anger. He would've just been a miserable, mean fuck like his dad, with no one in his life who needed more than that.

But Micah…Micah had given him a reason to be a man.

Still, Micah didn't need him anymore. He had a career, a home, a husband. Their dad would be dead soon, and nothing else would hold Micah here. His life was somewhere else.

Walker slid behind the wheel of his truck, but he only sat there, staring at the dash. He'd felt that, when they'd sold the ranch. Micah had wanted him to keep it. Walker had pretended he didn't want the memories, but that wasn't it. He couldn't run a ranch. Not even a small one. There were grazing contracts and water rights to be worked out. Profits and losses to track. Transportation arrangements. Orders to complete. He'd most likely have to hire a hand or two, at least during calving season. That was all kinds of paperwork he'd never even heard of.

Walker couldn't do it, so they'd sold the land, and it had really been his only chance at something different. Everybody moved on. Walker wouldn't.

He started home, feeling so pulled in two directions, he could feel it in his chest. His heart beat hard. He wanted to not see anyone for days, yet he was fighting the urge to head out and party. Live it up. Flirt. Get in another fight. It had felt good to break that bastard's nose the other night. The guy had deserved it. Lots of people did.

Yet, as he pulled onto his street, the first thing that entered his mind was that he wanted to see Charlie. Screw everyone else. And screw being alone. She'd snuck out and made him feel like crap, and all he wanted was to sink back into her again. To lose himself. He wanted her hands and her mouth and her laugh. And if she snuck out in the morning without a word, he'd want her again. And again.

She'd blown his mind last night. Inviting him to be rough. Demanding it, even. Nothing could've kept him from obliging. In that moment, everything in him had wanted it. For her. For him. Shit, she was under his skin already, and he was pissed as hell about it, but he still felt a shock wave of disappointment when he saw that her windows were dark.

But as he got out of his truck, his disappointment stuttered into surprise and a wicked grin spread over his face. Charlie's lights weren't on…but his were. She was in his place. Waiting for him. Maybe naked. In fact, maybe she'd stripped down and gotten into his bed to wait for him, and then the long night had caught up with her and she'd fallen asleep, and now she was curled up, cozy and warm and gorgeous in his sheets, and he could take off his clothes so quietly she wouldn't even notice until he slipped into bed and started touching her…

Yeah. That would be good.

But he'd take just naked.

Walker hurried up the stairs, trying to tread the line between moving as fast as he could and being quiet. Much as he wanted to play it cool, he knew there was a ridiculous smile on his face when he opened his door. Screw it. He was already half-hard. There was no way to hide his enthusiasm.

"Happy to see me?" she purred.

Only it was the wrong she. "Nicole?" His feet refused to move all the way into the apartment.

"Hey, Walker," she said softly. Her blond hair shone like gold in the dim lighting. She wasn't naked, but she'd definitely made herself comfortable. Her jacket lay across the back of his couch, revealing that she wore nothing more than a black silky dress, the fabric so thin it was obvious that she wasn't wearing a bra. He could see the outline of her breasts, her nipples almost as visible as if she'd been topless.

"Nicole?" he repeated, thoroughly confused by the switch from his imagination to reality. When he didn't move, she came to him, a secret smile playing across her lips.

"I heard you came to the ranch to see me," she said softly as she reached to touch his face. Her thumb feathered across his bruised eye. "I'm sorry they hurt you."

Walker pulled his head back until her hand dropped.

"Don't be mad, Walker. I didn't know he was going to send his man after you. But…I'm glad you wanted to see me."

Walker suddenly became aware that he was standing in his open doorway with an ex-lover who wasn't exactly dressed modestly. He moved in and shut the door. Nicole took that as a sign that she should slide her arms around his waist.

"Nicole…" He eased away, shaking his head. "I didn't go out there to see you."

She moved closer again, smiling up at him. "You just happened to be in the neighborhood?"

"No. I wanted to see Roosevelt."

Yikes. That knocked the smile right off her face. "The dog?" Her hands fell to her sides. "You're kidding, right? You're just saying that to be mean. You told me you wouldn't come on the property to see me because it felt wrong. But you're fine with throwing it in my husband's face to see your *dog?*"

"I thought your husband was out of town."

A little snarl warned him he was missing the point. He'd heard that snarl many times before in his life.

"I'm sorry, Nicole. Again. I meant it when I said it was over. I don't need this kind of complication right now."

"No?" She huffed and spun away to stalk to his couch, her high heels like hammers on the floor. "What kind of complication do you need, huh? The brunette kind? The sneaky embezzler kind? Or some other kind I don't know about?"

Walker sighed and wearily shrugged off his coat. "I can honestly say I have no idea what you're talking about."

"Your new girl," she snapped as she struggled into her jacket.

He hung up his coat and set his hat on a table, then reached out to help her into her jacket. "My new girl," he repeated flatly.

"Charlotte? Isn't that her name?" She grabbed her purse and finally turned to face him.

"I'm not sure she'd like to be classified as my new girl. She's a friend."

"Big surprise. You're good at making friends, aren't you, Walker? But maybe you should be a little more choosy."

"You're not making any sense. Charlie is someone I grew up with."

She stared at him for a long moment, head tilted to the side, mouth tight with anger. "You don't know?" she finally asked.

"Know *what?*"

She flashed a bitter smile. "Wow. Really? Well, let me put it this way. I don't think she's that girl you grew up with anymore."

Walker scrubbed a hand over his beard as the stress of the day finally slammed into him in a wash of bone-deep exhaustion. "Maybe you should just go."

"You don't believe me? Look her up. She was brought back to Jackson to help her brother recoup the money he owes people."

"That's absurd. She doesn't even like her brother."

She smiled again, sadly this time, and reached up to cup her fingers to his chin. "She's a criminal, Walker. That's why she's here." She leaned up on her tiptoes to press a kiss to his mouth. He was so confused, he could only stand there and let her. "And I'm the one who got you fired."

"What?" He drew his head back until she let him go. His mind was nothing but a dark, blank space with chaos swirling through it. "What did you say?"

She shrugged. "You said you wouldn't sleep with me because you were working for my husband. So I complained that you'd been disrespectful and I got you fired. But I guess it wasn't about your job, after all. That was just a convenient lie."

He took a step back to put more distance between them, trying to calm the wild anger that was building. "You got me fired and now you're calling *me* a liar?"

"I was just helping you with your scruples. It must have been uncomfortable working there, knowing how close you'd come to fucking me." Nicole headed for the door. "Bye, Walker. Don't forget to do a search for your new girlfriend online. It's pretty interesting stuff."

After the door slammed behind her, Walker stared dumbly at it.

Nicole had gotten him fired. No wonder people were talking. And no wonder she'd been so pissed that he wouldn't sleep with her after.

Jesus, he'd never even said a cross word to the woman. Why would she have done that? Did she not understand the importance of a paycheck? Or maybe she did. Maybe she'd wanted him dependent on her. *Christ.*

And now she'd really lost it. Accusing Charlie of being a *criminal?* That was a pitiful accusation. Ridiculous.

Walker threw a frozen dinner in the oven and hit the shower, too tired to truly process what Nicole had said. He stood under the scalding water for what felt like an hour, feeling the kinks begin to melt from his neck and shoulders. By the time he dried off and sat down with his pan of lasagna, he felt almost awake. Unfortunately, his brain was working now, and he started to worry about Nicole's ridiculous claims.

He opened the browser on his phone and typed in Charlotte Allington. And Walker felt his heart sink.

CHAPTER EIGHTEEN

SHE MADE IT through dinner with her brother without losing her temper this time. Barely. He'd been late, and since the reservation had been for eight, Charlie had been tired and grumpy and starving by the time he'd gotten there.

But she'd made herself be pleasant. She'd even buttered him up a little, asking about his business and how things were going. First, because he might have helped her get a job, and second, because she might need information from him. She even held her tongue when he ordered a second Scotch. And then a third.

By the time dessert came, she was ready to get home. "So, Brad...I hear you might have had more to do with me getting this new job than you let on."

His eyebrows rose. "I...might have put in a good word for you. Sure."

"I have to admit, I was surprised by that."

He shrugged and swirled the ice in his glass.

"I know we haven't always gotten along well, and I'm sorry I lost my temper the last time I saw you. You're just so...gruff sometimes."

"Yeah. I suppose. My wives have had more creative terms for it."

"Right. Well. I really wanted to thank you for suggesting me to Keith. I didn't realize you knew him so well."

"We've done some business together."

"Development stuff?"

He watched her for a moment. "Of course. But I think we were out to dinner when I gave him your name. Networking. You know."

"Thank you for networking me. I don't know what I would have done without this."

"Sure. It seemed like you'd be a good fit."

"Why?"

He shrugged. "That's what you do, right?"

"Right. But I didn't think you two were close. You said you didn't really know anything about Dawn."

"I don't. Keith and I do business. If the wives are ever involved they talk among themselves."

God. She was never going to understand this man. It was as if they'd been raised in different centuries. But that didn't mean she had to be rude to him. "Well, I'll get dinner as a thank-you."

"Nah. I got it. You didn't even have a glass of wine."

"Thank you," she said, trying not to sound as relieved as she felt. She'd been comfortable for years. A single girl with a good job and no commitments. She hadn't had a budget. She'd paid her own way. She'd even managed to acquire a comfortable savings. And thank God for that savings. It had allowed her to put a retainer down on a very good lawyer. The rest of it had gone on credit cards. Several credit cards. But she'd pay those off soon. As quickly as she could. The new apartment was her only extravagance now.

She thanked him again when the bill came, but decided to press the issue one more time. "You're sure there's nothing about the Taggerts I need to know about?"

"What is it that's bothering you?" he asked as he threw down some cash and stood.

"I don't know."

"Are you sure it's nothing specific? Because you've asked several times now."

She almost told him what she'd seen, but before she even opened her mouth, she felt stupid. *I think Keith is sleeping with another man's wife. A man you may know!* Yeah. Call the National Guard.

"No. It's nothing."

"Come on, Charlie."

"Dawn's just making me miserable, that's all. She seems to be suspicious about something her husband is up to."

"Well, I don't want to piss you off again, but..."

"She's a woman?" Charlie said archly.

He shrugged as he handed his ticket to the valet. "You want a ride?"

"No, thanks. I'm good."

That was a better ending than last time, but she didn't have the consolation of a big box of salad to carry home. The price of civility, she supposed.

She should have pressed him harder, asked him about the land deal, but her instincts were screaming not to put all her cards on the table. She was also trying to make peace with him, so she gave him a hug and set off for home.

It was almost ten by the time she got to the Stud Farm, and Walker's windows were dark.

"Damn." She'd played this all wrong. Now she didn't know whether she should feel guilty for the way she'd left that morning or pissed that he hadn't bothered getting in touch. She'd play it cool either way, she supposed, but she'd really like to know how he was feeling about the whole thing.

A stupid worry. He most likely wasn't feeling anything at all about it.

She kicked off her heels and collapsed onto her couch with her laptop. While she was reading an email from an old friend in Vegas, her in-box chimed again. When she saw Keith's name, she gasped in surprise, thinking her brother had already called to tell Keith that she'd been asking about him.

But no, the email was only work related and had gone to every manager. He wanted to know if any of them were aware of local charities that might be looking for sponsorship. Every public relations opportunity is worth exploring as Meridian Resort starts its first year as a part of the Jackson Hole community.

An immediate, exciting thought popped into her head: Ability Ranch. This could be her chance, her reason to press the issue with Walker one last time.

She pulled up the website for the Ability Ranch and frantically read through every page, paying special attention to the page about donations and sponsorship, then she wrote back to Keith with the idea.

A few minutes later, her in-box dinged again. That sounds promising. Go ahead with contacting them since you already have a connection. Or if you're not comfortable with that, I can forward this to Public Relations.

She immediately wrote back that she'd be thrilled to take on the responsibility of contacting the Ability Ranch about sponsorship opportunities. In fact, it would probably be best to visit in person, get a feel for the place.

Charlie looked up at her door, wishing she and Walker were close enough that she could just barge into his apartment and jump on his bed and wake him up. Was he really asleep? Was he just watching a movie?

She grabbed her cell and pulled up his name, hesitating before she hit Text.

She squirmed. She shook her head. Then finally, grimacing, she texted Are you awake?

Nothing happened. She waited. She drew a breath and then another. Five minutes later, heart still pounding with excitement, she forced herself to relax. Okay. Text me in the morning? I need to ask a favor. Night, Walker.

If she could just talk him into going out to the ranch with her, at least she'd know he'd seen it. She would've done her very best to point him in the direction of somewhere he belonged.

And if he wouldn't go, she'd go herself. She'd talk to

the staff, and gather up a stack of brochures and flyers, and she'd very subtly shove them all under his door.

It wasn't right that he thought of himself as "just" a cowboy. It simply wasn't okay. She was the one who'd started off bright and then burned out too young. Shit, it had been her destiny. But Walker...he'd gotten a slow start, sure, but he would build to something great. She could see it in him every time they met.

For the first time in a long while, Charlie felt like things were going well. She was slowly puzzling things out at work, Dawn had backed off, Charlie was on better ground with her brother and her life was going well. And soon? Soon she was going to be sure that Walker's life was even better.

Tomorrow couldn't come quickly enough.

CHAPTER NINETEEN

WALKER FELT NUMB. He felt…disconnected. His pulse stayed slow as he drove Charlie north on the highway out of town. He didn't get angry. He didn't demand an answer. He'd been with her for fifteen minutes, and he'd said all the right things, but he couldn't remember a word he'd spoken.

The morning was oddly still for the mountains. There was always a breeze here, and usually way more than that, but today the whole world was holding its breath, waiting to see what Walker would do.

He was waiting, too. So far, his brain hadn't offered even a hint of an idea.

Charlie had neglected to tell him a lot about her life, and even though there was no solid evidence that Nicole had spoken the truth about her, everything pointed right in that direction.

Walker hadn't known what to think last night. He'd tried just going to bed, but his mind had spun with thoughts of the stories he'd read online. Of a massive embezzlement scheme that had involved Charlie's lover, a married man who'd seemingly promoted her to help with his crimes. The charges against her had been dropped, but several other employees had been implicated. It hadn't been a one-man operation. She might have been involved.

When she'd texted him, he'd ignored it, hoping he'd know what to say in the morning. But dawn had come and gone with no help from his brain.

Had she done something wrong in Tahoe? And was she still doing it here? If Nicole was right and her own brother had brought her on to the job…

Damn.

"I'm still surprised you agreed to do this," she said, her hand spreading over his knee. "I thought I'd have to beg."

"Save your begging for other things," he said automatically, throwing in a wink before he could stop himself. He felt a little dizzy with the strangeness of it all.

"I know you don't want to work there, but I really need your knowledge about ranches to tell me if it's a worthwhile setup. I hate to throw the resort's money at a charity that's not worthy."

"It's no problem," he said, the words sounding far away. "I hadn't picked up any work today." Was this really about a charity for her? Or was this another scheme to steal money?

He glanced at her, still utterly confused. It was Charlie. She smiled at the road, her eyes bright with anticipation, her hand a warm brand on his thigh. Her pretty brown hair fell over her shoulders in waves.

He thought of the scent of that hair when he tucked

his face into her neck. She couldn't be bad. She wasn't. It made no sense.

But she'd had a tough life. Her dad had never been around. There'd been gossip about her mom going through men the way other women went through clothes. And she'd said herself that her brother was an asshole. So maybe Walker didn't know enough about her to judge.

You never really knew people, after all. He'd lived eighteen years with his mother, and he couldn't say he'd known much about her beyond that she was good at gardening and sewing and she didn't like cussing or muddy boots in the house.

But Charlie had been… When she was his tutor, she'd been that high school girl in cute movies. Smart and innocent and awkward and ready to break into the world and learn her way. She'd seemed untouchable. Too good for Walker and his hands that had already been calloused and stained with dirt. Could she possibly have stumbled down such a steep path in those few short years?

"Do you miss Tahoe?" he asked. He glanced toward her, but she kept her eyes on the road.

"No."

"Not at all? It must have been more fun than Jackson."

She shrugged. "I'd had my fill of Nevada, I guess."

"The resorts there are a lot bigger. It must have been a different kind of job, with the gambling."

"Yeah."

"I'd think this would be boring."

She finally turned to look at him. "There's nothing wrong with a little quiet. Especially when I have you to entertain me."

"Happy to be of service." He didn't mean for the sharpness that edged his last word, but it was there.

Her hand tightened on his knee. "I'm sorry I left without a word yesterday. I had to get in early, and I didn't want to wake you when I knew you were working."

"It's fine."

"I wasn't... I mean, I didn't know if I should bother leaving a note."

Their eyes finally met. Hers were wide-open and clear, as if she'd never hidden a thing from him and never would. Yet she never, ever wanted to talk about Tahoe. Damn her.

Walker cleared his throat and faced forward again.

"Ah," she said. "See? I was right."

No, she hadn't been right. He hadn't wanted a note, though. He'd wanted her. Snug against him, hot and naked and soft with sleep. That's what he'd wanted. To wake up to her just like that.

"Here it is," he said, relieved to change the subject.

"Oh!" She pointed at the sign ahead, iron and old wood spelling out Ability Ranch in simple letters.

Right away, he spotted a huge indoor riding arena and a large stable next to it, bigger than any he'd ever worked in. "Wow."

"It's big," Charlie breathed. He shot her a look and

she met it, and suddenly the worst of the tension between them dissolved.

"That sounds familiar," he drawled.

"Shut up, naughty!" she shrieked, smacking him on the arm. He loved hearing her laugh. If everything had been fine, he would have stopped the truck and pulled her in for a kiss until her laughter turned to sighs. For him.

Instead he drove on, all the way to the large parking area next to a building with glass doors and a bulletin board posted next to them.

"I'm going to run into the office," Charlie said. "Are you good with looking around?"

"Absolutely." There were plenty of vehicles in the lot, and he could see horses being led from the stable to the yard, so he helped Charlie out of the truck and set off toward the stables.

They were damn impressive. The aisles were wide and clean. Doors were thrown open on every wall to let in sunlight. There was a faint scent of manure, of course, but it was far outweighed by hay and the comforting smells of leather and horseflesh. The horses hardly reacted at all as people moved past the stalls. Only one seemed skittish, but the gelding was hardly alarmed; he was just obviously ready to get out of his stall.

Hell, Walker would've been ready to give the place a thumbs-up based on the stalls alone. Looking over the stables was like checking out the bathroom at a restaurant. If the barn was meticulously clean and maintained, you didn't have to bother looking any further. Management ran a tight ship.

He continued out through the far door to the gate of the outdoor riding area. There were four horses in the yard and a dozen kids. All the kids were in wheelchairs. All of them wore helmets and held grooming brushes.

Walker shot a look over his shoulder to be sure Charlie wasn't standing there, waiting to see his reaction to the scenario she'd set up. But no. Charlie was still off somewhere, setting up a charity donation or possibly stealing money from these kids.

Cursing under his breath, he started to turn back to the arena.

"Walker Pearce? Oh, my God, is that you?"

Startled, he searched the area for the voice, then finally spotted a woman crouched down by one of the kids, a horse's hoof cupped in her hand. He didn't place her for a moment, but then he smiled. Her black hair was in long braids beneath her cowboy hat, and her full lips were painted as red as ever. "Marlene?"

"Hey!" She stood and gestured another adult over before walking toward him. "Get on in here, Walker."

Marlene had taught riding at the Fletcher Ranch for a few months when Walker had first started. They'd had a couple of friendly nights together and then she'd moved on. He hadn't seen her since then, which would've been odd in another town this size, but not in Jackson. Not only was it spread out, but it was packed with strangers for a good eight months of the year.

"What the hell are you doing here?" she asked, going up on her tiptoes for a hug.

"Just checking the place out for a friend. How've you been? Holy shit!" He grabbed her left hand and looked down at the giant rock on her finger. The pale metal band stood out against her dark skin.

"Ha!" Her grin was clearly self-satisfied. "I got hitched a year ago. He's pretty good to me."

"I guess so. Congratulations. You living in a big house up on the mountain now?"

"Maybe," she answered with a smile that screamed *Yes!* "What about you? Have you settled down?"

Before he had to answer, she turned back to the kids. "Hold that thought. We'll catch up later. Come on."

"What are you doing here?" he asked, following her back to her group.

"They're learning how to groom. You want to help?"

He glanced over his shoulder again, but it still didn't seem to be a setup. "Sure."

"They all know to stay away from the back of the horse, right, kids?"

"Yes, Miss Marlene!" they answered.

"Still, keep an eye on them, and remind them to be careful of the horse's blind spots. Otherwise, just show them how to groom the horse. Hooves and hide. They may not be able to do all of the currying and brushing, but this is about building a relationship with the horse. Learning responsibility. It's not about a perfect job."

"Sure. Got it."

He headed over to the next group of kids.

"Say hi to Mr. Walker," Marlene called.

"Hi, Mr. Walker!" they shouted. Luckily, the horse's ears barely twitched. Walker couldn't help smiling at their eager little faces.

"Not so loud around the horse hooves, kids."

They giggled and the girl with the currycomb went back to carefully stroking the horse. "You can be a little firmer, darlin'. He has a lot of hair and you've got to get the dust out."

"Yes, Mr. Walker," she whispered.

Christ, this girl was adorable. She was tiny and delicate and missing both her legs from just above the knee, but she put her whole body into the effort while Walker held his breath and hoped she didn't fall out of the chair. That helmet looked as if it might make up half her body weight and could pull her over at any moment. Her little blond braids swung with the effort she put into the work.

"What's your name, sweetheart?"

"Jessica."

"Okay, Jessica, let's try a dandy brush now, and I'll show you the direction he likes to be brushed the best." Walker curled his hand carefully over her tiny one and showed her how to do it. She beamed and ignored Walker to pat the horse with her free hand.

"He's so sweet."

"He's very sweet," Walker agreed. The horse looked to be somewhere in his late teens, so he might be more tired than sweet, but he certainly tolerated the children well.

Walker glanced over at Marlene to see that she had one kid currying and brushing while she showed the other two how to pick hooves. He knelt next to the fore-leg and ran his hand down the horse's leg. "Boys, the first thing you do is ask the horse for its hoof."

They both giggled.

"I'm serious. You don't want to be rude, do you?"

They giggled again and shook their heads. Walker noticed that one of the boys had wild curls sticking out from beneath his helmet. "My word," Walker said, taking off his hat. "I thought I had a lot of hair. How'd you even get that helmet on, kid? Did it take three stable hands to wrestle it down?"

The boy collapsed into his chair, snorting with laughter while Walker shook his head.

"All right. Now see how I run my hand down the horse's leg?" He repeated the movement, then wrapped his hand around the gelding's cannon. "That lets him know you're here. When I press back a little, he'll lift his hoof."

He showed them the brush pick and explained why it was important to keep the hooves clean. "And what do you think this part is called?" he asked, pointing to the center of the hoof.

The horse sighed as if it had heard this joke a million times before.

Both boys shrugged.

"Here. Press it, but be gentle."

The closest boy tentatively put his finger to the hoof.

"Ribbit," Walker croaked.

The kids tried hard to keep their laughter muffled, but a few squeals escaped.

"That part of the hoof is called the frog."

"The frog?" They all reacted as if it was the funniest thing they'd ever heard.

"I don't know why it's called a frog, but that's what it is. That's the soft part of the hoof, and you run a pick along that triangle to scoop out any dirt. Don't worry," he added when he saw them wince. "It doesn't hurt. Then you brush off the debris. Here. You try."

He handed the pick to the second boy, almost jerking back when he realized the boy's fingers were curled into his hand in a tight spasm. But the kid managed to grasp the pick anyway and he brushed away the dirt that Walker had loosened.

"All right, then," Walker said. "Now check the shoe to be sure it's good and tight."

Minutes later, he looked up as Marlene laughed at something. For a moment, the sun blinded him, but then he saw her standing there with Charlie and another woman and they were all watching him.

Walker sprang to his feet so quickly that the horse shied. "Mr. Walker!" one of the kids scolded.

"Sorry."

Even before Charlie spoke a word, he saw her smile and knew this had been a setup all along, and he'd been sucked in as if he'd jumped willingly into a black hole.

"Don't you think he'd be amazing at this?" Charlie was saying to Marlene, speaking loud enough for Walker to hear.

"He's a natural."

Charlie nodded. "I know."

Walker patted one of the kids' helmets. "Keep up what you're doing," he murmured. "And don't move behind the horse." Then he walked over to break up this little meeting.

"Charlie, are you done here?"

"I am, but I was just talking to Miss Marlene about you. She says they're always looking for more instructors here at the ranch."

"Thanks," he said past lips that felt so tight they'd gone numb. "But I already have a job."

"Well, sure, but wouldn't it be more fun to work here?"

He looked at Marlene and forced himself to smile before he lost his temper. "Oh, I'm no teacher, I'm sorry to say."

"But, Walker," Charlie gushed, "you don't have to have a degree or anything. You just need a high school diploma and a certificate from a safety course that they do right here! Isn't that amazing? You can take classes right here for a few weeks and you'd be ready!"

She was practically bouncing on her toes. Walker wanted to walk away and never see her again. Ever. His heart beat so hard that it was difficult to hear his own voice. "Thanks, but I'm pretty busy."

Marlene smiled, so he was almost sure she couldn't see the rage on his face. "I understand, but you really are good with the kids. If you're interested, you can get the certificate and do some volunteer work. No pressure. But, Walker…not everyone falls into this as easily as you do, and you know everything there is to know about riding. So think about applying for a position. I mean it. You'd be doing a great service. The kids love you."

"Sure," he said. "I'll check into it."

"Promise?" Marlene pressed.

He lied without any guilt at all. "Absolutely."

He spun and walked away, leaving Charlie to catch up, though he couldn't stop himself from holding the arena gate open for her. Still, he strode off as soon as she was through. Her footsteps pattered behind him through the stable.

"Oh, my God, Walker," she called breathlessly. "I told you it would be perfect. Look at this place! It's so beautiful, and you looked so happy with those kids. I thought they were going to climb right up on top of you and make you take them for a gallop around the yard."

He walked faster and hit the unlock button the moment he spotted his truck in the lot.

"Walker," she said breathlessly, jogging up behind him.

"You had no right to do that," he growled.

"I'm sorry. I really did need to check out the ranch, I swear, but I admit that I hoped you would take to the place if you saw it."

"Oh, yeah?" he snarled. "That's what you'll admit to?"

"Walker!" She grabbed his arm, and he swung around so suddenly that Charlie stepped back.

"Damn it, I told you I couldn't do this. I told you I wasn't qualified. But you didn't want to listen."

"If you'd only consider—"

"No," he snapped. "I won't consider it. You don't know anything about it."

She looked startled for a moment, but then she shook her head and frowned at him. "Are you kidding me? I've known you since you were sixteen."

"You don't know me!" he shouted.

"Hey," she said, her voice low with shock.

Walker took a deep breath, trying to control himself. He didn't yell at women. That wasn't who he was. "Look. I'm not doing this. It's not the place for me. I don't belong here. Leave it alone, Charlie."

"How can you say that? I'm sorry I manipulated the situation, but you obviously belong here."

"I. Do. Not."

"What are you afraid of? Not being good enough? Everyone thinks you're amazing."

"I can't do this," he said, putting his hands on the hood of his truck. "Stop asking. Please." His heart beat harder. And harder. He pressed his fists against the shiny black paint.

"Walker. You love people. You've said it yourself. All you have to do is take a safety course for a few *weeks*. I know you don't want to think about reading and writing, but it's a temporary problem that could lead to a whole new life."

"Charlie…"

"Why can't you just try?"

"Damn it!" he exploded, swinging around to face her. "I didn't graduate, Charlie, all right? It's not so simple and pretty and tied up with a bow. I don't have my fucking high school diploma!"

She drew her chin in, her eyes blank with shock. "What?"

"I never graduated!" The words hung in the air between them, real now. As real as a dust cloud she'd kicked in his face. He'd said it. To Charlie.

"But…" She shook her head. "You did graduate."

"No, I didn't. And you need me to admit that, apparently, because you can't take no for an answer. You need me to say that out loud, not just to you, but to half the fucking people I know. I can't teach children anything because I didn't even graduate from high school! There. Are you happy now?"

"Walker… Just… We were at the same graduation ceremony."

"Yeah. Since I'd already been held back my sophomore year, they let me walk the stage out of pure pity."

She shook her head again.

Walker felt his lips draw back in a grimace of a smile. "I was supposed to take one more class that summer. I didn't."

Her eyes had gone wide. "But…why? Walker, why didn't you do it?"

He turned away and walked toward the door of his truck. "I was working."

"Why didn't you tell me?"

He froze, hand reaching toward the handle of the door. "Really? You're kidding, right?"

"I'm not kidding! Why wouldn't you just tell me that?"

"Ha." He stared down the road toward the highway beyond and all the cars flying past. "Surely you know it's not easy to talk about the most humiliating parts of your life."

"We're friends. We've always been friends. You can trust me."

"I can *trust* you?" He spun around to face her. "This is how you convince me I can trust you? By tricking me into coming here and making a fool out of me in front of everyone?"

"I didn't make a fool out of you! No one knows."

"I guarantee Marlene's going to call. We used to sleep together, FYI, so she has my number and she won't drop the subject. So either I'll have to tell her I don't have a diploma or I get to be the asshole who doesn't want to help these kids!"

Worse than that, Charlie had shown him one more thing he'd never be able to do. He could hate her for that alone. But there were other things to be angry about, thank God. Plenty of things.

"Walker, I didn't know that about Marlene, obviously. I didn't mean to embarrass you. But you can get a GED. You don't have to—"

"We know each other so well you think I should trust you with my secrets?"

She closed her mouth and eyed him for a moment before responding. "Yes. I do."

"Okay, Charlie. Here's another secret. I saw Nicole yesterday."

The pleading look disappeared from her face and Charlie stood straighter. "What? You saw her where?"

"In my apartment."

"Oh." Her chin went up. "I see."

He felt immediate regret for the way her face stiffened and he shook his head. "She wanted to tell me something about you."

"Yeah, right. What could Nicole possibly know about me?"

He stared hard at her, willing her to give him a little truth. But she offered nothing. "Is that the way you want to play this?"

She lifted her hands as if she were an innocent woman with nothing to hide. "I have no idea what you mean. The only thing I know about Nicole is that she's a married woman you were messing around with."

He smiled at that and huffed out a harsh laugh. "Yes. Another terrible secret. Do you have any secrets you'd like to share with me? Since we're such good friends? Because I heard some secrets about you, Charlie."

Fear flashed in her eyes. Real fear. She'd finally realized he knew something.

When she looked away, he knew it was all true. She wasn't the Charlie he'd thought she was. Maybe she never had been. Maybe she'd done well in school by cheating and working the system. Maybe she'd gone to Vegas because that was the natural place for someone to learn all the inside tricks.

"Wow," he huffed. "Just… I can't believe all the shit you've been giving me. How I need to improve my life. How I can do better. You're just…unbelievable."

"What did she tell you?" Charlie asked quietly.

"Why do you want to know? So you can counter it? How about you just tell me what the truth is, and I'll let you know if it matches up?"

Her lips parted, but she only shook her head and took a step back. One tiny step that told him she wanted to hear his secrets but she'd protect hers with everything she had.

"You were arrested for embezzlement," he started. And Charlie froze.

THIS DIDN'T MAKE any sense. Why was this happening now? Here? And why did it have to be happening with Walker? His blue eyes were cold as ice as he stared her down.

"That part is true, right, Charlie?" he bit out.

She whispered the only thing she could think to say. "The charges were dropped."

"But you were sleeping with the embezzler."

"Alleged. Yes."

"The alleged embezzler. Who was your boss."

"Yes," she admitted, helpless now. Trapped.

"Your married boss."

She nodded. "Yes."

"Who promoted you to head of security after you started sleeping with him."

"Yes." This time she felt her lips move, but hardly any sound came out.

"And you were fired from that position for helping him embezzle money."

"No. I mean, yes. That's why I was fired, but I didn't help him."

"Right." He looked past her toward the mountains and drew in a deep breath. "But you didn't stop him from taking the money."

She finally felt a glimmer of hope about this. She'd made a lot of mistakes, but she could tell the absolute truth about that. "It wasn't like that. I swear. I didn't know what he was doing. Maybe I should have, but I didn't. I didn't even know he was married."

Walker raised a doubtful eyebrow. "Yeah, that kind of thing is real hard to pick up on when you're working with someone for months."

"I didn't know!" she yelled, starting to feel a little crazed that no one would believe her.

"Sure. Well, that gives you the right to look down on me, then."

"I don't look down on you, Walker."

"No?" He chuckled, and the cool sound sent goose bumps down her arms. "You sure do a good job of pretending, then. For the past week, all you've done is make clear that I'm not good enough. Not good enough at working. Not good enough at applying myself. Not good enough at choosing who I sleep with. And certainly not good enough for you."

"That's—" She reached toward him, but Walker pulled his arms back so her fingers wouldn't touch him.

"Oh, to be clear, I'm good enough to play with. That much is obvious. But I'm not the kind of guy you'd ever bring home to Mom, right?"

What the hell was he even talking about? "I've never said that!"

"'You're not my boyfriend, Walker.' 'It's not serious.' 'You know how it is with Walker.' Oh, and 'Feel free to do Nicole, too. I don't care. You just can't have us at the same time.' If you were trying to make me feel warm and fuzzy, you did a really shitty job. It felt strangely like you were letting me know my place. You're good enough to fuck, cowboy, but don't go getting attached."

Her mind was spinning so fast she could barely grasp what he was saying. "I wasn't trying to keep you in your place! I was letting you know I knew mine."

"*Your* place? That's a little comical considering I've always treated you with respect. Jesus, Charlie. I've always known you were too good for me. *Better* than me. *Always*. From the first moment I met you. But I guess I was damn wrong about that, considering what you are now."

"But...I'm not..." She shook her head, trying to stop whatever he was thinking about her. "I'm not anything but myself. I just... I screwed up, yes, but I'm not that person. I don't want to be that person."

"So what the hell are you doing here?" he snapped.

"Here?" She looked around in shock at the Ability Ranch, trying to find one coherent thought to grab on to. "I'm sorry. I honestly didn't mean to hurt you. Even if I've been deceptive and stupid and *wrong,* I never wanted to hurt you or anyone."

"So you admit it?" Even beneath his beard, she could see the way his jaw clenched with fury.

"I already did."

"You're helping your brother steal money from the resort?"

His flat words hung in the air between them. Blinking, she tried to decipher them. "What?"

Walker tipped his head up and smiled bitterly at the sky. "All this time you've been trying to work on me, *improve* me, but at least I'm not a damn lying thief. I may be dumb as a rock, but I've got a soul."

"I'm not helping anyone stealing anything!"

"Yeah. Considering that everything else Nicole told me was true, I'll take that with a grain of salt."

"Nicole told you I was *stealing?*"

He shot her an impatient look and reached for the door of his truck. "She told me your brother brought you in to pull off the same shit that went down in Tahoe. I don't know what you call it to make it right with yourself, but I call it stealing. Come on. I'll drop you off at the apartment and get out of your life."

"My brother..." she repeated. It didn't matter that Walker got in his truck and closed the door, because she couldn't say anything else. She couldn't exhale, couldn't speak, couldn't move.

Her brother had brought her in to embezzle money? That didn't make any sense. She couldn't just embezzle unknowingly via osmosis. She'd have to be in on it.

But it did make more sense than Brad helping her out of the goodness of his heart. And Nicole would be in a position to know. She was sleeping with Keith *and* her husband had sold the land to Brad at what seemed like a steal.

What the hell was going on?

Walker started the truck with a roar. Charlie jumped almost a foot, her heart scrambling into her throat, but she still couldn't do more than stare at him past the glass of the windshield.

He rolled down his window and stuck his head out. "Come on. Let's get this over with."

She watched him. His normally warm eyes were distant now. His deep voice was rough and damning, when it had once been so sweet and rumbly in her ear.

"No," she said. "I'll find my own way back."

"Get in the truck, Charlie. I'm not leaving you here in the middle of nowhere."

"There are plenty of people here. I'll find a ride."

"Get in," he snapped.

She looked back at the ranch and thought of trying to explain her predicament to someone. But she was so embarrassed. Mortified at what Walker thought of her. She couldn't deal with more of that today, so she forced her feet to carry her to his truck and she got in.

They didn't say a word to each other. He didn't even look at her.

Charlie felt her fingers trembling and pressed them to her thighs. The fear was back. She'd left it behind sometime this past week, but it was back now, like a beast lurking in the dark, stalking her, waiting.

Was she being set up? Was this what her life had come to? Bad enough that she had to work at a place she hated, but now she was being set up, too? There couldn't be another explanation for it. She wasn't in on it. She wasn't helping. She was just...an easy target. A pawn. Something to be used and tossed away. By her own brother.

But just because Nicole had said it didn't make it true. Maybe this was a move in a game that Charlie wasn't part of. Maybe Nicole had said it just to win Walker back.

"It's not true," she repeated, her voice cracking around the words.

Walker didn't respond.

Because even if it wasn't true, some of the other stuff was. The things she hadn't wanted him to know.

He was right. She hadn't trusted him, but she'd expected him to fall in line behind her lofty demands. Do this. Do that. Make yourself better. And pay no attention to the woman pulling the levers behind the curtain.

But he didn't understand the why of it. She hadn't wanted him to know, but only because she'd wished she was better for him. She'd been ashamed, just as he had been, but with so much more reason.

Walker had been the last person on earth who'd believed in her, and she hadn't been able to let that go. And now he was lost to her forever.

CHAPTER TWENTY

THE MOMENT WALKER pulled away from the curb, Charlie rushed upstairs to grab her laptop. Email and internet access alone weren't going to solve this mystery. In fact, she wasn't sure they'd be any help at all, but her computer might come in handy.

Instead of settling down with it, she ran back downstairs, tossed her laptop in the car and took off for her brother's house. "What the hell? What the hell?" she chanted the whole way.

His place was in Teton, of course, not in the town of Jackson. An important developer like him needed slope-side access and a prestigious address in addition to a very slim and well-mannered wife. Charlie had never visited her brother's home, but she'd gotten the obligatory architecturally focused Christmas card every year.

In fact, she recognized the place from the cards when she finally pulled up, but the big For Sale sign out front was new. Charlie pulled carefully onto the steep, curved driveway and got out. Even before she knocked, the house felt deserted. It was too quiet and too dark, even in the noon sunlight.

Shit. Noon. She'd be missed at work soon. She'd emailed both Keith and Dawn to let them know she'd be in after checking out the Ability Ranch, but coming in after noon was stretching it.

Charlie shifted from foot to foot, waiting for an answer to her knock. She rang the doorbell and knocked again, but she knew it was hopeless. Her brother had probably been kicked out, and his soon-to-be-ex-wife was obviously not home.

She called his cell phone and left a message when he didn't answer. "Please call me as soon as you get this. It's important." Then she sent a text with the same message.

Damn him.

He couldn't really have done this, could he? Yes, he'd always been an asshole, but this was just malicious, even for the sake of money.

After pacing back and forth for a few minutes beneath the portico of his ridiculous house, Charlie did the unthinkable: she willingly called her mom.

It was always the other way around. Her mom called Charlie. Usually to ask for a hundred bucks or so, to get her through the month. Back when she was flush with cash, Charlie had been happy to send it. It had been like paying an insurance premium. She sent the money, and her mom wouldn't call again until she needed more. No late-night phone calls to lament about her latest true love. No unexpected visits on the arm of some new loser who'd never been to Vegas before. Charlie sent money, and the reward was silence.

The phone clattered as her mom picked it up. "Charlie? Is that you, honey?"

"Hi, Mom. How are you?"

"I'm good, honey. I'm really good. Is everything okay?"

"Everything's fine. Have you heard from Brad lately?"

"No, not since Christmas," her mom answered. "Why?"

"I'm just trying to track him down here in Jackson. I guess he's moved out of his house. I don't suppose you have a new address?"

"No, nothing. But I think Jacqueline is still living there, so you could drop by."

"Thanks. I'm sure he'll call back in a few minutes. Bye, Mom."

"Wait!"

Charlie winced and eased her thumb back from the end button.

"You're sure everything is okay? Are you doing well?"

"I'm good."

"I don't suppose you've met a cute man, have you? You know how much I love to hear love stories."

Yes, she adored stories about men. So much so that she liked to start her own new story every few months.

"You know, I met somebody at a singles' night last week," her mom continued with a happy sigh. "He's trying to start his own business, but you know how tough that can be. I—"

"I've got to go. But good luck with that." Charlie hung up before her mom could go on. Her friends in Vegas had accused her of being mean to her mom when she would come visit. They'd thought her mom was sweet and funny. She was.

She was also unwise and foolish and perpetually unable to see anything beyond the creations of her own mind. Every love was true love, no matter how many true loves she'd met that year. Every man was a soul mate. Every boyfriend a potential fiancé.

Charlie's childhood had been a revolving door of new daddies or special friends. Most of them had been mysteriously in transition between jobs and places to live.

Yeah, her mom was sweet, all right. Sweet enough to never see the truth about anyone or anything. Christ, singles' night was a big improvement. She'd had two "boyfriends" last year who'd just been con artists working the internet. But the pictures they'd sent had been *so gorgeous*.

Charlie closed her eyes and shook her head. She'd been so determined to make a secure life for herself. So determined never to be stupid or clingy or taken advantage of. Maybe she'd gone too far the other way.

She tried her brother one more time. It went to voice mail. If he was avoiding her, she had no way to track him down.

"Shit!"

Now what was she supposed to do? Go to work? Pretend everything was fine? She had no idea who was involved. It might be Keith. Or Dawn. Either of them. The only one Charlie could be sure of at this point was…

"Nicole," she muttered.

That was a beast she didn't particularly want to poke. The woman was married and having at least one affair, and Charlie had no idea what her husband knew. So instead of tracking down Nicole, she used her phone to look up the address of her brother's development company. It was a P.O. box, of course. *Damn.*

She didn't see much choice. She'd have to at least drive out to Nicole's ranch. She certainly couldn't ask Walker for the woman's number.

Walker.

Her throat went thick and her eyes burned. Walker thought she was disgusting now. Beneath him. And she probably was. It wasn't as though she'd been totally innocent about what sleeping with her boss had meant. She'd eaten up the attention of getting such an important promotion at such a young age, even though she'd been suspicious it had been more about the sex part of performance than the job part. She'd known she hadn't deserved that title.

But God, it had been exciting, being the golden girl for a few months. And knowing that she was just getting started and nothing could stop her.

And now even Walker looked at her with a sneer. He'd been happy enough to mess around with his boss's wife, though. Maybe she should skip the ranch and just check Walker's apartment.

Her tears dried at the sudden rush of anger, and Charlie slammed the door of her car and took off for the Fletcher Ranch. Screw all these people. It wasn't her job to protect Nicole's marriage. Or Dawn's marriage. Or Walker's ego.

Fucking men. Maybe she didn't need to ask any more questions. What else could it be except that Fletcher and Brad and Keith were mixed up in some shit together and they were screwing every woman in their lives over, physically and metaphorically? The men were either working together or trying to ruin each other, and they didn't care who got hurt.

She tried her brother again, then snarled at the road when he didn't answer.

She'd been right. She should just open a cozy little shop somewhere. A store that only sold girl stuff so asshole men wouldn't accidentally wander in. Pretty teapots. Or kitten posters. Or knitted dildo cozies. Yeah. The last was probably the best idea, because she was never going to have sex with a man again. Ever. Not even Walker, who could turn her on with one fucking look and make her come harder than she ever had before.

"Shit," she croaked, the tears coming again. She couldn't even hate him, because he was a good guy. A sweet guy. And he touched her as if she meant something to him, even if she didn't.

I always knew you were better than me.

Charlie pulled onto the county road that would lead her closer to Fletcher Ranch, but she didn't keep driving. She eased the car to the shoulder and put it in Park, too blind from tears to see.

Was that what he'd thought? Was that what she'd encouraged him to believe? That she was better than him?

She wanted to call him. To apologize or yell at him that he was wrong or beg him not to think badly of her. Just to hear him. To know that he'd talk to her. But there was nothing to say yet. She couldn't even deny what Nicole had told him.

Charlie wiped her eyes on the sleeve of her sweater and rummaged in her purse until she found a tissue. Screw Nicole's marriage. Charlie needed to talk to her.

She drove the last fifteen minutes to the dude ranch with no tears. No panicking. Just a determination to end this awful purgatory she'd found herself in. She'd either get clear of it or go straight to hell. At least it would be over.

She looked around as she drove past the ranch gates, imagining Walker working here for years. He must have fit in perfectly here, the ideal handsome cowboy to go with the perfectly maintained corral and the pretty flowerpots in the windowsills of the lodge.

She drove into the small parking area and was met by a blond man in scruffy jeans and a cowboy hat who was toting rope toward the corral. "Howdy, miss. Can I help you?"

"Hi. I'm looking for Nicole Fletcher?"

"Sure. If she's here, someone at the lodge will know."

She thanked him with a smile, telling herself he

couldn't be the guy who'd hit Walker, because his nose looked unmolested. She hoped she would run into that guy. She hoped his nose was still twice its normal size and painful as hell.

The girl at the welcome desk smiled brightly at Charlie's question. "Oh, sure! Nicole is helping set up for a wedding reception tomorrow night. We're all super excited about it. Who doesn't love a wedding?"

Well, Charlie didn't, but she always made sure to have a good time at them anyway.

She followed the hallways of the lodge down to a far room. The place was beautiful, with Western touches like elk-antler chandeliers and dark red carpets patterned after Navajo blankets, but there were signs of luxury in the expensive wood doors and molding. Charlie noticed it all in passing. She headed straight for the farthest doors and the woman's voice echoing into the hallway.

Charlie wanted her to be a villain, but when she spotted Nicole in the banquet room, she was laughing with a group of employees as they laid out tablecloths. She wasn't haughty and bossing them around. They seemed to like her. The conversation sounded like talk among friends.

Nicole's laughter died when she looked up and spotted Charlie. There was no mistaking the alarm that chased over the woman's face. Charlie didn't need surveillance training to identify that emotion.

Nicole smothered it, but the woman was no poker player. Her eyes darted from employee to employee, as if she expected them to immediately figure out some secret she wanted to keep hidden.

"Do you have a minute?" Charlie asked drily.

"I…" Her eyes kept skipping around the room. They settled briefly on a door set into a far wall, as if she wanted to run. But then she pasted on a smile and chirped, "Of course!" before rushing toward Charlie and pulling her through the doorway.

"Please just go," she hissed as soon as they were out of sight of the room.

"I need to know why you said that to Walker."

"Shh! Just… I was mad. And I'd had a couple of glasses of wine before I went over. I didn't know what I was saying."

"So you made up something about me?" Charlie asked.

"Yes!" Nicole smiled with relief as she led the way to an empty meeting room and pulled Charlie in. "Yes, I was lying. I was jealous that Walker was seeing someone else, and I lied about you."

"Yet you brought up my brother."

Charlie almost wanted to laugh at the fear that shaped Nicole's mouth into a surprised O, but it was too damn unfunny. "Your brother? How could I know anything about your brother?"

"Really? You're going to pretend you don't know anything now?"

Nicole shook her head in a parody of innocent confusion. Her blond hair settled perfectly back into place.

"You know. Brad Allington? He's the guy who paid

your husband millions of dollars for a piece of land three years ago."

"Oh, shit," Nicole breathed. She hadn't expected that. She started shaking her head and didn't stop. "I don't know anything about that."

"So what do you know about?"

Her head shook again. Charlie leaned closer. "Tell me what you know, or I'll tell your husband you're fucking Keith Taggert."

Her eyes went wide, fear flashing in their depths, but her mouth didn't open.

"Okay," Charlie drawled. "I'll tell Keith that you were also messing around with Walker."

She shook her head. "No. I didn't have sex with him."

"Not quite. Do you think Keith will appreciate that small detail? You're hoping to leave your husband and snag Keith, right? That's cool. If he's open-minded about these things, he won't mind about Walker."

She closed her eyes for a moment and took a deep breath. Then another. When she opened her eyes, she tossed her hair back and her shoulders stiffened. "Fine," she said, sneering, pretending it meant nothing to her. "I'll tell you what you want to know. What does it matter? Your brother's an asshole anyway."

Charlie smiled. "Finally a little bit of truth. Now… how about the rest of it?"

CHAPTER TWENTY-ONE

It was supposed to be simple, Nicole had whined.

Oh, sure. These things were always supposed to be simple. People forgot that life was one giant chaos machine that would insert itself into your plans whether you planned for it or not. So a simple moneymaking scheme hatched among a gang of thieves had turned into a bitter divorce and frozen assets and investment losses.

"Idiots," Charlie spat as she sped back toward town.

She didn't even give a damn about that. They could be criminal idiots together as often as they wanted to, but their backup plan had apparently been pulling Charlie into the mix for a little temporary ass-covering.

Before she got close to Teton, she pulled off the road near a Wi-Fi hot spot and sent a few work documents and emails to her personal account. Not quite legal, maybe, but she wasn't taking any chances with Keith. The laptop had important information on it, and it was company property. If she confronted him at the resort, he could confiscate the laptop before she had a chance to review her emails and documents.

The question was…would she confront him?

The rational part of her brain was telling her no. *Don't confront him. You haven't done anything wrong. They can't pin anything on you. Just keep your head down. Or better yet, give two weeks' notice and get out.* That rational voice in her head told her that confronting Keith wouldn't do her any good.

But the irrational part of her brain, which seemed to make up the vast portion of her mind at that moment, told her she didn't have to put up with this. That she couldn't put up with this. That she needed to take a stand.

After all, keeping her head down hadn't done her any good in Tahoe. More than that, this time she actually knew. She knew they were engaged in something illegal, and she couldn't just walk away.

But, her rational brain poked in to say, *it's only another case of rich-on-rich crime. Those people and their money are none of your business.*

"That's true," she whispered to herself as she pulled up to the resort. Rich people stealing from their rich investors. That had nothing to do with her.

Except that they'd pulled her into it.

She had no idea what she was going to do when she got out of her car. And no idea as she got off the elevator. And still no idea as she entered her office and closed the door.

But she got a glimmer when her door flew open a few seconds later and a self-righteous executive manager stepped in. "Where exactly have *you* been?" Dawn snarled.

"Out."

"Oh, is that right? And did you happen to see my husband while you were *out?*"

God, they were back to this again? Charlie did not have the time or patience for this today. Or ever again. "No," she managed to choke out.

"I checked the video, you hussy. I saw him go into your apartment!"

"What?" Charlie shot out of her chair. "Are you kidding me?"

"Oh, please. If you think—"

"Lady!" Charlie screeched. "I am not screwing your husband! Now show me the damn video!"

That snapped Dawn out of her rage. Unfortunately, Charlie was just starting hers.

"Unbelievable," she muttered as she brushed past Dawn, who blinked several times and drew her hands close to her chest as if to make herself less of a target.

Charlie headed straight to the surveillance room. "When?" she demanded over her shoulder.

Dawn seemed to be regretting her outburst now. "Oh. I'm not sure. It was probably… I was probably mistaken. I'm sorry, Charlie. Just forget I said anything."

"That is not going to happen. So either tell me when you saw it or I'll spend all day looking and I'll announce to everyone what I'm doing." She nodded at the man currently sitting frozen in front of the monitors. "Hi, Eli."

"Um…hello, Ms. Allington."

Dawn snapped, "You can go, Eli!" and he stood and slipped past them. "Listen," she continued as soon as he'd left. "I'm sorry I yelled at you. I've been under a lot of pressure."

"Just tell me already."

Dawn looked over her shoulder as if she were afraid her husband were standing there. Or she was hoping he'd come save her from her idiotic outburst. But no one arrived to offer rescue, and Dawn slumped in defeat. "Around twelve-thirty."

"This afternoon?"

"Yes."

Charlie muttered, "We just can't keep our hands off each other, I guess," and pulled up the correct camera feed.

There he was, giving a perfunctory knock on her apartment door, as if he already knew she wasn't there. Then he used a key and slipped right inside. "When does he leave?"

"I don't know. Someone came into the office. I had to shut it down. I didn't want...I didn't want anyone to know."

Charlie rolled her eyes and started reviewing at the highest speed possible, but something skipped by in the frame and she had to cut back almost immediately. Keith had left her apartment only two minutes after entering. "Two minutes," she said, playing it back again. She shot a glare at Dawn. "Even a little hussy like me isn't that good. Unless there's something disappointing about Keith you'd like to tell me."

"There's no need to be crude!" she snapped.

"Are you sure? I feel like yelling a whole lot of crude things right now. Your husband was in my apartment without my permission!"

"He's... I'm sure... If..." A hundred different things seemed to be spinning through the woman's eyes. She closed them for a moment, then nodded. "He's technically your landlord. I'm sure there was some problem he needed to address."

Charlie let her head drop into her hands. "Are there any cameras in my apartment?"

"What? Of course not! What are you talking about?"

"Just go," Charlie whispered. "Leave me alone. Please."

For once in her life, Dawn seemed to decide that staying quiet was her best course. She stood there for one long moment and then she thankfully, mercifully, left Charlie alone.

Charlie kept her eyes closed. This place was a madhouse. That bastard had gone into her rooms, violated her space. For what?

She opened her eyes and looked at the monitor. Two minutes. What had he done? Put in a listening device? That seemed a little extreme even for her paranoia. Sure, she'd *considered* it, but was that really a possibility?

Two minutes. Had he been looking for something? She looked at the time code again. It was after she'd called her brother. After she'd left a frantic message for him. He must have called Keith. And Keith had dropped by to look for damning evidence. For her computer.

Movement caught her eye, and Charlie looked up at the monitor to see Keith's car pulling into the employee parking lot. She jumped to her feet and raced to her office. The computer was still there. She locked her office door and started backing everything up to her personal online account.

Screw these people. She was getting out of here.

She watched the upload marker tick up too slowly. She didn't even know if anything important was in those files; she only knew that Nicole had said they'd planned to blame her if anything went wrong. What could they pin on her?

A knock interrupted her thoughts. She glanced at the computer. It was only 60 percent backed up. If Keith opened the door right now… But no. It had only been three minutes since he'd pulled up. Unless he'd raced up the stairs at superspeed, it was someone else. "Who is it?" she rasped.

"Eli, ma'am." She had a few minutes yet. She slumped and told Eli she'd find him later.

Then her mind kicked into high gear.

By the time Keith unlocked her office door five minutes later, she was ready.

CHAPTER TWENTY-TWO

CHARLIE KNEW HER hands were shaking, but there was nothing she could do to stop them. Her only option was to hide them beneath her desk as Keith took a seat in one of her chairs.

"I was worried about you, Charlotte. So was your brother. Where have you been?"

"For two people who were so worried, it's odd neither of you tried to call and talk to me."

He smoothed down his slightly mussed hair. "Well, I was wrapped up in a few things and—"

"I can't work for you anymore," she interrupted, not feeling one bit of worry as she said it. It was the absolute truth.

"Of course you can." She saw it then, finally. The cold, hard stone of the man beneath the layers of innocuous warmth. The core that had made him so successful by forty-five. "I spoke with Nicole. She seems to be confused about a few things. She drinks. She gets reckless. She's hot-tempered. She says things she doesn't mean."

"Like that you and my loving brother are using me to embezzle money out of your own resort?"

Keith offered an easy smile. "There's your answer right there. Why would I embezzle money from my own place?"

"You have investors. And when Brad's wife filed for divorce, she really screwed up that little deal you made with Nicole. You both needed the money, so Brad brought me in."

His smile didn't waver. "That land deal was totally aboveboard. It was well documented. I have no idea what you're talking about."

"Really? The real estate appraisers might have a different take on that."

His smile finally broke. Apparently Nicole had left out a few things when she'd spoken to him. Charlie had interrogated people before, and she'd sat in on some pretty intense questioning in Las Vegas. Nicole had been a piece of cake.

Thanks to Nicole, Charlie knew all about the land deal. Nicole had wanted a secret stash of money so she could eventually leave her husband, so when her husband had started talks with Keith Taggert about the land sale, she and Keith had hatched a plan. Nicole would pay off the appraisers to low-ball the land value. Brad, who wasn't known for having the best scruples, would be brought in as a middleman to buy the land, with the plan that he'd sell it to Keith at a much higher cost just a few months later. And then they'd all split the profit and live happily ever after. Keith would basically take money straight from his investors to line his own pockets, Nicole would slip her portion into a secret account, and Brad would make a nice little sum for his troubles.

But Brad's wife had filed for divorce and frozen all the assets only two days after Brad had sold the land to the Taggerts' resort. There was no way to slip 1.5 million dollars out of that sticky net. Keith Taggert had been counting on the money, and he hadn't been willing to wait years for the divorce to be final, especially if the settlement meant there'd be less cash left to divvy up.

So Brad had offered up a temporary alternative to keep Keith happy: Charlie. Too bad she wasn't interested in playing.

"I'm not going to be part of whatever plan you have, so you can drop it, Keith. I'm done here."

"I don't think so."

"Well, you're wrong."

He watched her carefully, his eyes emotionless. "You're under a noncompete for six months. But if you leave, it'll take you a hell of a lot longer to find work than that. Your reputation is already shit. I'll just make sure it's fresh shit."

"Oh, I don't think you'll risk that, Keith. Not with what I know."

Now he leaned forward, elbows on his knees and hands clasped loosely in front of him, as if he didn't have a care in the world. "No one will believe you."

"No? What about Dawn? Will she believe it when I tell her about you and Nicole?"

He smiled. "Do you think Dawn is going to leave

me over the possibility of an affair? What would she do
with her life then? Be a coupon-clipping single mom
watching all her old friends drive by in cars she can't
afford anymore? Please."

"No wonder she feels so shitty and helpless," Charlie snapped. "You're an asshole. And I'm out of here."

She stood and started to close the laptop, but Keith
grabbed it before she could.

"I believe that's my property."

"Fine. Enjoy it."

"You don't have to do this, you know. I meant what
I said about loyalty. You stay with me for a couple of
years, and you'll move up. It doesn't have to be this
way. I'm not some grasping hotel manager stealing
from his employer like that guy in Tahoe. There's no
risk here, Charlotte. For you or for me. You just do your
job, I do mine and everyone benefits."

"On the backs of your investors."

He shrugged. "They make their money, too."

"Just a little less of it than they've earned."

Keith smiled and held up an appeasing hand. "Look.
I understand. This is a shock, and you're feeling used.
Your brother should have let you in on this. I told him
to. Honestly. I told him to ask if you wanted in, and
we'd all work out a deal. So let's do that."

When she didn't answer right away, Keith nodded
and dropped his voice. "Listen, Brad treated you like
shit, and I shouldn't have let him get away with it. He's
your brother, so I deferred to him, but I was wrong. I
have no trouble admitting that to you. I'll make it up to

you, Charlotte. A little bonus when the resort opening goes off without a hitch. Ten thousand dollars. I know things have been tough for you since Tahoe. It doesn't have to be that way anymore. We're in this together, and you deserve your portion."

She was tempted. For one awful moment she was tempted to just say yes. Just give in. Just stay. Take the easy way.

Because he was right about her prospects. She wouldn't be able to work for another resort or hotel for six months, even before word got out that she'd left on bad terms. And if word did get out, no matter how it went down, her career would be over forever. She'd be forced to start over, with nothing but a pocketful of debt and an education that couldn't be applied to another field.

If she said no, it'd be the biggest step she'd ever taken on the road toward living in a run-down trailer in Florida with a string of men who just needed a few bucks to get their lives back on track. She'd be unemployed. Again. Unemployable. Again. Hopeless. Again.

And she'd probably be under investigation. Again.

Damn it all to hell.

She stood and grabbed her purse. "Fuck you, Keith. I'm not a criminal, and I never have been, despite what everyone wants to think."

His face twisted from a smile to a sneer so quickly that she stepped back despite the desk between them. "If you breathe a word about this to anyone, I'll make sure you take the fall. Be very clear on that. You keep your damn mouth shut or this will all be on your head."

"You can't pin anything on me. All I've done is install a few cameras and train some security personnel. Unless you're prepared to prove I'm a magician, you're shit out of luck."

"Wrong. You've already embezzled thirty thousand dollars. In just a few weeks' time. That's pretty impressive for a young woman like yourself, but then again, you do have experience."

"What? That's absurd." She actually laughed. But Keith looked so pleased with himself…

And then it hit her. Nicole hadn't known what Keith and Brad had planned, but Charlie could see it perfectly now. "The expense report. The budget."

Keith didn't even bother answering. He just smirked.

"I didn't prepare those."

"Maybe, maybe not. But you were the last one logged in to them. And somehow, amid all those new expenses and new hires, a few dozen payments made their way to an online account. Maybe it wasn't you. Maybe it was. An investigation would take months to sort out. Just like that last one did. The police would be involved. You'd have to hire a lawyer. And of course, it would all end up in the papers for anyone to find with a quick search."

"You asshole."

"Hey. I'm not forcing this on you. That isn't how it needs to go down. Like I said, keep quiet and there won't be any hard feelings. It's simple. All right?"

Charlie stuffed the few personal items on her desk into her purse and grabbed her phone. "Tell my brother I never want to speak to him again."

"No problem. I'm sure he'll be broken up."

Her heart raced as she walked past him. It kept racing as she walked to the elevator and glanced fearfully up at the cameras. What else could they make up about her? What else would they claim? It wasn't as if it was difficult to set people up. She'd heard of that happening in Vegas. A few grams of coke in someone's bathroom, and suddenly the police were there and it was all being documented.

Jesus. There was nothing she could do about them. She just needed to get out of here and leave this behind.

Charlie wiped the sweat off her temple as she stepped off the elevator and rushed to her car. She glanced in the rearview mirror as she pulled away from the resort for the last time, half certain someone would be following her. But no. She drove away unmolested. If she'd left anything there, it could stay. It wasn't as if she'd be welcomed back.

She'd expected to feel relieved at escaping, but she was scared. Really scared. This man was holding an axe over her head, and there was no telling if he'd drop it or not. Even if she kept quiet, he could still use that information. After all, he might not like the feeling of waiting for her axe to drop, either.

Charlie wanted to call someone. She wanted someone to meet her somewhere and hug her and tell her it would be fine. A friend. A lover. Anyone.

But she had no one. Everyone had left her, or she'd
left them. Her brother, her mom, every boyfriend she'd
ever had. Even every party-hopping friend. She wasn't
good at love. She never had been. She'd never wanted
anything to do with it.

Her life was superficial. She'd set it up that way.
And now her years of being young and successful and
carefree were over, and she was alone. After all, if you
didn't believe in love, it wasn't going to be waiting for
you when you needed it.

She started to drive to her apartment, but what
would she do there? Sit on her couch and worry? It
had been a refuge from anxiety just a few days ago,
but it couldn't protect her from anything now.

For a moment, she considered finding her brother to
confront him, but she'd meant what she said. She never
wanted to speak to him again. What could he possibly
say that could make it better? Maybe he'd expected
nothing bad to happen to her, but there was no denying that the emergency parachute in this little plan had
been blaming everything on Charlie. Because she was
already vulnerable.

Her own brother had seen her down on her knees
and instead of helping her up, he'd pulled his foot back
to kick her. Hard.

What kind of person was he? Their childhood had
taught Charlie not to believe in love, but it had apparently taught Brad not to give a damn about anyone except himself. A reasonable reaction, she supposed, but
that didn't mean she could ever forgive him.

Her last desperate thought was to turn to Walker. In fact, she actually took the turn that would lead her back to the Stud Farm and Walker's apartment. She could knock on his door and throw herself into his arms so he'd have no choice but to hold her. And then explain that, yes, everything Nicole had told him was true, but Charlie really hadn't known anything about it. *Really.* Again.

But how much would that matter? Even if she proved the truth to him, he was still right about her. That she'd treated him like a project. That she'd lied to him about herself. She couldn't deny any of that.

Charlie pulled up to the curb and looked at his window. His arms would feel so good around her, and she knew she could get him to give in. He was too kind not to. But as good as it would feel in that one short moment, she'd rather die than know he was touching her out of coerced pity.

She sat there for a long time, thinking it through. Thinking of going to bed tonight, and every night, having to worry that she might wake up the next day to the police knocking on her door.

That had been the most terrifying experience of her life. Being brought in to the police station. Facing the hostile questions of a very blunt district attorney. Having no idea what was going on or even what they thought she'd done.

She'd cried there. In front of those people. She'd cried and apologized and begged them to tell her if she was going to jail. For weeks, she'd lived with that fear. It had paralyzed her. Defeated her. She hadn't even had time to process the hurt and betrayal she'd felt about her lover. That had been so far secondary, she had barely cared at first.

And now she was here with those same fears. Keith wanted her to live like that again. Not just now, but forever. That was the whole point of his threat, after all. To make her afraid. To make her obey.

Her hands trembled against the steering wheel. With some of that fear, yes, but it was building into something else. Fury. Hate. Determination.

She wanted to call her cousin. Nate was a sheriff's deputy. She could lean on him. Let him help.

But this was a small town. She'd heard all the stories about the kinds of deals that were made behind closed doors in Tahoe. It wouldn't be any different here. It would go to the D.A. who would be best friends with someone with a lot of money invested in another deal Keith was doing, and… Yeah. She knew how that went. How it always went.

A few leaves drifted down to settle on the hood of her car. It was a beautiful day. A peaceful day. The world marched on around her. It didn't care if she was scared or not. It didn't care if she played it safe or took a chance.

Reaching into her purse, she took out the phone she'd used to record the conversation with Keith. That recording would protect her. And exonerate her. But only if people got a chance to hear it.

The rational part of her brain croaked to life again,

telling her to think about it. Take her time. She could make that choice just as easily in a week as she could now. She should consult an attorney. Be careful. *Think*.

But look where that had gotten her before. Out of prison, yes, but still afraid to stand up to anyone. Afraid to walk away from being mistreated. Afraid to be herself. And lying to a good man like Walker Pearce.

Charlie pressed her forehead to the steering wheel. She knew what she needed to do. She knew *exactly* what she needed to do. And it was the thing that scared her the most.

CHAPTER TWENTY-THREE

FAT FLAKES OF snow drifted through the air, weaving a lacy sheet that barely obscured his sight, even fifty feet out. Walker slipped off his hat and let the air cool his head for a moment as the latest herd of cattle milled about, confused by the half day's push down the mountain.

Walker had been in the high country for a full week now, camping out and catching an extra few hours of work whenever he could. He'd finished up the roundup for his new boss, but there was plenty of work to be found. Hands got hurt or didn't show up, and there were nearly a dozen ranchers who needed to get their cattle out of the national forest before the deadline hit.

He loved the beauty of these mountains, and the weather had been decent. Most of the days had been bright and crisp with groves of turning aspen blazing across the hills. The nights had been good, too, with the kind of camaraderie he'd missed since he'd left the ranch. He'd caught up with a few old friends and made some new ones. He'd shared beers and heard stories that had almost made him feel that his life was normal. Almost.

The only bad part about it had been all the time he'd had to think. Time for everything he'd heard and said to Charlie to eat at him.

He couldn't help feeling bad now, for the words he'd thrown at her and the way he'd treated her. What if she'd been telling the truth? Granted, that was a little hard for him to imagine. A woman who'd do all those things would certainly have no qualms lying about it. But he shouldn't have bothered throwing it all in her face if he wasn't even going to listen to a response.

People had done that to him his whole life, and he'd always hated it. His dad, certainly, but even teachers in school who'd wanted to help him, lecturing him about all his problems and never wanting to hear his take. And women. Women always assumed the worst about him, even the ones who liked him, like Charlie. He wasn't that damn bad. He knew how to keep his dick in his pants. Hell, most of the time, he didn't mean a damn thing with his flirting. And he'd never messed around on anyone. Not once.

So yeah, he knew a thing or two about being yelled at by someone who just wanted to yell. He'd certainly given it his all with Charlie.

She was probably guilty. She'd halfway admitted it. But what if she wasn't?

His horse shifted restlessly under him, and Walker stroked her neck. He had to hold his place and keep the cattle grouped up while the hands near the road started loading them up. Given a chance, the animals would start edging away from the road and the lowing of the cattle being loaded up. So Walker held his horse steady and whispered a promise of an apple when they were through.

He'd apologize to Charlie when he got home. If she'd made a mess of her life, that was her problem. And whatever she'd gotten caught up in, she'd meant nothing cruel when she'd dragged Walker out to the Ability Ranch. She'd done that out of the goodness of her heart. Her meddling, know-it-all heart. Charlie honestly thought he belonged at that place.

And the thing was…maybe she was right. Or she might have been right if Walker had been born just a little smarter. Because the Ability Ranch was another thing Walker couldn't stop thinking about.

He wouldn't mind helping out around there. He could maybe drop in and work with the folks teaching the classes every once in a while. Except then he'd have to explain why he couldn't do more. Why he couldn't work there full-time.

His face burned at the very thought. Out here, no one ever asked for a résumé or even an explanation. Even at the dude ranches, they only made you fill out some basic information for a background check and payroll. He could put down where he'd gone to school and they didn't give a damn whether he'd graduated with honors or skipped every class.

But the Ability Ranch would be different. He couldn't just wing it there. No. He'd have to explain. He'd have to watch their faces as he admitted to being a thirty-year-old dropout who struggled to read and write.

Shit. He couldn't do that. It'd kill him.

Walker was the one shifting restlessly this time, and the horse danced a few feet to the side.

"Sorry," Walker murmured. And he was sorry. Because even admitting his fears to himself made him ashamed. Those kids at the Ability Ranch had a lot more to deal with than dyslexia and pride, and here he was, telling himself he couldn't do something simple like ask for help or admit his weakness.

Maybe he should be more worried that he was a jackass and a coward than the fact that he didn't have a diploma. "Shit."

He frowned and eased his mount forward a few feet as the first heads of cattle were loaded up.

A truck pulled up next to the trailer and a man got out to speak to one of the cowboys down below. Walker watched as the guy nodded and then swung his mount around to ride up the trail.

"Walker!" he called when he got closer. Walker moved the last dozen feet to meet him.

"Hey, there's an emergency back home. Your dad is in the hospital and your brother's flying in this afternoon."

Walker cursed and looked away for a moment before nodding. "All right. Thanks for the information."

"You should get going."

"Naw, it's fine. It's already three. If my brother said

he'd be there this afternoon, he'll be at the hospital sooner than I will."

"Yeah, but…it sounded pretty bad. I didn't want to scare you, but they said your dad's on a ventilator. That's serious stuff."

Walker nodded and said thanks again, but he walked his horse back to his post. Micah could take this one. There was nothing Walker could do anyway. If the old man was dying, he'd go more peacefully if the son he hated wasn't there. And if he wasn't dying, then Walker would get there tonight and spell his brother for an hour or two.

Walker had enough to deal with. He shouldn't have to deal with his dad, too. He hadn't even seen the man for two years before Micah had decided he had to go into a home.

It wasn't fair, goddamn it. None of it was fair.

But then he remembered that last moment at the hospital, when his dad had so sweetly asked for his wife. A woman he thought he'd only been married to a year. *Jesus.*

Walker pushed the cattle down the hill, his jaw aching from the way he clenched his teeth. It wasn't fair, but it was fucking life, wasn't it?

He broke away and rode down to the trailer. "I guess I'll head out, after all," he said, and took off for the campground to head back down.

He couldn't let Micah face that alone. He couldn't let Micah watch by himself as their father died. Walker might be a failure and an idiot, but he wasn't the man his father was. He was better. He had to be better.

DESPITE THE LONG hours of waiting next to the hospital bed, Walker didn't cry when his dad died. He didn't feel even a lump in his throat. But he held Micah while he broke down, and Walker was glad to be there for his little brother. It'd been a long night, but in the end, it had been over mercifully fast. Faster than James Pearce had deserved, maybe.

He and Micah spoke to someone in hospital administration to make the initial arrangements, and then Walker drove his brother to his favorite diner for some much-needed food. The morning sun seemed too bright after that endless night in the hospital room.

"Shit," Micah sighed into his coffee. "I can't believe he's gone. I always thought he was too mean to die."

"Ha. Isn't that my line?"

"Hell no. You think it wasn't hard for me to watch how he treated you? And I know you protected me, but I still got my share of whippings."

Walker laughed. "Remember that time you snuck the truck out to go drinking? I think you were fourteen."

"Oh, shit. I couldn't sit right for a week."

"Spare the rod, I guess."

Micah snorted. "I suppose. It's a miracle I didn't develop a taste for leather daddies and canings."

"Jesus, Micah. I don't know what either of those things is, and I don't want to. I'm a nice country boy."

"Nice, my ass."

"Also something I don't want to know."

They both broke into deep laughter, which surprised even Walker. But it felt good. Cathartic. Like having a wake and letting someone go. There wouldn't be a service. Their dad didn't have any friends around, as far as they knew, and no family. They'd have him cremated and then interred at the local cemetery, so this place was as good a location for a wake as any.

"Do you remember that dog?" Micah asked.

"Which dog?" They'd had a couple over the years.

"That little terrier. Damn thing was smaller than a barn cat."

For a moment, Walker drew a blank, but then he frowned in surprise. "God, I think I do. It died when we were little, though. You were only five or six, I think."

"Killed by a coyote. Dad always acted like the dog was a nuisance, but he let him sleep inside at night and sometimes he'd feed him scraps under the table. Do you remember that? It was the weirdest thing. That big man and that scared little dog. And when it died, Dad took it out to bury it behind the barn like it was just another chore, but I heard him crying."

"Dad?"

"I know. I snuck around the back of the barn, and he was sobbing as he dug that grave."

Walker shook his head. "I swear, I don't even know what to say to that. It makes no sense."

Micah nodded and sipped his coffee. "It doesn't

make anything better, I know, but…I think Dad was the way he was because of Grandpa Pearce."

Walker blew out a long breath. "That man was a true bastard."

"Yeah. Meaner than Dad. I think Dad was terrified of him."

Walker felt a shock at those words. "You think? He just always seemed angry. I can't picture him scared."

"I know, but whenever Grandpa Pearce came around, Dad spent all his time in the barn. He even skipped meals if he could. However mean Dad was, however badly he treated you, I think he got it worse as a kid. From his dad and his older brother. That's what he learned. It's what he knew."

"Well, he could've learned better if he'd bothered. I'd never treat a kid that way."

"I know that. You'd be a great father. If you ever managed to settle down."

Walker didn't know what to say in response. The thought of having his own kids filled him with a joy so deep it scared him. But the idea that he might pass his learning disability on… That scared him in a deep and different way.

But even if he didn't have his own kids, maybe he could make up for the way his dad had lived. Maybe he could make that better even for himself.

Walker cleared his throat and shifted the last of the pancakes around on his plate. "Speaking of settling down…"

Micah raised an eyebrow.

"I've been thinking of getting that GED."

"Holy crap, brother." Micah reached across the table to slap his shoulder. "Yes. Don't think about it. Just do it."

"It's just… It's hard for me, Micah. It might take a while."

"Because of your dyslexia? They make accommodations for that. I told you a long time ago that you can listen to the test on audio instead of reading it."

"You did?"

"Hell yes, I did. How can you not remember that?"

Walker scrubbed a hand through his hair and told himself not to change the subject no matter how much he wanted to. "I don't know. I don't like to talk about it. Not even with you."

"You just have to go to the community college and talk to someone."

"At the college?"

"Yes, they've got classes. They can give you extra time on the test. Jesus, Walker, just do it already. I've never seen somebody drag his feet more about anything."

His brother said it so simply. As if it were no big deal. "Fine," Walker said, pretending it was easy to face. "Christ. You're like an old lady about this."

"You think? Because I'll take you out back and whip your ass if you don't get it done." Micah froze as soon as he said the words. "I'm sorry, Walk. I didn't mean it like that."

Walker just rolled his eyes. "Please. You couldn't

whip my ass if you tried, Mr. Administrator. I'm a man's man."

Micah grinned. "No. I've definitely got you beat in that department."

And just like that, it was easy again. The horrible conversation was over. Walker would get his GED and then they'd never have to speak about it again.

They finished their food and drank another half a pot of coffee, and Walker let himself wonder if he could do something different with his life. Something he'd never expected.

"I'd better find a hotel," Micah said, suddenly looking exhausted despite all the coffee.

"No way. You'll stay with me."

"I'll be here for a few days. I'm not sleeping on your damn couch that long."

"Fine. But at least come hang out tonight. We'll order pizza. Watch a game."

"Sure. Drop me off at my car?"

Micah excused himself to use the restroom, and Walker threw the tip down and headed for the cashier to pay. A stack of newspapers caught his eye with an unusually large headline across the front. Nothing like the normal celebrations of local parades and kids getting awards. This was real news.

Local Business Developers Under Investigation for Fraud

Walker grabbed a paper and handed over an extra dollar before moving slowly outside. Brow furrowed, he forced himself to concentrate on the tiny print. Even as slow a reader as he was, it didn't take him long to find the names Keith Taggert and Meridian Resort. And then another name: Brad Allington.

He breathed out a curse and kept reading. This had to be about Charlie. It had to be. But he scanned the whole front page and didn't find her name.

"Shit!" He closed his eyes for a second and then started over.

"Hey, brother, I was going to pay for breakfast."

"Hold on," he muttered, and held up a hand when Micah kept talking. "Just give me a second."

He tried reading faster, but that didn't work, so he slowed down again and just read the first sentence of each paragraph. Finally he found it.

An employee with security ties to the resort first brought this story to the attention of the paper via a voice recording. Owing to the explosive nature of the allegations, the paper contacted the district attorney's office about—

"What's going on?" Micah pressed.

"Holy shit," Walker breathed. "It's Charlie. It has to be."

"Who's Charlie?"

Walker looked up at his brother and shook his head. "No one."

"No one? You look like Dad's ghost just walked up and smacked you in the forehead."

"She's…no one," he tried again, but Micah stared

him down, suddenly looking every inch the older brother despite that he was younger by two years.

Walker spilled the whole story.

Five minutes later, they were sitting on the curb staring out at the highway together.

"Well, damn," Micah said.

"Yeah. Damn."

"You really like this girl?"

Walker nodded, his head slightly dizzy when he moved too much. "Yeah."

"If this is true—" Micah tapped the story, which he'd read quickly through and then summarized for Walker "—you're going to have some apologizing to do."

"Yeah," he said one more time, aware that it was likely the understatement of the century.

"Then drop me off at my car and get to it."

"Sure. But… What if she doesn't want to see me?"

His brother offered a hand and pulled him up. "Then I guess you'll have to suffer in silence until she does."

"Thanks. That helps a lot."

"Come on. You're the expert on women, Walker. Not me. If anyone can effectively beg forgiveness, it's you."

Walker felt so dazed he had to concentrate on driving to keep his mind from drifting. Had Charlie really done that? And had he pushed her into it?

He'd taken off at five o'clock the morning after their argument, and he hadn't been back in town since. He hadn't even been in cell phone range. One week on the mountain and all hell had broken loose. A hell he might have set in motion.

Micah looked at him as they pulled up to the hospital. "Whoever this girl is, whatever happens, she's right about the Ability Ranch, you know."

"She might be," Walker conceded. "We'll see."

"If that's why you're looking into the GED, then you already know she's right."

He shrugged, feeling worse about it than ever. "Probably."

"All right. I'll call you later."

"You think we should check about Dad?"

"I'll call the mortuary," Micah said. "You go on and find her. I'll see you tonight." He shut the door and walked toward his car.

"Micah!" Walker called, rolling down the window. His brother turned around. "Thanks for taking care of him. When I didn't want to. When I refused to. Thanks for that. I'm the older brother. I should have done it."

Micah just watched him for a moment, and then he smiled. "But you did everything else. You had to leave a little for me. I love you, Walker. Now go on. Make me proud."

Shit. Walker felt the burn of tears in his eyes as he pulled away. But he managed to blink them back, too overwhelmed by panicked worry to indulge in anything deeper right now.

Her car was there when he arrived at the Stud Farm, and even though he'd feared he wouldn't be able to find her, the fact that she was there felt like terror. Now he really would have to face her. He'd have to apologize. He'd have to walk away if she slammed the door in his face. Whatever anxiety he'd felt about his educational failings was nothing close to this, but he'd face it for her.

He ran to the building and took the stairs two at a time, the newspaper still clutched in his hand. The building was empty. No reporters milling about or police parked at the door. It seemed anticlimactic, but his heart was thundering like crazy when he stopped in front of her door and raised his hand.

Two deep breaths and then he did it. He knocked. And she opened the door right away.

Her face was pale. Her eyes shadowed with exhaustion. Her hair was mussed as if she'd just woken.

"Charlie?" he whispered. "Are you okay?"

Charlie took one step forward. Her lip trembled. And then she fell into his arms, sobbing. Walker just picked her up and held her. "I'm sorry," he said, and she cried harder. His own tears finally fell.

CHAPTER TWENTY-FOUR

"I'm sorry," he murmured again against her hair, pulling her tighter to him on the bed.

"You don't have to keep saying that," Charlie insisted, though she took the chance to kiss his chest one more time.

"I do have to keep saying it."

"No. Anybody would've believed the worst. The whole thing was set up because it was so believable."

"I'm not anybody," he insisted. "I should've known."

She just kissed his chest again, wishing she could sneak her hands beneath his shirt and feel his skin. But she didn't know if that's what this was now. After he'd shown up, she'd cried herself into such a mess that she'd kicked him out so she could shower. She'd stood in there for what seemed like an hour, letting the water wash away her tears, then she'd gone to his place to crawl under his covers and hide.

He'd joined her after his own shower. Even though he held her, she didn't know what it was. Even if it was only pity, she didn't care. She'd been so alone all week. So utterly alone. Now she wanted to crawl inside him and feel safe. Thank God he seemed happy to play the part of protector for a little while.

When Rayleen had first told her he'd be gone for a week or two, Charlie had felt relieved. She wouldn't have to face him or apologize or even explain. But then things had gotten intense. And scary. And she'd gotten so tired.

After she'd played the audio of her conversation with Keith for the editor of the paper, there'd been no turning back. A reporter had made a copy of the audio and contacted the D.A. right away to find out if they had a comment. Charlie had known that would happen. The point hadn't been to keep the law out of it, but to get the truth in the public eye so Keith's connections couldn't sweep it under the rug or paint her as the bad guy.

But of course, her past had come into it. And then the interviews with police and attorneys. The phone calls from the paper. She'd been afraid then, and she'd wished for Walker. Just as a friend. Just as a presence who brought her a little peace.

"I should have told you earlier," she said. "About Tahoe. I'm so sorry I didn't. I just—"

"Stop, Charlie. You don't need to apologize."

"I do. Because I kept it from you on purpose, Walker." Her throat burned and tried to close. She hoped he wouldn't feel a few extra tears on his shirt. She'd already cried so many. "I wanted you to see me the way I used to be, before everything went so wrong. I lied to you. Even about this place. I had a room at the resort, but I didn't want to tell you I was being bullied and harassed, because I didn't want to be a woman who'd put up with that."

"Hush. It doesn't matter. I called you a thief. I think we're even."

"You think?" she asked, smiling past her tears.

"Damn close, at least."

His chest rose beneath her and then he blew out a deep breath. She raised her head to look at him, but his hand guided her head back down. "Since we're telling truths…"

"You don't have to tell me anything else. You should sleep, Walker. You haven't gotten any sleep, and your father—"

"Let me say it before I lose my courage. While you were in the shower, I called the Ability Ranch."

"Oh," she gasped, then covered her mouth to stop herself from interrupting again.

"I talked with my brother this morning. About my dad. About my issues. And I can't let the man keep beating me now that he's dead."

Her fingers stroked his skin. "I'm so sorry."

"I almost let him make me into what he called me. I see that now. Thanks to you. So I called the ranch. I talked to Marlene. I told her I needed to get my GED, but I'd like to help out while I worked toward that. Once I take the safety certification training and get my GED…I think I'll have a job."

"Oh, Walker. You… I'm so proud of you. You have no idea. I know how hard that was. I—" God, she was crying again. Sobbing, really, when she'd thought herself all sobbed out.

"Come on, woman. It's not that big of a deal. You can just say 'I told you so,' and move on."

"Shut up," she choked out as he laughed at her. "It's a big deal. A really big deal."

He tucked in his chin and smiled at her. "Now you're just bragging. You and my brother can crow about your victory tonight. If you'll stay. I'd like you to meet him."

"Really?" Something warm and scary bloomed inside her chest. Something she didn't want to feel and told herself not to. "You want me to meet your brother?"

"Yes. Only if you want to, I mean."

"Of course I want to."

He smiled at that, but then he let his head fall back to the pillow. "But there is one complication about working at the Ability Ranch."

"What's that?"

"I just thought… I mean… I want to try to do this right."

"Do what right?"

"Well…if I start working at the ranch, I'll be working with Marlene, so…"

"So." She felt a twinge of pain, remembering the woman's gorgeous eyes and wide smile.

"Yeah," he finished weakly.

She tried to ignore the jealousy that stabbed through her. "You mean maybe you two would have a thing again?"

"What? No! I meant I'd be working with a woman I once dated."

"I don't know what you're saying!" she cried out in exasperation.

"I just mean I wouldn't want it to upset you. And if it would, maybe I shouldn't work there."

Charlie managed to beat the jealousy back entirely at those words. "Are you kidding? If I were going to get upset about all the women in your past, Walker, I never would've slept with you. You've had lovers. So have I, I promise. Even if this were more—"

"It is more," he interrupted.

"More?" she repeated, certain he didn't know what she'd meant.

"Yes. More than sex, damn it. More than nothing." He rose on his elbow and met her eyes. "It is for me."

"Walker…" What was he saying? Surely not that. Not this soon.

"We're friends, Charlie. We always have been. I like you. I admire you. You make me laugh and think. And you turn me on so much, my fucking hands shake when I touch you. That might not be love, not yet, but it isn't nothing, Charlie. Is it?"

She wanted to look away, but she couldn't. "Love?" she whispered.

"Maybe. Someday. Would that be so awful?"

"With you?" she asked.

Walker winced. "That's what I was thinking, yes."

Love. With Walker. That damn natural disaster was suddenly looming over her, changing the pressure in the air. Love. Just the possibility of it made her heart shake with fear.

But fear wasn't the only feeling. Not at all. She'd always loved so many things about him, after all. That part was already real.

"Maybe I haven't been the kind of guy you could count on, Charlie. Maybe that's why you didn't confide in me or ask me for help. But I will be that man. I swear it."

She thought of the way she'd felt when she'd opened the door. When she'd seen him standing there. Relief had washed over her so suddenly that all the little twigs of bravery and strength she'd stacked up over the past year had been swept away. She'd been left standing there completely raw and crumbling. And Walker had scooped her right up. That had been all she'd needed to let go. His arms. The rumble of his voice telling her it was okay.

"I know I could ask you for anything, Walker," she whispered. "It wasn't like that. If…" She swallowed her fear and tried again. "If this was more, I'd be fine about Marlene. And anyone else in your past. I could deal with that. If…you loved me. Maybe."

She hadn't realized how tight his jaw had been until the tension left it.

"I mean, as long as I don't have to hear anything about it. How amazing the sex was or—"

"No one is more amazing in bed than you, Charlie."

That stopped her words on a laugh. "Ha! You and your flirting. You're the worst."

"You don't believe me?" He flipped her over onto her back and loomed above her. Taking her hand, he drew it down and pressed it to his cock. It was already hard. "You drive me crazy. Everything about you. Everything," he whispered as he closed the space between them and took her mouth.

God. She'd thought she'd never feel this again. She'd thought it was over, and now he was offering *more.* She kissed him eagerly, desperately, her hands digging into his shoulders so he wouldn't change his mind and pull away.

"I've never loved anyone, Charlie," he murmured, "and you're the last woman I'd ever deserve."

"That's not true."

He pushed her shirt up and put his mouth to her breast.

She gasped his name and pulled him closer. "That's not true," she sobbed.

"It's true. But maybe…" He slipped her pants down, his hand sliding over the mound of her sex. "Maybe someday…" He freed his cock from his pants, sliding a knee between her legs so she'd open for him. "I could be."

By the time he slipped on a condom, she was panting, but she still wasn't prepared. She wasn't ready for the sure stroke of his thrust and the shock of being so utterly filled with him. She cried out, and he swallowed the sound with a kiss.

"This is more," he said as he pulled back and thrust again. "It's more than anything else."

She framed his face in her hands and kissed him, raising her knees to his hips to take what he offered.

"It's better than anything else," he growled.

"Yes," she gasped.

He took her deeper. Invading her body and her soul. "It's better."

"Yes. It's better. *Walker*." She twisted her hands into his hair and tugged his head up until she could meet his gaze. He pressed his hips hard against her and held himself there, deep inside her.

"You're better," she said. "And, God…Walker, I love you so much."

His eyes widened for a moment before he closed them. It was slow after that. Slow and deep and careful, as his tongue stroked hers and his hands touched her everywhere. Everywhere. Finally he pulled her on top of him, and let her set the rhythm. He slipped his hand down her belly, and his thumb brushed her clit, and Charlie was lost.

She was lost in the feel of him, the fullness, the stroke of his body in hers as she took him faster.

"You're so beautiful," he growled. "You're so fucking beautiful, Charlie. I love you. Goddamn it, I love you."

She came with his words in her ear. Those terrifying words wrapping around her, getting inside her, making her believe that this was *better*.

Both their hearts were thundering when he pulled her down to his chest and wrapped his arms around her. She was crying again, her tears sliding down his neck, but there was no way to stop them. She was terrified. She had nothing. No job. No future. And now there was *this*. Love. Awful, overwhelming love.

And she wanted it.

"You've made a stupid mistake, Charlie," he whispered into her hair.

"What?" she croaked.

"You shouldn't have convinced me I'm good enough for you. Now I've gone tame and you'll never get rid of me. I'll never leave you alone."

She curled her arms around his wide chest, still shocked at the size and heat and strength of his big male body. It was all hers now. Other women might have had their shot, but they'd blown it. "So you're mine now?" she asked.

"I'm all yours, Charlie. One good ol' cowboy in your hands, whether you want him or not."

She squeezed him tighter, listening to his heart beat slow and sweet against her ear. "I want all of you," she whispered. "Just the way you are, or however you want to be, Walker. Just you."

EPILOGUE

THE BRIDE HAD insisted she wanted a small wedding. In fact, she'd insisted she wanted no wedding at all, but she'd given in with suspicious ease.

First, they'd planned for a small reception at the Crooked R, but so many people had begged for an invitation that the plans had changed. And changed again. Now the wedding and the reception were being held in the huge, high-ceilinged event room at the Ability Ranch. The tall windows framed the snowy Tetons and blue sky above them. Despite the sun, an occasional gust of wind blew sparkling waves of snowflakes off the roof, but there wasn't a hint of cold inside. Inside, the air shimmered with happy conversation and laughter and waves of anticipation, but when the first notes of the fiddle sounded, every voice went quiet. The groom removed his black cowboy hat and handed it off to his best man, Cole Rawlins.

The bride had refused to wear white, but she looked stunning in a pearl-gray dress. A sapphire necklace and earrings played up her blue eyes and upswept white hair, and it was clear that the pink in her cheeks couldn't be attributed to rouge.

For a moment, Rayleen looked scared, her eyes darting over the large crowd of people rising from their chairs for her.

Charlie wondered if Rayleen was now regretting her earlier speech about not needing anyone to give her away because she'd been supporting her own damn self for years. But she visibly steeled herself, set her mouth in a serious line and started down the aisle to the sweet notes of "Here Comes the Bride."

Charlie squeezed Walker's hand and smiled when he pulled her a little closer to his side. "She looks beautiful," he whispered, just as Charlie was thinking it.

Rayleen did look beautiful, and when Charlie turned to peek at Easy standing just in front of the dais, she caught the wistfulness of his smile as he watched his bride approach.

Rayleen stared straight ahead, as if she were afraid to meet anyone's eyes, and Charlie noticed that the bouquet in her hands trembled slightly as she passed.

"Miss Rayleen," Easy said softly, holding out his arm as she reached him.

The bride murmured something that ended with "…foolishness," but she took Easy's arm all the same. In fact, her knuckles turned white where she gripped him as she stepped onto the dais.

Grace, Rayleen's only attendant, took the small bouquet of white lilies from the bride's hand and gave her a kiss on the cheek. The audience seemed to hold its collective breath for a moment, waiting for Rayleen to either bolt or loudly declare that she'd changed her mind and wasn't letting some half-dead old cowboy take over her life. But Rayleen only drew a deep breath and faced the pastor.

The ceremony went off smoothly, though when the pastor accidentally uttered the word "obey," Rayleen shot him a look of such promised violence that he choked on the sentence and immediately corrected himself. Easy snorted, and then Cole tried to swallow a laugh and failed so miserably that he had to duck his head for a long moment.

But Rayleen held her tongue up until the moment the man intoned, "You may now kiss the bride."

"Pah," she scoffed. "I'm not going to let Easy show off in front of half the town, just because some old—"

Her words ended in a squeak when Easy swept her close, bent her over his arm and kissed her senseless. When Easy finally stood her straight again, he only smiled. Rayleen smiled back.

The crowd cheered, filling the room with a happy roar as Rayleen patted the back of her hair and pretended she wasn't blushing. Easy held her hand and kissed her on the cheek for good measure.

"Well, all right," she grouched when the cheers finally died down. "Let's have the damn party, then."

The fiddle sang out the wedding recessional march, but instead of exiting down the aisle with her groom, Rayleen tugged him toward the bar on the other side of the room. "I need a damn whiskey," Charlie heard her mutter as they passed.

Walker pulled Charlie into his arms as the crowd

began to drift toward the tables set up for the reception. Charlie didn't feel any compulsion to move.

"God, you look delicious," she groaned, tilting her head up for a kiss. She'd made the same complaint three times on the drive over, manhandling him until he'd been groaning, too. If they hadn't been running late, she would've made him pull the truck over for a quickie, but she'd have to be satisfied with molesting him on the way back to town. As it was, she slipped her fingers into his recently cropped hair and pulled it.

"Stop it," he growled, tugging her hand down.

"Why?"

"You know why. You're too good at getting me... interested."

He stepped a few inches back.

"But you look so hot," she whined, giving his shoulder an insolent shove. He did look hot. She'd never seen him in a suit before, and combined with the short hair and newly close-cut facial hair, he looked like a damn movie star. The rugged kind of star who just got hotter and hotter the older he got.

"You look pretty hot yourself, Charlie." His eyes swept down her tight blue cocktail dress. "But I'm still managing to restrain myself." When she shot him a doubtful look, he answered with an innocent smile, as if he hadn't slipped his hand into her panties on the way over.

"I am going to ruin you on the drive home," she promised. His innocent smile faltered. "Come on," she said. "Let's go congratulate the happy couple."

She thought she heard him moan in frustration, and that made her smile all the brighter as she approached the large crowd that had assembled around Easy and Rayleen. Easy was shaking hands. Rayleen had her back turned and was instructing the bartender on how to serve whiskey properly.

Walker shook Easy's hand and added a slap on his shoulder. "Congratulations on snatching her up before I could," he said.

Easy laughed. "Thank you, but—"

Before he could finish his sentence, Rayleen swung around with drink in hand. "As if I'd have given you the time of day, Walker Pearce. I like a man who hasn't put all of his business on the internet."

Charlie nearly fell over laughing. "My God, Ms. Rayleen, I think I love you," she said, before she pulled the old woman in for a tight hug. "Congratulations. Easy is such a good man."

"Aw. He's all right," Rayleen answered, blushing again.

"So all right you decided to pen him in for good?"

Rayleen shrugged, but Easy shook his head. "Naw. I told her she could have one sample and then she'd have to buy the bull."

"One sample?" Rayleen cackled. "That was more like four. Four and a half if you count the time we—"

"Woman!" he barked. "My point is that I told you that was all you got unless you agreed to do it proper."

"Proper. Sure." Her blue eyes rolled. "You didn't want it so proper a few nights ago."

At that point, Charlie wondered if both Easy and Walker might faint if they blushed any harder, but Charlie worried she might pass out from laughter. "I see why you didn't wear white."

Rayleen shrugged. "Everything's pretty gray now anyway. Can't imagine I'd fool anyone."

A flash went off just as Easy shot his bride an exasperated look.

"That one should probably go on your wall," Eve said as she aimed her camera one more time. She'd donated her photography skills as a wedding gift, and she was obviously enjoying herself. "Everybody gather around," she said, gesturing to Walker and Charlie, as well as Grace and her boyfriend, Cole. She called out for Merry and Shane as well, and then began snapping pictures of the group. A few seconds later, Charlie's cousin Nate joined the group with Jenny, and Eve's boyfriend eased the camera from her hands.

"You get in there, too," he insisted. "I'll take the photo."

"But what about you?" Eve protested.

"You know how much I hate having my picture taken." When she looked as though she'd protest again, he kissed her forehead and shooed her into the frame. "Everybody smile."

"Ridiculous crap," Rayleen muttered, but Charlie noticed she hid her drink and smiled all the same. Her smile turned to laughter when Easy kissed her temple. Charlie found herself blinking back tears. It was so sweet. Such a cute couple surrounded by so much love. It made Charlie feel…certain. That love was real and good. And that every couple here had it in spades. It was the first wedding in a long while that was filling her up with more than booze.

In fact, it was long after the opening notes of the local country band before Charlie even found herself with a glass of champagne. The sun was setting, sending jagged rays of orange and pink from behind the darkening mountains. Charlie wandered the edges of the crowd, smiling at the happy dancers. The evening was perfect and beautiful, and the bride and groom swayed happily together to an old Patsy Cline cover.

For a strange second, Charlie imagined herself with Walker like that. In that moment. Married and hopeful and happy for all to see. The thought made her dizzy. She'd never considered that with anyone. She'd never even brought a date to a wedding, worried that the celebration would somehow rub off and snap her dormant serial-marriage gene into activity.

But now…she wanted to be near Walker. She wanted to hold his hand and watch the happy couple and…she wanted to hope.

Five minutes later she'd begun to suspect that he'd gone to visit the horses when she finally spotted him just past the glass doors. He was only a shadow in the evening sun, but there was no mistaking his silhouette, even with the new haircut. She knew his body, after all. The curve of his shoulders, his narrow hips and strong thighs. And when his head turned, the bold line of his nose. God, he was beautiful. Charlie followed him outside.

"Hey, darlin'," he said, turning to her with an open smile.

"What are you doing out here?"

Before she even had time to shiver in her thin blue dress, Walker had slipped off his suit jacket and eased it over her shoulders. Warmth took her over and seeped into her skin.

"Just taking it in," he said after he'd tucked her under his arm so they could watch the last colors disappear behind the mountain. The light hovered for a long moment as if the sun was showing off just for Charlie and Walker.

"I love this place," he whispered.

"I know," she said past her tightening throat. He put in so many hours here. He volunteered at every after-hours event. At first, she'd thought it had been because he was working toward a position, but he'd been hired on full-time two months before, and his devotion hadn't wavered. Walker simply adored the work. It filled him up until he came home to her glowing with it.

He loved the kids, of course, but she thought it was the work more than anything. The purpose of it. The joy. Heck, he'd spent the past two weeks working with veterans, and nothing had changed except that he occasionally met them at the saloon after a long day of lessons.

"It's almost seven," he whispered, his hand sneaking down to rest on her hip.

She nodded and closed her eyes, snuggling into his side. "Maybe we can stay a little longer."

"You said you needed to work."

"I know, but… What the heck. What's the point of being the boss if you can't take a night off every once in a while?"

Walker turned to her and touched a finger under her chin. She looked up at him, at the strong planes of his face limned with the last purples of twilight. "You're hot when you're in charge," he said.

"So you've said every day for the past three months."

"Hey, the truth is the truth."

She smiled and didn't deny it. It was pretty hot. She'd certainly been awfully horny anyway. She'd founded Pinnacle Security exactly ninety days ago, she'd fulfilled her first contract five days later and now she had thirteen clients, every one of them rich and willing to pay a lot of money for a custom security plan to keep their mountain estates safe. She designed systems that fed information not only to a local security company, but also to the estate management firm and the client's computer itself. The clients never seemed to actually check it, but they loved knowing they could even operate the cameras via remote signal.

Actually…the best part about her new job was that she no longer had a boss, and if she had anything to say about it, she never would again.

A flurry of excited barks gave Charlie the chance to back away from Walker before she got knocked over by the furry blur that launched itself at him. "I'm glad he's not a girl, or I'd be jealous," she said just before Roosevelt gave Charlie an equally enthusiastic welcome.

"Down, boy," Walker said. "Your mom is all dressed up tonight."

Roosevelt obediently plopped onto the ground while Charlie snorted at the words.

"You don't have to be jealous, you know." Walker gave Roosevelt a thorough head scratch. "He loves every single kid that comes through the gates exactly as much as he loves me. I don't think he'd come home with me now if he could. Too much attention here."

"I'm glad. I'm not sure which of us you'd rather cuddle."

"Hey, come on. I'd absolutely pick you. But then you'd have to get out of the way so Roosevelt could sleep next to me."

When she smacked his chest, Roosevelt jumped up, anticipating a new game, but the dog was distracted by a distant whistle from the barn and took off.

"He's so happy here," Walker said.

"Everybody seems pretty happy here," Charlie said, sliding her fingertips over his jaw to draw his attention. When he looked at her, Charlie kissed him. "I'm so proud of you," she whispered against his mouth.

He kissed her for a long moment before pulling back. "What about you, Charlie? Are you happy?"

She shivered as a gust of wind snuck snow-chilled air beneath the coat, and Walker pulled her into a hug. Charlie went willingly, laying her cheek against his chest and slipping her arms around his waist. The party looked so bright and warm past the glass. A separate world like yet another feed she was watching on yet another monitor. But strangely, all those people, all that joy…that was her life now. She wasn't removed from it. She wasn't observing.

She was a part of it, and for the first time in her life it felt as if she was the one being protected. "Yes," she whispered. "I'm so happy." She'd faced her biggest fear, finally.

This was love. With Walker. With all these friends. Her very own love story. And she wasn't scared at all.

* * * * *